WORSHIP YOUR QUEEN

BOOK THREE

PENELOPE SKY

HARTWICK PUBLISHING

Hartwick Publishing
Worship Your Queen
Copyright © 2017 by Penelope Sky
All Rights Reserved

CONTENTS

CREWE

ARIEL WALKED inside my office without knocking, a leather-bound notebook wrapped up in her arms. Her black frames sat on the edge of her nose where they always were since she preferred not to wear contacts. "Got a minute?"

I grabbed the scotch sitting on my desk and drained it in one swallow. "I suppose."

She sat down and crossed her legs before she opened the notebook. She scanned her notes, her head bent and her glasses threatening to slide off her nose. "How's your chest?"

Painful. Annoying. Weak. Take your pick. "Fine." It'd been a month since Joseph shot me. I was still going to physical therapy three times a week, trying to rebuild the muscle of my left pectoral. I couldn't use my left arm the way I used to, but once I got my strength back, everything would return to normal.

She didn't look at the nearly empty bottle of scotch sitting on my desk. "You know you aren't supposed to drink while you're on narcotics."

Like I gave a damn. "I'll be fine. What do you want?"

Her eyes narrowed at the way I snapped at her.

I was still in a lot of physical pain, and my mood had turned darker than a winter storm. Now I was constantly angry, wanting to punch any solid piece of furniture I came into contact with. But Ariel was the last person in the world who deserved my wrath. She was one of the few people who was truly loyal to me.

No one else was.

Especially that stupid fucking cunt.

I rephrased my words. "How can I help you?"

"That's better," she whispered. "You're invited to the golf tournament in London. No one knows you've been shot, so I had to accept the invitation. Will that be a problem?"

My swing may be off a little bit, but I'd make it work. "No."

"Good." She turned back to her notebook. "We have a buyer interested in purchasing the distillery. Should we give him an audience?"

I wasn't selling my business for any amount of money. "No."

"I thought as much…" She continued down the list. "Sasha called for you."

I knew what she was calling about. Ariel knew I preferred not to take personal calls from anyone—not anymore. "Tell her I'll pick her up at seven."

Ariel nodded. "I will. Also, Layla called about dinner tonight."

"Tell her I'll also pick her up at seven."

Ariel didn't blink an eye or show an instant of judgment. She preferred me this way, back to fucking without giving a damn. Booze and women were more powerful than the narcotics I was on. It stopped me from thinking about anything besides tits and pussy. "That's all I have for now. Do you need anything from me?"

"No. Thank you."

Ariel rose to her feet and gave me a look before she headed for the door.

We hadn't talked about what happened that night. When I opened my eyes in the hospital room, she was there holding my hand. She didn't ask me any questions or say she told me so. She understood I didn't want to talk about it, and she let it be.

And I was grateful.

I deserved to be told off for my stupidity. I deserved to be insulted for my poor judgment.

I deserved the bullet that pierced my skin and nearly penetrated my heart.

Ariel stopped at the door. "Crewe?"

"Yes?"

"Lay off the scotch."

I met her gaze without saying a word, unable to fulfill her request. The booze was the only thing keeping me sane. It was the only thing keeping me going. "I'll think about it."

LONDON

I FINISHED my shift at the hospital then walked home. I was running late because I had a date that night, and I'd barely have time to do anything with my hair or makeup. As soon as I walked through the door, I took a quick shower and managed my hair as best as I could. Then I left my apartment again and walked to the pizza place where we were meeting.

Will and I were set up by mutual friends. I'd heard nothing but good things about him, but I'd never met him in person. Instead of feeling nervous like I usually did on a first date, I didn't feel anything at all.

I walked inside and saw him sitting in a booth, wearing a t-shirt and jeans. He had dirty-blond hair and light-colored eyes, looking handsome but with a distinct boyish charm. He smiled when he saw me, a dimple in each cheek.

He was cute, but I didn't feel that thrill shoot down my spine.

I walked over to him and extended my hand. "It's nice to finally meet you."

He shook my hand. "You too."

I took a seat across from him and studied the menu. "So what are you thinking?"

"That you're very pretty," he said with a smile.

A chuckle formed in my throat, but I didn't let it escape. "I meant about the menu. What are you going to get?"

"Hmm…" He eyed the choices on the wall. "I'm not picky. I'll eat anything."

"Ditto."

"You wanna split one, then?" he asked. "How about the supreme?"

"I like the way you think."

He winked before he went up to the counter and ordered.

The second I was alone in the booth, my face fell and my thoughts turned to the man I hadn't stopped thinking about. Crewe was always on my mind, and even when I was asleep, he was in my dreams.

I thought I would have forgotten him by now, but I hadn't. I finally had my life back, the kind of freedom I'd gone six months without having, but it didn't feel as good as I thought it would. I found myself missing the stone walls of the castle, the comfortable bed I used to sleep in every night, and the view from the bedroom window. I missed listening to Crewe brush his teeth before bed and watching him shave in the morning when he got out of the shower.

Now I felt empty inside.

There was no excitement in my life, just the same mundane routine I did every day. On my days off, I spent time with my friends, but most of them were busy studying for their exams. I didn't have any family, so there wasn't anyone to open up to about my struggle.

I wondered if Crewe still thought about me.

Will returned with our number on a stand and two sodas. "It'll be fifteen minutes."

I tried to push Crewe out of my mind, but that was almost impossible to do when I was with other men. I hadn't slept with anyone, but I still felt like I was betraying Crewe in some way. And I felt bad for my dates since they were constantly being compared to the man I'd slept with for the past six months—a duke. "I hope my stomach can manage it."

"I can order some breadsticks or something."

"No, it's okay," I said quickly. "It'll ruin my appetite if I eat now."

"Yeah, me too." He stared at me and faltered, unsure what to say to keep the conversation going.

Crewe and I never had that problem. We wouldn't speak for hours, and that was perfectly fine. It was comfortable, actually. "So, you're an accountant?"

"Yeah. I've been working at my dad's office, but I'm gonna open up my own soon. Just wanted to get a few years of experience before I did that."

"Not a bad idea."

"You're a physician assistant, right?"

I nodded.

"You gonna start medical school again in the fall?" He knew exactly why I dropped out of the program to begin with. Some of the other men I dated treated me like fragile glass, damaged goods. Other men were brave enough to date me, but they had their guard up the whole time.

I didn't appreciate being looked at like that, like there was something wrong with me. While Crewe shouldn't have kidnapped me, our relationship was consensual. I had the power to say no whenever I wanted. None of my dates would understand that because I didn't want to discuss my time in Scotland. "That's the plan. But I like what I do now."

"Sounds like a good gig. Plus, you're getting paid."

I nodded. "It is nice to buy food and shoes—those are the two things I can't live without."

He chuckled, but it didn't seem genuine.

I was already bored, and we hadn't even gotten our food yet. None of the guys I met were interesting. They were all the same—educated, nice, and predictable. They lacked the attraction and passion Crewe possessed. Crewe was dark and dangerous, but in a good way. He had infinite layers to his persona, layers I'd never had the chance to peel back. He could make an entire conversation out of a simple look.

He never bored me.

As each week passed, the truth became clearer. Crewe was supposed to leave my thoughts, but his presence only grew in my mind. When I was alone in bed at night, I hardly slept because I missed his powerful body next to mine. My thighs squeezed together because I missed having him between my legs. I even touched myself and thought of him as I did it.

It was getting harder to deny the obvious—that I missed him.

A lot.

Will made small talk about our mutual friends and told me a bit about his family.

I nodded along without really listening, wishing I were home in my apartment with my vibrator—thinking about Crewe. I missed the way his scruff used to rub against my collarbone as he kissed my neck. I missed the way that same facial hair would rub against my inner thighs when he kissed me between my legs. I missed his big, manly hands all over my body, the way they would grip my tits as he fucked me at the edge of the bed.

"Are you alright?" Will stared at me with both eyebrows raised.

I had no idea what he just said. I was zoning out, picturing Crewe's perfectly chiseled body on top of mine. "Yeah, I'm fine. For a second, I thought I left the stove on in my apartment…but I'm pretty sure I didn't."

Will bought my story and continued talking about his aunt, a professor at NYU.

I went back to thinking about Crewe.

Over a month had come and gone since I saw Crewe get carried away on a stretcher. I knew he survived the ordeal and he was going to be okay, but that didn't stop me from worrying about him. I hoped he was making a good recovery, that he wasn't drinking too much, and that he wasn't more bitter and angry than he was when we first met.

I wanted to talk to him, but I didn't think that would go over well. The circumstances hadn't changed between us, so there was nothing to say. There was nothing to fix. I just hoped these feelings would go away.

Unless I really did love him.

Did I?

I was home on a Saturday morning when Joseph called me. We talked here and there, but never about anything that happened with Crewe. Our mutual anger hadn't dwindled, but we put that aside because all we had was each other.

"Hey," I said into the phone.

"What are you doing?" He spoke with a dead voice that was calm, borderline tired.

"Sitting on the couch watching TV in my pajamas." Nothing I wore was as comfortable as Crewe's t-shirts. I wished I'd gotten to take one home with me.

"How'd your date go?"

There wasn't much to tell. "Okay. We had pizza then went our separate ways. I don't think he'll call me again." And if he did, I would turn him down. There was no chemistry, no interest whatsoever. I felt like I was having dinner with a brother more than a possible lover.

"That's too bad."

I wasn't too disappointed. "What are you up to?"

"My plane is about to land in New York."

"Really?" A smile formed on my face even though I was still mad at him.

"I'm doing business in town. Was hoping I could see you."

"Sure. You wanna grab lunch?"

"How about I pick something up and bring it to your place?"

I forgot that he was living a criminal life like Crewe. Crewe hardly went out meals. In fact, we'd never been on a real date. He probably had to lay low at all times. "Yeah, sure. I like Chinese."

"That makes two of us. I'll pick it up on the way."

———

I showered and cleaned the apartment before he arrived. There was no evidence that I looked like hell, usually sitting on the couch with two open bags of potato chips. I vacuumed and destroyed all signs of my laziness. If he'd witnessed it, he would definitely crack a joke or two about it.

When he knocked on the door, I opened it and let him inside. Normally, I would hug him right away, but the memory of what he did to Crewe was still heavy in my mind. He nearly killed the man I spent half a year with. I wouldn't forget that anytime soon. "Hey."

"Hey." He carried the plastic bag of food to the table. "You wanna eat now?"

"Sure." I opened my wallet and pulled out some cash. "How much do I owe?"

"Shut up and eat." He sat down and pulled out the two trays of food and chopsticks.

I opened mine and began to eat, unsure what to say to him. It was the first time we'd been alone since he dropped me off at the airport a month ago. We talked on the phone, so he knew I had a job and a fairly normal life. "This is good."

"It's awesome. I haven't had Chinese in nearly a year." He scarfed down his food, grabbing large chunks of food between those two small sticks.

I hadn't had it in just as long.

"So, how are things going?"

"Good. I really like my new job. Everyone is nice."

"That's cool. Your friends are glad to have you back?"

"Yeah, but they walk on eggshells all the time, like if they say the wrong thing, I'll lose my mind."

He watched me as he chewed his chow mein, the stubble along his chin thick because he hadn't shaved in a while. Joseph and I didn't share a lot of characteristics, but we had the same eyes—green like our mother's. "They're just being sensitive. Can't blame them for that."

"I know. But no matter how many times I tell people I'm fine, they don't believe me. They tell me I need therapy."

"Therapy isn't a bad idea."

"I don't need therapy," I said coldly. "Crewe treated me well."

He shook his head. "I'm not a therapist, and I can tell you have Stockholm syndrome."

"I do not," I snapped. "Crewe always gave me a choice. He never made me do anything I didn't want to do. Everything between us was consensual."

"Except your freedom."

"Well…" I didn't have an argument against that.

"The guy kidnapped you. End of story."

"It's not black and white, Joseph." I stirred my food with my chopstick, suddenly losing my appetite. "I cared about Crewe. He cared about me. If I had the chance to talk to him about everything, he probably would have let me go."

"Doubtful."

"You don't know him the way I do."

"And I'm glad I don't."

I stared at my brother and felt my rage come to the surface. "I told you not to hurt anyone. I told you not to shoot Crewe."

"His men fired first. I didn't have a choice."

"Because you were ambushing his castle with guns and tanks."

He shook his head. "They still fired first. And I wasn't planning on shooting Crewe until I looked at him… Then the anger took over."

"He didn't deserve that."

"And I didn't deserve to have my sister kidnapped for six months. You just lost your mind in the process."

"I didn't lose my mind, Joey. Crewe is a good man."

He rolled his eyes.

"Have you heard anything about him?"

"What do you mean?"

"How's he doing? Is he working again?" The doctor told me he would live. I just hoped that meant he would live a normal life.

"As far as I can tell, he's back to normal. I haven't seen him with my own eyes, but I hear he's still running the scotch business with Ariel and taking care of his royal duties like the douchebag that he is."

I shot him a glare. "Don't talk about him like that."

He met my fire with his own. "What the hell is wrong with you? He stole you from your bed in the middle of the night and kept you as a prisoner. As in, he broke international law. Why are you protecting him?"

Joseph would never understand. No one would ever understand. "It was more complicated than that. Crewe and I had a relationship...we were friends. We were close." There were no words to describe what we had. I wasn't even entirely sure what the two of us shared.

Joseph set down his chopsticks in the center of his food and looked at me, his expression hard. It was a stare he'd given me countless times as we were growing up. It usually meant he was pondering what he was about to say. "London...did you love this guy?"

I told Crewe I loved him, but I thought it was just an act. I was tricking him into caring about me, being an actress in a play. But maybe those words weren't meaningless. Maybe I meant them from the bottom of my heart. "I...I don't know."

"You don't know?" he whispered. "The fact that your answer isn't a simple no is concerning to me."

"It's concerning to me too."

He'd hardly eaten his food, but he pushed it aside like he was finished with it. "London, I don't understand, and I'll never understand. I tried to make it right with Crewe by doubling the amount of money I owed, but he took you anyway. I'll always hate that man for the way he stabbed me. But...I'm trying to have an open mind about this. I just don't understand how you can care about a man who took away all of your freedom. Help me understand."

"I can't...it's complicated."

"Well, try anyway."

There was a lot of graphic content that would make Joseph upset, and I couldn't mention that. It would just make us both uncomfortable. "I hated him in the beginning. I fought him every chance I got him and put up a wall that he couldn't penetrate. But when he said he was going to sell me to Bones…I did what I had to do to stay with Crewe. So I slept with him." I didn't look at my brother as I told the story. He probably wasn't looking at me either. "I think that's when everything changed. I think that's when Crewe began to soften. He kept me for himself. And if I'm being honest, I enjoyed being with him."

Joseph turned his gaze out the window, like he wasn't listening at all.

"As time went on, we got closer and closer. We started to trust each other. And then it became a routine…a comfortable one. Crewe always treated me with respect, took care of me, and listened to me. He didn't feel like my captor anymore. Honestly, I miss him and that castle."

Joseph rubbed his jaw. "You miss him now?"

"Yeah," I admitted. "I've been on a few dates, and I don't feel anything. All I can think about is him. I can't stop thinking about the way we left things. I can only imagine how angry he is…how much he hates me. But I wonder if he misses me as much as I miss him."

Joseph sat back in the chair and crossed his arms over his chest. He released a quiet sigh of irritation. "I don't know what to say."

"You don't have to say anything. But Crewe never laid a hand on me while I was his prisoner. He never took me against my will. The most he ever did was raise his voice when I annoyed him. Honestly, I was safer with him than anywhere else in the world. I know I shouldn't feel anything for him, but it doesn't change the fact that I do."

"Well, I think you answered my question."

"What question?" Talking about Crewe made me forget why we started talking about him in the first place.

"That you love him."

It was hard for me to focus at work on Monday. I worked in the emergency room and helped out the physicians with patients with moderate illnesses. I had a lot of patients with pneumonia and one or two diagnosed with sepsis. The weather was changing in New York, and people were catching colds left and right.

I filled out chart after chart, and during my downtime, Crewe came back to my mind.

Did I love him?

I'd been so focused on playing him that I didn't realize how much my feelings had developed. I just assumed it was lust because the sex was good and he was handsome as hell. I didn't think anything more serious could develop under the circumstances.

But clearly, it had.

I'd been in New York for over a month, but I wasn't happy at all.

I was just miserable.

The only place I wanted to be was in that castle with that scotch-drinking man. I missed the bed I used to share with him. I missed the courtyard with all the roses. I missed the way he kissed my hairline when he was being particularly affectionate.

I missed everything.

When I got off work, I met Joseph for coffee because he was still in town. Since he was all I had, I felt obligated to tell him what my plans were. He was the closest thing I had to a best friend too, despite what he did to Crewe.

"What's up?" He carried his venti coffee to the table and sat down.

"I've been doing a lot of thinking…"

"That's never good." He sipped his coffee, wearing a black leather jacket with a gray t-shirt underneath. He definitely didn't look like an insurance salesman.

"I think I'm going to go to Scotland."

He gripped his coffee on the table and stilled like a statue. "What?"

"They have an open position in Edinburgh at the embassy. And while I'm there, I can talk to Crewe about everything—"

"You're going back to Scotland to tell Crewe you want to get back together?" he asked incredulously.

"I guess." I wanted to do more than that. I wanted to apologize for being responsible for the death of his men, for being the reason he was shot. I wanted to feel him in my arms and know he was okay. I hadn't stopped thinking about it, having nightmares about it.

Joseph shook his head. "I know bossing you around is a waste of time, but don't bother."

"What do you mean?"

"If you think Crewe is gonna welcome you back with open arms, think again."

"I doubt it'll be with open arms, but—"

"And he might kill you."

That was one thing I knew for certain would never happen. Even when he was bleeding out onto the floor, he cooperated with Ariel to protect me. I was the reason why he was shot, but he still put me first.

I knew he really loved me.

"He wouldn't hurt me," I said with confidence. "I don't know how he'll react, but it won't be violently."

"Even if you're right, he'll never take you back. You embarrassed him, lied to him, and humiliated him in front of all of his men. If the past has taught you anything, it's that Crewe always gets even. Even if he wanted to, he couldn't forgive you for what you did and move on."

"It's not like he's so innocent."

He chuckled. "Trust me, he doesn't see it like that."

His warning didn't change anything. If I didn't speak to Crewe and at least make an attempt, I would think about it forever. I would live in regret for not knowing what could have happened. "I'm going to do it anyway and hope for the best."

Joseph didn't hide his look of disappointment. His enemy captured me as payback, and now I wanted to go back to him. It was something he couldn't wrap his brain around. "You want me to go with you?"

"No," I blurted. "That'll just make it hostile. I have to go alone."

"Are you sure?" he pressed. "I can wait by the road. Who knows what his men will do to you."

"They won't hurt me." Crewe made his orders very clear. Even when he didn't owe me anything, he still looked after me.

"How can you be so sure?"

If I loved Crewe after everything he put me through, then he still loved me. That was something I believed. "I just am."

3

CREWE

"WHAT HAPPENED HERE?" Sasha sat on my lap with her legs straddled over my hips. Her huge tits were in my face, and her petite waist was perfect to grab on to. Her hand snaked up my chest to the scar over my pec. Thin black lines stretched over my pec from where the surgeons cut me open then put me back together.

"I got shot."

"Ooh…" Her fingers moved gently across the wound. "I'm sorry to hear that."

"Not a big deal. Just a battle scar."

"And quite the conversation piece." She spoke perfect English but had a heavy French accent. I liked listening to it when we were in bed together.

Meaningless sex with women acted as a great distraction. I didn't think about the woman who caused more damage than the bullet that nearly pierced my heart. And when I was pretty much drunk all the time, that helped too. Not to mention the painkillers I was still on. "Yeah, I suppose."

Someone knocked on my door even though it was almost nine o' clock. "Sir?" Dimitri's voice carried into the bedroom. "I'm sorry to bother you, but it's urgent."

I had a naked woman on my lap. Nothing was that urgent. "It can wait until tomorrow."

Dimitri's feet didn't fade away as if he walked off. His mouth was right by the door. "It's Lady London. She's here. Do you still want me to send her away?"

My entire body froze when I heard what he said. At first, I thought I imagined the entire thing, but my fingertips pressed into Sasha's hips, reminding me that this wasn't a dream. This was really happening. "London?"

"She's outside, sir," Dimitri said. "What are your orders?"

Sasha looked down at me. "Who's London?"

I ignored what she said. She wasn't even there. "I'll be down in ten minutes." I rolled Sasha off me and grabbed my boxers and jeans from where they lay on the floor. I yanked them on and picked a random t-shirt from my closet.

Sasha sat up in bed and pulled the covers to her chest. "Who's London?" she repeated.

I straightened my hair with my fingers as best as I could before I headed to the door. "I don't have time right now.

I'll be back soon." I knew London wasn't going anywhere, but my heart just spiked with adrenaline. I never expected to see her again, never hear from her again. But she was standing outside my door in the middle of the night.

What did she want?

The last time I saw her was when we got into the Jeep. After that, everything turned blurry.

When I thought about what she did to me, the anger emerged. I shouldn't even go downstairs to see her. I should slam the door in her face and demand my men to drag her off the property by her hair.

But that didn't slow me down.

I walked down the stairs, feeling my pulse pound in my ears like a pair of drums. My hands automatically formed fists, and my knuckles turned white. No matter how much anger burned under the surface, it didn't stop me from wanting to cross that threshold.

Stop me from wanting to see her.

I reached the front door and stared at the dark wood. Only a few feet separated us, separated me from the woman I once loved. She played me for a fool, manipulated me exactly the way Ariel warned. She humiliated me in a way Josephine never did.

And to think I actually loved her.

I took a deep breath and willed the anger to leave my body. I wanted to wear a stoic expression, an expression of nothingness when I looked at her. I didn't want her to understand how much she hurt me.

But I doubted that would last long.

I opened the door and stepped out into the night, taking the long stone steps to the driveway. I saw her outline in the darkness, her body wrapped in a black jacket. Her breath escaped like vapor because the October nights here were far colder than the ones in New York.

Her face finally came into view from the outdoor lights. Her brown hair was exactly as I remembered, slightly wavy from the damp air. She wore dark jeans with black boots, looking slender in the curve-fitting outfit.

I stood in front of her and looked at her head-on, doing my best to appear as indifferent as possible. It was cold outside, especially in just my t-shirt, but I refused to invite her inside my home—not when she was my enemy.

She met my look with those green eyes I used to love. Sympathy and pain were written in them, remorse for what she'd done. I didn't need to hear her apology to know it was sitting on the tip of her tongue.

I waited for her to speak first since I had nothing productive to say. The only thing that came to mind were cold insults that wouldn't further the conversation. Any shred of chivalry I had was long dead.

"Hi…"

I didn't say it back, purely out of stubbornness.

The wind was strong tonight, and her hair whipped across her face. When it got in her eyes, she tucked it behind her ear. "I was hoping we could talk inside. There's a lot of things I want to tell you."

"No."

Her eyes contracted when she heard the authority in my voice.

"I never want you to set foot inside my house again." I was surprised how well I controlled my tone. On the way to the door, I'd thought about strangling her. Now I was calm and collected, making my walls as thick as the Great Wall of China. "I don't give a damn about anything you have to say, and you're stupid for showing your face around here. Maybe you've forgotten all the men who died because of you—but my crew hasn't."

She finally bowed her head, breaking eye contact with me and tightening her arms around her waist. "I said I told Joseph not to come. I specifically told him—"

"Not to hurt anyone or kill me," I interrupted. "But you did plan for him to come. You were stupid to think my enemy wouldn't desecrate me the second he had a chance. You plotted against me on purpose, took advantage of my heart like the whore that you are." My temper flared, and now it couldn't be controlled. I didn't feel bad for insulting her, not when she'd insulted me worse.

The fire didn't leap in her eyes. "I told him not to come at all. I told him I was going to talk to you first."

"Talk to me about what? Tell me that you successfully tricked me into being pussy-whipped?"

"No. About treating me like a real human being and not a prisoner." Her own anger rose, but she kept it under control a lot better than I did. "Crewe, you said you loved me, but you still kept me chained up like a dog."

"There were no chains. I wish there were."

"You know what I mean. I wanted to ask if you would let me go…"

I clenched my jaw because I probably would have done it if she'd asked. The second she didn't want to be with me, I didn't want her either.

"I knew you would, but Joseph disagreed. That's why he moved in when he did."

This conversation was just making me angrier. "Why are you here? It happened, and it's in the past now. Why are we talking about this? And why didn't you just call me on the phone? Why are you showing up at my doorstep in the middle of the night?" I at least hoped she wanted me back, that leaving me was a mistake. The second I realized she just wanted to be relieved of guilt, it pissed me off all over again. I hated myself for wanting anything else in the first place.

"I wanted you to know that I never wanted to hurt you or your men."

"I'm so glad to hear that," I said sarcastically. "Really changes everything."

Her hair flew in her face again, and this time she pulled it over her shoulder. "I wanted you to know it wasn't all an act. I wanted to be free because I deserved to be free. I did what I had to do to get out."

"Congratulations."

"But when I told you I loved you…I meant it. I didn't realize it at the time, but now I do."

My hands were still by my sides, cold from the breeze and white from my grip. "You expect me to believe that?"

"Why wouldn't you? You were there, Crewe. You knew how I felt about you before I even said anything."

I shook my head and stepped back. "Everything was a lie. You successfully played me, tricked me into getting what you want. Now that you have your freedom, why don't you just go enjoy it and disappear?" I hated to think of how many men she'd slept with this past month. I shouldn't care, and the fact that I did pissed me off.

"Because I haven't enjoyed my freedom…not like I thought I would."

I stared at her and couldn't look away. My entire body shut down so I could take in everything without missing a single syllable.

"Crewe, I miss you. I thought I would be happy back in New York, but I'm not. All I do is think about you. I'm not saying I don't want my freedom, because I do. But I want both. I was hoping we could start over."

"Start over?" I asked with a strangled laugh. "I almost died on the operating table. No, we can't fucking start over."

Her eyes welled with tears. "I understand you're mad—"

"Mad doesn't do it justice. There are no words to describe what I'm feeling, London. I've never actually wanted to hurt you until right now. I want to slap you so hard that your neck breaks. That's how I feel."

She didn't take a step back even though she should. "I want to apologize for everything, but I can't. I did what I had to do to survive. The only thing I am sorry about is hurting you. I never wanted to hurt you." The tears continued to build on the surface of her eyes, but they didn't fall. "You know that, Crewe."

"I don't know anything, London. I don't know a damn thing." The longer we stood outside, the more immune I became to the cold temperature and my hardening heart. I let my guard down again, and of course, it bit me in the ass. I felt stupid for ever trusting her. "I never want to see you again. Do you understand me?"

This time, the tears fell. They streaked down her cheeks to her lips.

Instantly, I felt my broken heart tighten.

"Crewe, I admit things didn't work out the way they should. I should have talked to you about everything sooner. But you can't pretend to be the only victim in this situation. You've done things wrong too. You took my life away from me when it was never your right. I don't even know how I fell in love with you to begin with, but the fact that I have tells me this is real. So, you can't put all the blame on me. We're both guilty of a lot of things."

"Maybe I kept you as a prisoner in the beginning, but you were never a prisoner toward the end. I made my feelings for you perfectly transparent. I never lied to you or misled you about how I felt. You, on the other hand, perfectly deceived. That's worse, if you ask me."

"Again, I was just trying to survive. In the process, I began to love you. I didn't know it was going to happen, but it did. I could have run off with Joseph the second I got the chance, but I didn't. I stayed behind and made sure you survived. I didn't have to save Ariel, but I did because I know how important she is to you. I made a lot of mistakes, but I did the right thing when it mattered most."

The breeze increased, and I watched her shiver slightly. If this were a different time, I would wrap my arms around her and take her inside. But I couldn't look past my heartbreak or my embarrassment. She tricked me, and I honestly didn't know what was real and what was a game. I was too angry to even consider forgiveness. I was too pissed to even contemplate starting over. "The only reason why I'm gonna say this is because it's the only chance I'll ever have."

When she blinked, more tears fell.

"I really loved you. As in, I loved you in a way I've never loved anyone else. I trusted you. Fuck, you were my whole world. There was nothing I looked forward to more than getting off work and making love to you. I was happier with you than I ever was with Josephine, or anyone else that came before her. What we had was special. For the first time in my life, I was actually happy."

More tears came, a waterfall in the making.

"But that's over because it never really happened. Maybe you were sincere in your feelings, but I have no way of knowing when those moments occurred. When you told me you loved me, it was a lie. The second the words left your mouth, they were meaningless—"

"But they aren't meaningless now, Crewe," she said through her tears. "I love you. I know I do. It just took me some time to come to terms with it, to realize I couldn't run from it anymore. This relationship didn't start off in the right way. But that doesn't mean we can't give it a new beginning."

"I don't want to have a new beginning."

Her hands reached for mine, and her frozen fingers wrapped around my wrists.

I pushed her away before I gave myself the opportunity to enjoy her. "Don't fucking touch me."

"Crewe—"

"Get off my property." I wanted this to end. I wanted to go back to my life and forget she ever existed. I stepped back and turned to the entrance.

"I know you still love me."

I stopped and turned around, watching her hair blow in the wind.

"I know you do. Just take some time to think about what I said. I'm staying in Edinburgh for a month… I'll be around."

"I don't love you, London," I said coldly. "I stopped loving you the second Joseph pointed that gun at me."

She'd stopped crying, but her eyes were still shiny. "Ariel told me what she said to you."

My eyes narrowed as the betrayal swept over me. I never asked Ariel to keep that a secret, but I assumed she would have kept that information to herself.

"The only reason you got up was to protect me. After everything we'd been through, you still put me first. So don't pretend you don't love me. Don't pretend I don't mean anything to you. I know you're angry right now because this is the first time we've spoken, so I can be patient. I can give you some time. I'll be in Edinburgh until the end of this month. When you're ready to talk, I'm sure you'll be able to find me."

Her confidence just pissed me off more. "You shouldn't waste your time, London. I'm not coming after you. I have a woman in my bed waiting for me at this very moment. I've moved on with my life—as I'm sure you've moved on with yours."

She controlled her expression and hid the hurt that was burning under her skin, but I could see the devastation in her eyes.

I enjoyed hurting her, enjoyed getting back at her for hurting me. If she imagined I'd be crying over her, she was stupid. I didn't shed a single tear. I spent my time drinking scotch and screwing beautiful women.

Because I was still the scotch king.

It took Ariel five seconds to figure out London stopped by. "What did she say?" She walked into my office without knocking, her arms crossed over her chest and her eyes focused on me like lasers.

I would have told her it was none of her business, but since Ariel warned me about her to begin with, I felt obligated to share. "She wanted to apologize for lying to me. Then she told me she loved me and wanted to start over." I flipped through the expense report like our conversation wasn't important enough for my full attention.

"That fucking cunt." She ground her teeth together, looking angrier than I'd ever seen her. "What did you say?"

"What do you think, Ariel?" I looked at the totals in the back of the report before I closed the folder. "I told her to get off my property and disappear. End of story."

Ariel breathed a sigh of relief like she'd been expecting me to say something else. "Thank god."

Like I'd ever give London another chance. That ship had sailed. "I'm sure we won't hear from her again."

"Better not." She finally took a seat and crossed her legs. "Are you doing okay?"

I was insulted by the question. "I'm more than okay, Ariel."

"You haven't talked about it and—"

"Because I don't need to talk about it. It was a mistake, and it's over. Let's move on." I didn't need to be reminded how stupid I was. I put my life, as well as the life of everyone around me, in danger. Some of my men were buried in graveyards because of my poor judgment. It's not something I would easily forget.

"Does that mean you've reinstated Dunbar?"

Dunbar had been right about her too. I should have let him beat her to a pulp. "Yes. I gave him a two-week vacation as an apology."

"That was nice of you."

Not nice enough. "Is there anything else you need? I've got a lot of shit to do today."

Ariel glanced at my bottle of scotch, which was half empty even though it wasn't even eleven yet. "Nope. I'll see you later." She left my office without a backward glance, in a much better mood now that she knew London wasn't making a resurgence.

Even if I wanted to take London back, I wouldn't.

Not after what she did.

I had too much pride, too much stubbornness to let bygones be bygones.

But I did love hearing that she still wanted me, that New York felt empty without me in her life. It made me feel good to know that she actually loved me, that she flew all the way here just to see me.

She accused me of still loving her.

Which I didn't.

But I couldn't stop thinking about her, not while I was at work or while I was in my room alone. Sleep had been difficult since the day she left. The only time I slept somewhat well was when a woman slept over. But even then, it wasn't the same.

As soon as London left, I'd asked Sasha to leave. I didn't feel like being interrogated by a woman who wanted me all to herself a long time ago. I was in too foul a mood to please a woman for the night.

I just wanted to be alone.

But my mood hadn't changed. I was just as angry as the moment she left. I was even more angry that I allowed her to have this power over me, to make me feel so many different things at once.

And I was pissed that I hated seeing her cry. It made me feel like shit when it shouldn't. I enjoyed hurting her, but that desire faded away almost instantly. I wish I'd never mentioned Sasha when it was such a low blow.

And then I hated myself for caring about her feelings.

I was so fucked up in the head.

What was wrong with me?

A week went by, and I didn't contact her. I knew she was staying in Edinburgh, but I didn't have a clue what she was doing. She didn't come from money, so I didn't know how she was paying for this expensive trip across the world.

Especially since it was all a waste of money.

Even though she was always in the back of my mind, I refused to go to her. I refused to see her after everything we'd been through.

She claimed I loved her, but that was just wishful thinking.

I didn't.

At least, I wouldn't admit it to her or myself.

Dunbar just returned from vacation, and he was still cold to me. He obviously hadn't forgiven me for my error in judgment, and I couldn't exactly blame him. He lost friends when Joseph ambushed the castle with his men. It was their job to protect me and the keep, but that was an unnecessary war that could have been easily avoided.

If I'd thought with my brain and not my dick.

The next day, I was taking a trip to my distillery in Edinburgh. I knew London would be in the city, but I hadn't planned to acknowledge her existence. But that didn't mean I wouldn't think about her.

Because I always thought about her.

I completed my physical training in the morning, which was excruciating since the muscle had been so severely damaged, and then I sat in the back of the car as Dunbar drove me into the city.

All I had to do was call Dimitri, and I would figure out exactly where she was.

But I didn't make the request.

I stayed strong—learning from my past mistake.

4

LONDON

I COULDN'T SAY I was surprised by Crewe's reaction.

I didn't expect him to forgive me in a heartbeat and take me back in his arms. I knew it would take more time, greater effort. But I didn't expect him to be so merciless and cold. I knew he still cared about me. There wasn't a doubt in my mind. But Crewe was the proudest man I'd ever known.

Image was everything to him.

A week passed, and I didn't hear from him. I was working in a clinic in Edinburgh that wasn't too far from his new distillery. I didn't pick the location on purpose. That just happened to be where they stationed me. The pay wasn't amazing, but the cost of living was cheap enough that I managed. I had a small flat in the city, which allowed me to walk anywhere I wanted. There was a grocery store nearby, and of course, the view was incredible. I was living in one of the oldest towns in the world, but it didn't feel as historic as the castle I shared with Crewe.

As more time passed, the more I realized I may never get him back.

Everything was working against us, mainly his bitterness. I think all men should be a little proud, but he took it to a new level. It was probably his royal heritage that made him that way. I wasn't sure what else it could be caused by.

Joseph called me in the afternoon, the same time he called me every day. He knew I was in Edinburgh alone, and being the protective older brother that he was, he needed to check on me. "How's it going?"

"It's okay." I couldn't really enjoy my new surroundings when I was swallowed by misery.

"Hasn't called, huh?"

"No…"

"I'm sorry, Lon. But I told you he wouldn't."

"I think he just needs some time. I haven't lost all hope yet."

"Well, you should. He's not gonna change his mind."

I was prepared to let him go if I had to, but I didn't want to. I certainly didn't want to return to New York and try to start over, to find a man who made my heart flutter the way Crewe did. I couldn't fall for another man when I was already in love with someone across the world. "It's only been a week."

"It could be a year, and it wouldn't change anything." Joseph liked to make his opinion extremely well known, regardless of how it made me feel. He never beat around the bush, not even to protect my ego.

"Maybe I should try contacting him again."

"And what will that do?"

"Hopefully something." I had no way of contacting him. All I knew was where he lived, but I feared I wouldn't be so welcome there a second time. "Or you could give me his number…"

"I could, but I'd rather not."

Joseph would help me if I pushed him enough. "If I could meet him somewhere else, that would be fine. But he doesn't leave the castle too often."

"I'm sure he does. He has that scotch facility in Edinburgh."

"Yeah, but he usually sends Ariel to do that stuff for him." Crewe seemed to have recovered from his wound well, but he was probably limiting his outdoor adventures. "Unless you can tell me where he is…"

"You think I'm a spy or something?"

"I have no idea what you do, Joseph. And that's because I've never asked." I didn't want to know what his criminal activities were. Since he was my brother, it was better if I didn't know. I had to love him no matter what, and it would be difficult if I knew he was a murderer.

"Give me his number. Maybe I can get him to meet me somewhere."

"You know, chasing a guy like this seems kinda desperate."

I bit the inside of my cheek. "Just give me the number, Joseph."

After he finally handed it over, I hung up and called Crewe. Every time it rang, my heart moved into my throat. I could hardly breathe because I was nervous, utterly terrified whether he answered or he didn't.

"This is Crewe." He spoke with a rich voice that was smooth just like scotch. I missed the way his voice sounded when his lips were pressed against my ear. Just his voice alone could bring me to my knees.

"It's London."

Crewe remained silent, the sound of a moving car acting as the background. It sounded like he was on the road, probably in the back seat while one of his men drove him around.

I didn't expect him to say anything else, so I continued onward. "Where are you headed?"

"Does it matter?"

I didn't appreciate Crewe's coldness, but I would have to deal with it for the time being. "If you're on your way to Edinburgh, maybe we can have dinner."

"I am on my way to Edinburgh. But let's skip the dinner."

Maybe Crewe wasn't lying. Maybe he truly did stop caring about me. "You've gotta eat sometime, right?" I kept the conversation playful, knowing that would get to him better. I'd already cried my eyes out, and I couldn't do it anymore.

"In this instance, I'd rather go hungry."

He was ice-cold, and my heat couldn't force him to melt. "I'm working at a family practice clinic here in town. After working all day, it would be nice to relax over a bottle of wine. But you know I can't drink an entire bottle on my own."

"You're a beautiful woman. I'm sure you can find someone to share it with you."

I rubbed my temple at the brush-off. "Have dinner with me." Joseph was right, I did feel desperate chasing him like this. This man kept me as his prisoner for months, and now I was doing everything I could to get him back. He was the only man I'd ever fought for like this. Times like this made me wonder if it was worth it.

"I have a date tonight."

I didn't want to believe that was true because it killed me, but I didn't know why else he was going to Edinburgh later in the day. But there was a chance he was lying, trying to hurt me enough so I would hang up. "Make a rain check."

He chuckled. "I think I'll stick with what I've got."

"Or you could blow her off and come straight to my flat." Jumping his bones was how I got him to fall in love with me in the first place. Sex was always a way into Crewe's brain. It worked before, and maybe it would work again.

"And do what?"

He took the bait. "I don't want to give anything away...but I would probably be on my hands and knees most of the time."

Crewe was quiet, probably considering my offer.

I hoped he would take it. If I could get him in the same room, it would make it much easier for us to talk. A face-to-face interaction was always preferable to hearing his voice over the phone. I could read him much better when I could watch the expressions change in his eyes.

"I told you, I have a date."

"Well, I don't believe you." There was no way for me to know if he was lying or not. I just had to hope for the best. "And I haven't been with anyone else since I left you, not that it matters." Actually, it did matter. I knew that would mean something to him.

Crewe was quiet.

I knew he was thinking, considering.

"I don't care what you believe, London. I have to go."

I hated it when he called me by my first name. So impersonal. "Crewe—"

"Good night." He hung up.

After hearing the rejection of the dial tone, I tossed my phone on the table. I wasn't going to call him again when I knew it wasn't going to get me any closer to him. The only real chance I had was to get in the same room with him.

But how would I manage that?

I called Joseph back.

He answered immediately. "What did I tell you?" He didn't even bother hiding his gloating. "You need to let it go and move on."

I had another plan in mind. "I need to get in the same room as him."

"Unless you walk up to his door without getting shot, I don't see how that's gonna happen."

"You're going to help me."

"What are you talking about?"

"He kidnapped me and made me his prisoner. Now it's his turn to get kidnapped."

Joseph's voice rose a few levels. "Are you really suggesting that I capture the guy?"

"Yes. You're going to bring him to me so he and I can talk —face-to-face."

"Wow. You aren't kidding."

"No. And you owe me, Joseph."

"Don't go there," he snapped. "I did everything I could to get you back."

"You don't owe me for that. You owe me for shooting Crewe when I told you not to."

He sighed into the phone.

"When his driver takes him somewhere, I need you to intercept the car and drive him to me."

"You're crazy."

"Are you saying you can't do it?" Playing to his ego should work.

"Yes, I can do it. But I'm not going to do it."

"Yes, you are. And you aren't gonna hurt anyone."

"Now, that's impossible."

"It's not. No guns."

"You expect me to hijack his car without a gun and actually turn my back to Crewe, who's definitely packing?"

"He won't hurt you."

He laughed into the phone. "I shot the guy. Of course, he'll take his chance."

"No, he won't." I knew Crewe would never hurt someone I loved unless it was a matter of life and death. "Tell him why you've taken over the car, and he'll cooperate peacefully."

"You have no idea what he might do."

"Yes, I do." Despite being apart for the past month, I knew him better than anyone. "Trust me, Joey."

"Goddammit…how did my life get to this?"

"Because you fucked with Crewe Donoghue."

5

CREWE

TWO WEEKS WENT BY, and I didn't hear anything from London.

She was about to head back to the United States, getting back to the life she had before she got mixed up with me in the first place. A part of me wanted to call her now that I had her number, just to hear her voice, but I wouldn't allow myself to do that.

I'd made my decision.

And when I made up my mind, I didn't change it. She had my trust once before, but she blew it when she crossed me. I couldn't take back Josephine, not that I wanted to, and I certainly couldn't give London another chance.

I was too pissed.

And stubborn.

I was golfing in London that weekend, catching up with friends and some business partners for the charity event. Maybe hitting the links would get my mind off London. I hadn't gotten laid in weeks because I'd been too busy, so my dreams and fantasies constantly drifted back to her. I beat off to her memory more times than I cared to admit.

But that didn't mean I loved her.

And I would have kept seeing Sasha, but work got in the way. London's reappearance had nothing to do with me calling it off.

It was just a coincidence.

My men carried my two bags to the car as I walked to the entrance with Ariel.

"I've got your schedule ready. Mark will take care of everything when you land. I'll handle everything on this front."

"I had no doubt you would." I adjusted my watch on my wrist before I straightened my black jacket. "You know how to reach me." I walked out the door and saw my car parked in the roundabout in the midst of statues.

"Good luck on the course."

I gave her a quick nod before I opened the back door. "Don't need it. But thanks anyway." I got into the back seat and immediately pulled out my phone, planning to get through my emails on the drive.

Dunbar pulled onto the road and headed to Edinburgh, where my plane was waiting for my private takeoff. He didn't make conversation, but he'd always been a quiet man. Ever since London's betrayal, he'd never looked at me the same. He did his job and communicated with me as little as possible. Even a raise hadn't improved his spirits.

But as long as he did his job well, I didn't have room to complain. I wasn't a chatty person, preferring long stretches of silence to meaningless conversation. That was one of the things I adored about London. For a woman, she didn't have much to say. She could sit with me for hours without saying a single word.

The memory of us having dinner together on the balcony tugged at my heart.

But I pushed it away.

We came to a stoplight in town and sat at the light for over a minute. I didn't have to catch a flight at the airport like everyone else, so I didn't care if this delay put us back a couple minutes. I had a few emails from one of my regional managers, so I responded to those with my eyes glued to the screen.

Then the front window shattered.

"What the—"

A man slammed Dunbar's head against the steering wheel so hard he knocked him out cold. The horn honked, and the rest of the cars in traffic sped away on the sidewalk since they didn't know what was happening.

There was a gun under the seat, so I snatched it with lightning speed.

"It's me." Joseph pushed Dunbar's body to the passenger seat then got behind the wheel. "I'm not packing, so you can calm down. London sent me." He fastened his safety belt then drove through the light once it turned green.

The only reason why I didn't shoot him was because of London. Otherwise, he'd have a bullet in his brain right now. "What the hell are you doing?"

"Taking you to have lunch with her. When you're done, I'll drive you wherever you need to go."

Was this a joke? "You knock out my driver and expect me to spend time with your sister?"

"Hey, this was all her idea. I wanted to kill the guy, but she said no."

"Ironic," I said. "I want to kill you right now."

"She told me you wouldn't. And for some idiotic reason, I trust what she says." He didn't turn around and look at me even though he knew I was holding a loaded pistol.

I wanted to shoot him just to prove London wrong, but I couldn't do that. When I imagined how heartbroken she would be, it made me feel like shit. I turned the safety back on and stowed it under the seat. "Where are we going?"

"She made lunch at her apartment. I'll wait in the car, and when you're done, I'll take you to the strip."

I couldn't believe London actually arranged this. When she put her mind to something, she didn't give up. But I hoped she would give up soon because she was wasting her time. "Your sister is an idiot."

"You know, I would normally kill you for saying that, but this is the one time I actually agree with you."

I looked out the window and watched the buildings go by. I knew her apartment was somewhere in the city. I was tempted to look it up a few times, to make sure she was safe wherever she was living. Thankfully, Dunbar was unconscious and unable to tell Ariel what happened. If Ariel knew, she'd burst into London's apartment with a gun in each hand. She'd hated London before, but now she loathed the woman.

After a short drive, Joseph pulled up to the curb of a small apartment building. It was solidly built, but not in the greatest part of town. Must have been all she could afford on her salary. "She's in apartment 110."

I could just get out and wave down a taxi, but I didn't do that. A part of me wanted to have this lunch. A part of me enjoyed the fact that London went to such lengths to see me again. After not speaking for two weeks, I wondered if she'd given up on me. I wanted her to let me go, but at the same time, I wanted her to fight for me.

I got out and located her apartment in the complex. I stood in front of the door for a minute, thinking about how this lunch would go. My cock hardened when I pictured us ending up on her bed, screwing on the old mattress that had probably been there since the complex was built. It didn't matter how many women I slept with to get over her, they were never as good in the sack as she was.

I missed it.

Instead of knocking, I walked inside. She invaded my personal space by sending her brother to commandeer my car, so I didn't feel any remorse for barging into her place when she was expecting me. "I need some painkillers before I leave. Dunbar is gonna wake up with one hell of a migraine."

She stood at the kitchen counter and turned around when I made my announcement. Instead of looking annoyed, she stared at me exactly the way she used to, like she missed me after I'd been gone at work all day.

I loved that look, and that fucking terrified me.

"I'm sure he'll be fine." She grabbed the two plates and set them on the small wooden table that hugged the small living room. Her standard of living was poor, even by poor standards.

But I didn't have the audacity to insult her. I took a seat at the table and stared at her.

She sat down and poured me a glass of my own scotch, knowing I wouldn't have wanted water or anything else. She took the seat across from me, looking fine in the dark blue dress she wore. She was overdressed for the occasion, so I knew that outfit was specifically picked to impress me.

And it did.

It was the first time she'd ever cooked for me, and I stared down at the meal of chicken, salad, and rice. It smelled good, and it smelled even better because she was the first woman to ever make me anything. Josephine couldn't cook if her life depended on it. A life of royalty had made her inherently lazy and stupid. "This looks good."

"Thanks." She placed her napkin in her lap and began to eat like she hadn't just kidnapped me.

"Is this how you get all your dates?"

"Just the ones I really like."

I forced myself not to smile in response, but it was difficult to do. Even under the extreme circumstance, our chemistry was evident. She was the only person in the world who could make my anger disappear without even trying. I grabbed my fork and ate, surprised how good it was. "Looks like you can save lives and cook."

"I'm a woman of many talents."

I drank my scotch as I stared at her, taking advantage of the fact that her gaze was averted so I could look at her. She didn't get right to the point immediately, but I knew it was coming. She was giving me a false sense of security, a comfort that wouldn't last long.

"You're going golfing this weekend?" she asked, keeping the conversation light.

"Yeah. It's a charity event. I go every year."

"That should be fun. But it'll probably be cold."

I drank the rest of my scotch, downing an entire glass before I even finished my meal. London probably noticed, but she didn't make a comment about it. My health was none of her concern anymore. "It's always cold in London. I'm used to it."

"How are you at golf?"

I wasn't one to brag. "Not too bad."

"I've never played."

"It can get a little boring after the ninth hole." Now we were talking like we used to, the conversation flowing even though the topic of discussion was mediocre. It didn't matter how close Ariel and I were—we'd never had this kind of relationship. The only person I'd experienced it was with London. The fact that she sucked me in so easily only fueled my anger. "Let's get to the point, London. I have a plane to catch." I didn't eat all of my food even though I wanted to, just to make a statement. I wasn't going to eat her cooking and picture her making my meals. That was exactly what she wanted.

"The point?" she asked. "I just wanted to see you. There is no point." She did something different with her makeup, making her eyes darker and her lashes longer. I liked the smoky look, the prominence of her cheekbones and the fullness of her lips.

I poured another glass of scotch just to spite her.

She hid her annoyance, but I knew it burned under the surface.

"You know I'm leaving in a week. My position here at the clinic is over, and I need to get back to New York."

I knew her time here was running out. She gave herself a month to make it work with me, and not a day longer.

She set her fork down, not finishing her food either. She looked me square in the eye, unflinching, strong, and beautiful. "It's been a few weeks now. I'm assuming you've had a chance to think about what I said."

That's all I'd been thinking about. "It doesn't change anything. You know that."

She gripped her glass of scotch but didn't take a drink. "I can apologize as many times as you need to hear it, but you have yet to apologize to me."

"Apologize for what?" I asked incredulously.

"For keeping me as a prisoner to begin with."

I'd never apologize for that. I drank from my glass, dismissing her comment.

"My point is, neither one of us is innocent. But we love each other. Whatever we have is special, real. I know it is. I can see it in your eyes right now."

Why did I have to give myself away so easily? Why did she have to read me like a goddamn book? "It doesn't matter how we feel about each other. It's over. So go back to New York and leave me the hell alone." I pushed her away harder, trying to get her off my mind forever.

She didn't flinch. "Crewe, when I leave next week, I'm not coming back. When I land in New York, I'm going to push you from my thoughts and move on with my life. I'm gonna find someone else to spend my life with. I'm not going to mope around and miss you. If you want me, now is the time to say something."

My fingers gripped the glass tighter.

"I'm not bluffing, Crewe. Drop your pride and work with me on this."

Now that there was a timer set, I felt the weight of the situation. If I ever found out she got married and had kids, even if it were years down the road, I'd be devastated. Even when knew she tricked me, I couldn't let Ariel hurt her. I didn't know why I loved this woman after the way she deceived me.

But I did.

"This is the only offer I'm gonna make."

She stilled at my words, anxious for me to finish.

"And these conditions are nonnegotiable."

"I'm listening," she whispered.

"You come back with me—as my prisoner. You forsake your previous life completely. I'll fuck you when I feel like it, spend time with you if I'm in the mood, but I don't owe you anything else. I'm free to do what I want, when I want." I was offering her the life I offered her in the beginning— one without promises. If she wanted to be with me again, she'd be the one to make all the sacrifices.

Her eyes narrowed in disappointment. "You're asking me to be your slave?"

I nodded.

"To have no voice? To have no rights?"

I nodded again. "Take it or leave it."

She crossed her arms over her chest and gave me a loathing look, the same kind she used to give me when we first met —when she hated me. "You're being serious?"

"Dead serious."

"Then I'll leave it. No man in the world is worth it— certainly not you." She left the table and carried her dishes to the sink, dismissing the meal even though our plates were still full. Her back was turned to me, so I couldn't see her face.

I waited for her to say something else, to tell me what she was thinking. But nothing else came.

She walked back to the table, looking indifferent as she grabbed my plate. "You can go, Crewe. We have nothing more to say to each other."

I'd successfully pushed her away. I'd successfully made her give up. "You don't have any of your own demands?"

"You said it was nonnegotiable."

I could just walk out, but my ass didn't leave the chair. "Everything is negotiable."

She threw my plate in the sink, where it shattered loudly. She turned back around, all her love and affection gone. "I thought things were different, Crewe. I thought you actually loved me, and when someone loves someone, they treat them like a human being. The fact that you want to keep me under your thumb, to boss me around like you own me, tells me that nothing was ever real between us. I'm not a thing, a possession, a pawn in your world. Your constant need to own and control everything is despicable, especially when you think you can apply it to me. Now I know this never would have worked, that I should have left when I had the chance. I don't feel bad for leaving—because there was never a reason to stay."

***

I put on a good face for my weekend in London, talking to old friends, acquaintances, and people with astute business minds. When I was surrounded by like-minded people familiar with noble aristocracy, I was in my element.

But all I thought about was her.

I pushed her buttons—hard. Freedom was a hard limit for her, a topic she wouldn't negotiate, and I disrespected it.

But she disrespected me when she lied to me.

I shouldn't feel bad about what I did because I'd accomplished what I set out to do. I pushed her away so she wouldn't come back. She would finally leave me alone and leave our relationship where it belonged—in the past.

At the end of the weekend, I retired to my hotel room alone. When I was away from Scotland, I usually entertained myself with a beautiful woman. Sometimes she was a regular, and sometimes she was someone I bumped into at the bar. I wasn't picky when it came to choosing a partner. There were lots of degrees of attractiveness, and if she had a pretty smile and soft skin, she usually fit the bill.

But now I didn't want anyone.

I drank alone then went to bed alone. The last time I slept well was when London was with me. Ever since that night, I tossed and turned in the enormous bed with cold sheets. I didn't listen to her melodic breathing as she slept. Sometimes she talked in her sleep, and that always made me laugh.

But I didn't want anyone to join me.

Sasha helped with the loneliness, but she also made it worse sometimes. I constantly compared her to London, the woman I truly wanted to have. No matter how much she hurt me, my cock missed her pussy.

He missed her more than I did.

I lay in my bed and looked out the window. A stormy sky had just spread over the city, and slowly, drops of rain began to pelt the glass. The rain came slowly, and then it pounded against the glass as the storm picked up. Soon, it became background noise, the only soothing thing in my life right now.

I missed Fair Isle. I hadn't been there in a long time, too busy working in Scotland to return. I only slept with London once while we were there, and now I wished we could both hide away there and forget the rest of the world —with Finley, of course.

But that would never happen.

My phone rang on my nightstand, and I immediately snatched it because I knew it was important. Nobody would call me at this hour unless they had something valuable to impart to me. I didn't even check the screen before I answered. "This is Crewe."

"It's Dunbar," he responded. "I just wanted to let you know she left Scotland. Her plane took off a few hours ago."

I'd asked him to notify me if her situation ever changed. She said she was leaving in a week, but she obviously cut the trip short—because she gave up on me. I listened to the rain as I stayed on the phone, unsure how to respond. "Thanks for letting me know."

"Good night, sir." He hung up.

I kept the phone to my ear even though he was gone. I listened to the line go dead before I tossed the phone back onto the nightstand. My eyes immediately returned to the window, where the water stuck to the glass then dripped down.

She really left.

It was over.

I'd never have to hear from her again.

I could go back to my life.

It should come as a relief, like a toxin had been removed from my bloodstream. But instead of feeling joyful, I felt something else entirely.

Pain.

6

LONDON

JOSEPH CALLED ME. "How's it going?"

"Good." I tucked the phone between my ear and shoulder as I carried the grocery bags to the counter. I left the front door wide open because I didn't have enough hands. "I just picked up a few things to make dinner."

"Ooh…like what?"

"Nothing fancy. Grilled cheese and rice pilaf."

"Uh…those don't go together."

"Then you obviously haven't tried it. It's delicious." I walked back to the living room and shut the door. "Where are you now?"

"I shouldn't say things like that over the phone. But I can tell you I'm in Europe."

"There're fifty countries in Europe…that doesn't narrow it down."

"That's the point," he said with a chuckle. "So you've settled in?"

"Yeah. I'm working at the hospital again. I'm part time right now, but one woman is going on maternity leave, so I'm gonna take her position while she's gone. I'm sure it'll lead to full-time work eventually."

"Yeah, probably. You need anything? Money?"

Like he hadn't given me enough already. "I have plenty. Don't worry about me."

"You know I'll always worry about you."

"Well, don't."

He chuckled again. "So…are you doing alright?" He didn't ask about Crewe specifically, but that's who he was referring to.

"I'm fine." Once Crewe said those words to me, I let him go. I'd never forget what we had and how I felt about him, but I needed to move on. I shouldn't have to fight that hard to be with someone who wasn't so innocent. He made mistakes too—plenty. But putting all the blame on me was ridiculous. It didn't matter how much I loved him. I wasn't putting up with that shit. "I have a date tonight, actually."

"Already?" he asked in surprise. "Where did you meet this guy? Please don't tell me you're using Tinder. That's how people get chopped up."

"I met him at the grocery store just now. We both reached for the last bag of bread, and one thing led to another…"

"So you don't know anything about him?"

"Other than the fact that he's cute and eats bread, not really."

Joseph laughed. "I guess that's all that matters, right? Well, I'm glad you're moving on."

"Yeah. Crewe is too stubborn. I'm not wasting any more time with him."

"Works for me. Never liked the asshole anyway."

This time I didn't defend Crewe. "I feel like we're always talking about me. What's new with you?"

"Not much. Just work."

Work that I didn't want to know anything about. "Do you have a woman in your life?"

"A few. Nothing serious."

I could tell by his tone that topic wasn't up for discussion. "Well, I'll let you go. I've gotta get ready for my date."

"Wait, you said you were making grilled cheese and rice for dinner. So are you meeting him after that?"

"I was planning on eating that after the date." After we rolled around in my bed for an hour. The guy was hot, and I needed to get laid. It'd been nearly six weeks, and Crewe already had lovers in his bed. Plus, he was never coming back.

Joseph didn't pry anymore, probably assuming the worst. "Talk to you later."

"Bye."

I met Roy at a sandwich place a few blocks from my house. I picked the place because it was cheap and laid-back. I didn't like fancy dinners that required an expensive outfit and several courses.

Sandwiches were fine with me.

Roy was cute. I could tell he worked out because he had a nice body. He was a firefighter, which was an extra plus. He was easy to talk to and sweet. In fact, he was too good to be true. It made alarms go off in my head. "Can I ask you something?"

"Sure. What's up?"

"You're too good to be true, so what's your baggage?"

"My baggage?" he asked.

"Did you just get out of a relationship? Divorced? Something like that?"

He smiled despite the awkward question. "Actually, yeah. I just got out of a serious relationship three weeks ago. It's probably too soon for me to be dating, but I thought you were pretty, and I didn't want to pass up the opportunity."

He was super sweet. "Well, that's flattering. I just got out of a relationship too." It was nice dating a guy who didn't know anything about my past. He didn't stare at me like I was damaged goods—not like the guys my friends set me up with. "So that's perfect for both of us."

"Yeah, I guess so."

We finished our meal and just sat there and talked to each other. I already knew the basics and didn't need any more information. He clearly was a good guy, not a serial killer. And since we were both in difficult situations, I didn't feel like I was ruining any potential by being forward. "You wanna come back to my place?" I didn't beat around the bush because I wanted my message to be clear. I wasn't inviting him over for a drink or a movie.

I just wanted sex.

His eyes lit up at the question. "Definitely."

Neither one of us had to work the next morning, so Roy and I slept in. When we both woke up, we made breakfast and then watched morning cartoons like kids. The sex was good, and it was enough to get me off.

It'd been so long that it didn't take much.

I didn't think about Crewe because I wouldn't allow myself to.

It's not like he thought about me.

Roy hung around for an hour or two, and we got to know each other a little better. I didn't have any expectations of seeing him again, and I didn't have a clue what he wanted from me. If this was just a one-time thing, that was perfectly fine.

Roy showered and got dressed before he returned to the living room. "So, you wanna go out again sometime?"

After everything that happened with Crewe, I was just looking for a hookup. It would take me a while before I was in a place to actually fall for someone. Roy probably assumed that, but maybe it needed to be clearer. "I'm not looking for anything serious right now. Honestly, a booty call situation would be perfect."

When he smiled, he had a dimple in one cheek. "That's the answer every guy dreams of."

"Are you one of those guys?"

He shrugged. "I don't want to get into another relationship either, but I do like you. I think that's perfect." He stuck out his hand.

I shook it. "Works for me."

"Awesome. I guess I'll see you later."

"Yeah, sure." I walked him to the door and gave him a kiss goodbye. "Until then."

He crossed the threshold then turned around to look at me. "So…would it be too forward if I came by after work?"

"Not at all." I gave him another kiss before I let him slip through my arms and walk away.

When I walked back into the apartment, I didn't feel any remorse or guilt. I was moving on with my life, picking up one piece at a time. I would never find anyone who was remotely similar to Crewe, but maybe that was a good thing.

I needed something new.

I had a long shift in the ER that night. Lots of traumas, lots of ambulances. Every time I went to work, I thought about the night Crewe was shot. His blood had soaked my clothes, and I still hadn't gotten rid of them.

I had no idea why I kept them.

I stayed an hour over because there were so many patients to see. I didn't care about the overtime pay, just helping out the physicians on staff. When I finally grabbed my coat and walked out of the automatic doors, I was exhausted. Roy was supposed to come over when he finished his shift, and I knew that was at any minute.

I walked up the sidewalk and headed back to my apartment, noticing the piles of snow on the ground. The snow came early this year, making the air cold and dry. I stuffed my hands in my pockets and walked.

I knew there was someone behind me because I could feel his footsteps. He gradually came closer to me, and when we passed a lone streetlight, I saw his tall shadow stretch across the concrete.

No one was around, and it was a bad side of town. Maybe I was just being paranoid, but after being drugged and taken across the world, any unusual behavior was alarming to me. This guy may have seen me in the hospital and thought I was cute. He bided his time until I got off work to make his move.

I discreetly dug into my pocket and pulled out my keys. I inserted the biggest one between my knuckles, prepared to stab him in the eye if he made a move. I held my phone in my other hand, gripping it tightly by the base, ready to be used as a weapon.

He sped up and came closer to me, close enough to touch me.

I spun around with both of my weapons up and ready. "Get the fuck away from me." I stepped back when I recognized his face, my hands slowly lowering.

Crewe.

In a thick winter coat and dark jeans, he wore dark colors to make him blend in with the night. His face was cleanly shaven, and his eyes held his surprise at my violent reaction. "I didn't mean to scare you."

"Then why did you follow me like a stalker?"

He stepped back and put his hands in his pockets. "I appreciate the way you protected yourself."

"Thanks…I guess." I put my phone and keys back in my pocket, but my heart was still beating so fast from the adrenaline. The fact that my stalker was Crewe terrified me in a completely different way. I didn't have time to think about what any of this meant. He was standing right in front of me, looking at me with those brown eyes I used to find solace in. "Why are you here?" When I said goodbye to him in Scotland, I meant it. I moved on.

He stared at me in silence, his usual response to all my questions.

"What the hell do you want, Crewe? I spent the last month in Scotland waiting for you. If there was something you wanted to say to me, you had your chance to say it. But now you don't." I turned around and walked up the street again, wanting to get away from the man who played with my heart like a toy.

"London." He followed behind me, his voice close against my ear.

"Good night, Crewe."

He grabbed me by the elbow and yanked me against the brick wall of the insurance building we'd just passed. His body crowded mine until I was flat against the wall, my back feeling the coldness from the bricks.

His brown eyes looked menacing in the dark like this, in the middle of a questionable neighborhood long after midnight. His arms pinned mine against the wall, as if he suspected I might hit him. He pressed his face close to mine, his warm breath falling over my cold skin. "I'm here now, so you're going to have to deal with it."

I tried to shove him, but he was too heavy. "That's not how this works. I stayed there for a month and tried to work this out. I don't want to be a prisoner again, so I'm starting over here. I started seeing someone, and I like him. You missed your chance."

That was the wrong thing to say because his expression turned maniacal. "Who?"

"What does it matter? How's Sasha, by the way?" I didn't have a clue if that was the woman he was bedding, but I didn't know any of their other names.

His eyes narrowed, but he didn't answer. "Honestly, I don't know why I'm here. I'm still fucking pissed, but I can't stop thinking about you. I can't sleep. I can't get over you. Everything is just so…bleak. I don't know what to do."

"You came all the way here to tell me that?" I asked incredulously. "You could have just called."

"I didn't call for the same reason you didn't call. I wanted to see you. Every time you tried to talk to me, I pushed you away. You'll never understand how much you killed me inside. When I had a bullet stuck in my chest and I was bleeding everywhere…it didn't hurt nearly as much as what you did."

My anger died away when I heard the sincerity of his words. I already knew I'd hurt him because I saw his expression that night, the way he looked utterly hopeless. He didn't even have the motivation to save his own life. That was how much I killed his spirit.

"When I sold you to Bones, he brought this collar…"

My eyes concentrated on his face as I listened to every word.

"He wanted to hook it around your neck for the entire trip back to Italy. When I saw it…I couldn't do it. I didn't keep you because I had a better idea of how to use you. I kept you because I just couldn't do it. I couldn't condemn you to a life of misery when you didn't deserve it." He lowered his face, breaking eye contact with me. "I never put that micro pulse inside your brother's head, I just made you think I did. Because I could never hurt you like that. I would never hurt someone you love. And I don't know when these feelings began to develop…but I knew they started long before you felt them for me."

My hands relaxed against his arms, and instead of pushing him away, I began to pull him closer into me.

"When I was engaged to Josephine…"

He was engaged?

"I thought I loved her. I thought we could have a great life together. But being with you has shown me how much of a mistake that would have been. I was so angry when she left me for Sir Andrew, but after I had you… I thought it was the best thing that had ever happened to me. I've never felt close to anyone like I do with you. It's like…I don't feel so alone."

Josephine left him? I didn't know any of this.

"I've had a hard time accepting everything that happened because it hurt me so much. When I said I loved you, I meant it. The idea of you not meaning it…hurts me more than I can put into words. The fact that any of it was a lie hurt. But you're right, I'm not so innocent. I didn't start off this relationship in the right way. I kept you as a prisoner for most of it. So…I'm just as guilty. You did what you had to do to survive. And I respect that." His hands released my arms and moved to my waist. His fingertips dug into me the way they used to, with desperate need and unbridled passion. "I know I was an ass to you. It's hard for me to forgive someone when they cross me…just a mentality I have."

"But you know I didn't mean to cross you. I told Joseph not to come—"

"I know. And you saved Ariel when you didn't have to. You saved me. I know. I'm just a stubborn man."

"*Very* stubborn man."

He didn't smile, but his eyes lit up slightly. "I thought I could forget about you and move on with my life, but I can't. That's why I'm here. I left Scotland without thinking any of this through…unsure what my goal was. But now that I'm here, I know exactly why I flew across the world to see you." He pressed his body farther into me, sandwiching me against the wall. He rested his forehead against mine and looked down at my lips. It was dark and cold, but the combination of our bodies kept us warm.

"Then what do we do?"

"I don't know," he whispered.

"My life is here. Your life is there. It's already so complicated." When I was in Scotland, I would have stayed if he asked me to. But I moved on from that possibility and settled in New York, assuming that's where my future was.

"I know. But we'll make it work…somehow."

"How?" I pressed. "Because it can't go back to what it was. I'm not gonna sit in my room all day until you're done with work. I need my own life, my own goals. I need to be a free woman, not someone at your beck and call. We need a new start, one where my conditions are met."

He stepped back so I could see his face. "Start over?"

"Yes. You know, where we go on dates and get to know each other. Not where you boss me around all day. I need to be my own person."

"So…you would live somewhere else?"

"Preferably."

"Okay…does that mean you're giving me another chance?" He looked at me with hope in his eyes.

When I said I wasn't coming back, I meant it. But now that I was looking at Crewe, getting lost in his scotch-colored eyes, I didn't want to say no. I didn't want to be stubborn. "I'm willing to forgive and forget if you are."

The smile that was in his eyes finally reached his lips. He came closer to me, his hands gripping my sides once again. He pressed his lips to my forehead and gave me an affectionate kiss, an action that contradicted his nature. "Forgive and forget."

"It's not much, but this is what I call home." We entered my small apartment, and I left my jacket by the door. I was still in my scrubs, so I didn't exactly look my best. I usually wore a tight dress—exactly what Crewe liked.

He didn't look around, his eyes on me. "It's nice. Smells like you." He slid off his thick jacket and placed it next to mine on the coat hanger. His strong shoulders came into view through his t-shirt, as well as the rest of his powerful physique.

I suddenly remembered I hadn't even washed the sheets from the night before with Roy. And he was still under the impression we were hooking up tonight. It was three in the morning, so maybe he already went home.

But what if he didn't?

"You want anything to drink?" I walked into the kitchen to stall, needing to keep him away from my bedroom. Crewe probably wouldn't know some other man had been there just hours before he arrived, but that felt deceitful. I would never want to hop into a bed another woman had just rolled around in.

"Scotch, if you have it." He took a seat on the couch.

I didn't, but I probably wouldn't offer it to him even if I did. "How about water?"

"I guess that'll do." I carried two glasses to the coffee table and sat beside him, feeling my heart race as fast as it did when I spotted him on the sidewalk.

Crewe looked at me, looking like a handsome man I'd found in a bar. He didn't look like Scottish royalty, like a man who'd inherited a castle and a lifetime of wealth. He just looked like a man I'd given my heart to. His hand moved to my thigh, his strong fingers squeezing my muscle gently. The look he gave me wasn't nearly as intense as it normally was, but it hinted at the old affection he used to show me. It was the first time I looked at him and didn't see the anger on his face. "You want to head back with me tomorrow?"

"Back to Scotland?"

"Yeah. If you need some time to wrap up things with your job, I can wait. I can do most of my work from my laptop."

He expected me to drop my life and take off with him again —typical. "I have a life here now, Crewe. I have a job I like, and I'm starting classes again in the fall. I said I wanted to start over, not go back to how we were."

His gaze turned searing, pregnant with disappointment. "Then how do you expect to do this? You know I can't move here."

"And I can't move there either."

His eyes narrowed even further. "You were prepared to live there when you stayed in Scotland."

"I know. But you let me go. I meant what I said, Crewe. That was your only chance. You had four weeks to change your mind, but you didn't."

He pulled his hand off my thigh, his gaze turning hostile. "Now look who's stubborn."

I let the jab wash over my skin. "I've already sacrificed enough for you, in case you've forgotten. How would you feel if I asked you to walk away from your business, your home, and your friends just because I said so? I know you, Crewe. You couldn't give up your life the way I gave up mine. You would never be happy."

"Well, I won't be happy with you living all the way here by yourself."

"I'll be fine. Don't worry about me."

"Now that I've seen you walk home alone at night, I don't believe that."

"If you attacked me, I would have stabbed you in the eye."

"And I would have taken you just like I did last time," he said coldly.

This conversation was taking a steep nose dive. "Those are my terms, Crewe."

"If this is a relationship, we both get terms."

"Yes, you're right. But I'm not leaving. I'm finishing school like I planned."

"And how will we see each other?"

"When I have breaks, I'll fly out and see you. When you have time, you can fly out and see me."

Now he looked like he wanted to strangle me. "Is this a joke? I'm not doing a long-distance relationship. Those never work. I want you in my bed every single night. I want us to be together, not on different continents. Your stubbornness is annoying."

I scoffed. "You're one to talk."

Crewe clenched his jaw tightly. "You're a bright woman. You know your plan is unrealistic and unattainable. That's not a relationship. That's a long-distance booty call. I'm always down for a hookup, but not like this."

I wasn't stupid. I knew what I was offering was a little ridiculous. But I was tired of being the one to sacrifice everything for the relationship. I gave up six months of my life for this man. I wasn't giving up anything else. "I don't have a better idea."

He leaned back into the couch and sighed, his annoyance filling up the apartment like the heater on a cold day.

I didn't look at him because I didn't want to see his anger. I'd looked at it enough times.

He sat up again. "What do you need, exactly?"

"What?"

"What are the specific things you need? School, right? What else?"

"Independence. My own apartment. My freedom…"

"Okay, you can have all of that in Scotland. We can enroll you in a medical program there, we can get you a flat, and you can do whatever you want. How about that?"

It was the only reasonable compromise I could think of. But it still wasn't what I had planned. "That would mean I'd be living there forever…because then I can only practice medicine in the UK. I can't just transfer that back to America. I'd have to retake a few classes."

Crewe stared at me with an unreadable expression. "We're both making sacrifices here."

"What sacrifices are you making?" I demanded.

"Everything. You think I want you to live alone? You think I want you to be at school all day? If I had it my way, we would go back to exactly how we were. So yes, I am making sacrifices."

"But this isn't going to last forever. I'm moving all the way there and going to school, and then when you get married, I'm going to have to move back and redo a year or two of medical school."

"Who said anything about marriage?" he asked.

"You told me you have to marry someone of your stature. I'm obviously not the right match."

He rubbed his fingers across his chin and sighed. "That's the last thing on my mind right now. Let's not worry about what's gonna happen down the road. Let's just focus on now."

"That's kinda difficult for me to do…"

He rested his hands on his thighs and brought his hands together. He bowed his head and stared at his hands, the corded veins extending up his forearms and across the back of his palms. "All I know is…I've hated being without you. And if I feel that way now, I'm sure it'll be worse as time goes on. I really can't picture myself with anyone else right now. So I say we don't worry about it."

It was nothing concrete, but it was sweet nonetheless. "Okay."

"Okay? Does that mean you'll move to Scotland?" He didn't keep the hope out of his voice.

I couldn't believe I was going to make the sacrifice, but there were no other options. I could stay here, but the city didn't feel the same anyway. I wanted to have my life the way it was before Crewe took me, but that wasn't possible. So much had changed. I wasn't the same person I used to be. "Yeah…it does."

He grabbed my hand and gave me a squeeze. "It's gonna be an uphill battle for us, so at least we figured that part out."

"Uphill battle?"

"Ariel will never approve of this."

I respected her as his business partner, but I didn't understand why she had so much power over him. "This is your personal life, not hers. I don't understand why her opinion matters to you."

"It matters because she warned me about you—and she was dead on about it."

I looked away.

"It matters because you distracted me from what's important. It matters because some of my men died because of you. It matters because everything changed the second you walked into my life. They don't trust you, so they don't trust me. That's why it fucking matters." He pulled his hand away.

I didn't know what to say. I'd already apologized for everything that happened, and I didn't see the point in doing it again. Now we needed to concentrate on moving forward. "Then how is this gonna work?"

He didn't respond for nearly a minute. "It'll just take some time. She'll get over it—eventually."

"And Joseph?"

"What about him?"

"I can't have my brother and the man I love hating each other."

He stared at his hands, his shoulders straight but heavy. "I don't know what you expect me to do about that. It is what it is. He's not gonna change, and I'm certainly not going to change."

Maybe a reconciliation would come in time. Joseph stole money from Crewe and then shot him. It would take Crewe a long time to let that go.

He leaned back against the couch and looked at me, his brown eyes no longer annoyed. He stared at me the way he did on the sidewalk, like he'd rather be doing something other than talking.

I knew what was coming next, but I didn't know how to circumvent it. We couldn't sleep in my bed, not when it was covered in Roy's cologne. "Where are you staying?"

His eyes immediately narrowed. "With you."

"I mean, what hotel?"

"It's down the road. Why?"

"How about we go there?"

"Why would we go there if we're here?" He patted the cushion of the sofa. "This place is comfortable enough for what I have in mind."

I missed sex with Crewe, along with all the other perks of our relationship. I would love to get lost in him again, to feel that heavenly stretching his body caused. But the sex wouldn't feel so good if he figured out a man had been here less than twenty-four hours ago.

Like the universe was out to get me, there was a knock on the door.

At this time of night, it could only be one person.

Crewe's eyes darted to the door, and that typical look of threat grew in his features. His eyes turned dark and empty, hiding all of his thoughts like he'd just erected a wall. His arms flexed in reaction, and his shoulders rounded in preparation for the problem that just emerged. "Are you expecting someone?"

"Uh…yeah." I had nothing to feel bad about, but this was still the most awkward situation in the world. I knew Crewe had been with other women, but at least I didn't have the displeasure of looking at them.

His eyes narrowed in a sinister way, understanding the implication of words immediately. "Would you like me to answer the door?" His jaw was clenched harder than I'd ever seen it. It was a miracle he could make out words at all.

"No." I jumped out of the chair and headed to the door, wishing the couch wasn't so close to the entryway. The couch faced the opposite way, but all Crewe had to was turn around if he wanted to get a look at Roy.

This was bad.

I hustled through the doorway and shut the door behind me.

Roy was in gray sweatpants and a t-shirt, his hair still damp from a shower. He'd just gotten off work and probably stopped by on the way. "Hey. You're still up?"

"Yeah, I got off work late."

"Cool." He smiled, one dimple forming on his cheek.

"But…I'm gonna have to take a rain check with you. A permanent one. I told you I just got out of a relationship… but now I'm back in the relationship."

"Oh, really?" he asked. "The guy finally got his head on straight. Good for him. You're a serious catch."

I'd just blown him off, but he had a great attitude about it. "I'm sorry about this…"

"Don't be. I knew it was too good to be true." He released a hollow chuckle. "Well, good luck." He extended his hand.

I shook it. "Thanks. You too."

He walked away and disappeared from the hallway.

When I walked back inside, I was surprised to see Crewe where I left him. He had an angry side to him, and I was surprised I hadn't witnessed it. He was possessive and jealous, but he kept his rage under control. "He's gone."

Crewe rose to his full height, over six feet of muscle and man. His jeans made his ass look great, and the sleeves of his shirt were tight on his arms. His body was just as sexy as his face. When he faced me, he still wore that grim expression of anger. "Let's go to my place."

He must have figured out why I didn't want to stay here. At least I didn't have to spell it out for him. "Just let me grab a few things…"

———

We got out of the car and stood on the sidewalk of the hotel he was staying at. Hardly anyone was on the sidewalk at this time of night, but to the left stood a man in a black trench coat with a black beanie over his head. He was taping a paper to the pole of the streetlight.

Crewe whispered something to the driver and slipped him some money.

I kept watching the man, wondering what he was posting at this time of night. When he was finished with the paper, he walked toward me and held out a sheet. "I'm sorry to bother you…have you seen this woman?"

I took the paper and examined the woman's features. She had dark brown hair and a pretty face. She was an engineer for the city but went missing a few weeks ago. Her name was Pearl. "I'm sorry, I don't."

Crewe emerged from nowhere and placed his body between the two of us. "Can I help you?"

"He's just trying to find his friend," I said.

"Have you seen her?" The man held the paper out to Crewe. "She's a really good friend of mine…disappeared on a trip to Mexico. I keep thinking she might turn up, but there's been no luck."

"Sorry, man." Crewe pulled me into his side and guided me to the entrance of the hotel.

"I hope you find her," I said over my shoulder before we walked inside and took the elevator to the room.

His hotel room looked like more of a penthouse. It was bigger than a home for a family of four, with more amenities than he would ever use, but dukes seemed to travel in style. It had a full kitchen, two living rooms, and three bedrooms.

What did he need all of that for? "It's nice."

He carried my bag into the master bedroom and set it on the edge of the bed. I would have carried it myself, but he insisted on handling it. He slipped off his shoes and immediately began to undress. Once the shirt was off, his perfect torso was revealed. It was lined with grooves of strong muscle, delicious skin, and the large scar that sat above his heart.

I stilled as I stared at it, seeing the strange lines that stretched out around it. The scars were more noticeable because of his white skin. It contrasted like white font on black paper. It was difficult to look at because I remembered exactly how it had appeared when the blood was soaking into his shirt as he lay on the ground. I'd ripped his shirt in half to stabilize the wound as much as I could, but nothing could stop the profuse bleeding.

I was surprised he hadn't bled out and died.

He undid his jeans and pushed them to his ankles. When he was in just his boxers, he walked to the bed and yanked the sheets back.

I couldn't look at him anymore. Tears formed in my eyes when I remembered the horrifying night. When I got him to the hospital, I didn't know if he was going to live. I thought the love of my life was going to fade away before we even had a real chance to enjoy each other.

I hated to let anyone see me cry, especially Crewe. It was an act of weakness, and I never let anyone see me that way. I moved into the hallway and found the bathroom. I darted inside and shut the door behind me, getting a moment of privacy so I could let my tears fall. Even though Crewe made a full recovery, I would never erase the memory of the moment his body jerked and fell to the floor. The strongest man I knew had been crippled by a bullet, and when he lay there dying, he had no motivation to get up again—because of me.

I sank to the floor and leaned against the wall. I hadn't even turned on the light, and only the crack under the door gave me illumination. Instead of letting myself sob my heart out, I controlled my breathing and steadied my tears, knowing Crewe would check on me if I took too long.

His bare feet appeared at the door a few seconds later, and he lightly rapped his knuckles against the door. "Lovely?"

Another tear escaped when I heard the nickname. It'd been so long since he'd called me that. Lately, it'd only been London—and it wasn't the same. "I'll be out in a minute." I did my best to keep my voice strong so he wouldn't realize I was sitting on the bathroom floor with tears in the back of my throat.

Crewe opened the door and invited himself inside. He didn't do a double take when he noticed me on the bathroom floor, as if he already suspected I was there. He kept the door halfway open so some light could come into the room. His thighs were muscular and toned, looking athletic as he moved in his boxers. He moved to the spot beside me against the wall and sat down, his long legs stretching out before him. Naked or clothed, he looked just as beautiful.

I stared straight ahead, not wanting to look at his scar again.

"Talk to me," he whispered. He placed his arm around me and pulled me into his side, letting my face move to his shoulder.

I closed my eyes when I felt his warm skin against my cheek. My face automatically turned, and I pressed a kiss to his shoulder, tasting the skin I used to devour every night. My arm hooked through his, and I closed my eyes, comforted by his presence.

The bathroom had beige tile with matching sinks. A large walk-in shower stood in the corner, and a nice display of towels hung on the rack. The sounds of our breathing echoed in the enclosure, and the light from the hallway stretched across our feet.

"I just…I was so scared I was going to lose you."

"I'm right here, Lovely."

"I know. But when it was happening, I'd never been so scared. It was like losing my parents all over again, but worse. It was worse than when I thought I was going to Bones. It felt like the end of everything."

"It'd take a lot more than a bullet to kill me."

"But it almost did kill you. And seeing all the blood…and the fact that you wouldn't get up."

"I was devastated," he whispered. "But you got me up."

"No, Ariel did."

"Because she threatened to kill you. I had to get up. I had to do the right thing for you. I've always put you first…even if you don't realize it."

"I do." I kissed his shoulder again. "I'm so sorry about everything, Crewe. I never wanted you to get hurt. If something happened to you…I wouldn't have been able to go on."

"But nothing happened to me." He turned his head and pressed a kiss to my forehead. "I'm here—with you."

CREWE

I GOT the best night of sleep in a long time.

My arms were locked around her body so she couldn't slip away from me in the middle of the night. I wasn't afraid of her slipping away, but my subconscious was. I was tired of the loneliness, tired of the nightmares.

She was my cure.

I woke up the following morning and saw her wrapped tightly around me, clinging to me as if she had the same fear. She was in my t-shirt and her panties, her long and slender legs brushing against mine under the sheets. I didn't move because I didn't want to wake her up. I entertained myself by watching her sleep, watching her chest rise and fall rhythmically.

When I returned to Scotland with London in tow, I knew that would cause a rift between Ariel and me. None of my other employees cared for her, not when she was the reason some of the men lost their lives. The only person who did like her was Finley, and that was because he hardly interacted with her.

Honestly, I had no idea what I was doing.

I didn't know how this was going to work or for how long. Taking an appropriate wife had been a priority because I did need to have children, and not just to continue my line. Kids were something I'd wanted for my own reasons.

To regrow my own family.

I didn't have parents or a brother. I was all that remained of my bloodline. If I had sons and daughters, I could share my legacy with them. Hopefully, I could look at them and see my own parents' features looking back at me.

Since London wasn't a suitable partner, that set me back. She didn't have any wealth or connections to bring to the marriage. I wasn't even sure if she wanted to have children. She didn't seem like the kind of person who wanted to put her career aside to be a mother. She was just as ambitious as I was.

Maybe I could spend a year or two with her before I had to let her go.

Or maybe I was just setting myself up for torture.

I really didn't know.

She woke up a moment later, her big and beautiful lashes opening to reveal the emerald eyes that haunted my dreams.

She took in my features slowly, the recognition gradually dawning on her.

She needed a moment to understand this was real.

"Morning." She slid her hand across my cheek, feeling the stubble that had grown overnight.

"Morning." I dug my hand into her hair and kissed her, feeling the electricity immediately surge down my spine. I didn't make love to her last night because I was too furious about her nighttime visitor. I didn't like thinking about the last time he was in her apartment, the last time they fucked.

So I didn't ask.

But I hadn't been able to get it off my mind. I kept picturing a man's hands all over her body—a pair that didn't belong to me. It made me more than angry—more than jealous. In fact, he broke my heart.

But I had no right to be angry. She told me there hadn't been anyone else when she stayed in Scotland. If I hadn't taken so long, nothing would have happened. The second she came to New York, she resumed her life without thinking about me.

She wasn't bluffing.

So it was my fault.

I'd been with other women too, so my hands weren't clean. But that didn't make it hurt any less. I wanted to be with her when there wasn't another guy in the picture, sitting on her doorstep for an obvious booty call.

My cock was hard, but I tried not to push it into her hip, giving her the wrong idea. If she went down on me or rode me, I wouldn't have the strength to say no. But I didn't want to extend an invitation.

She stretched her arms above her head before she hooked her leg over my hip, pressing my cock right against her own hip.

Now there was no hiding it.

"When do you want to leave?" I asked.

"Leave for what? Breakfast?"

Of course, she was thinking about food. "No. For home."

"As in, you want me to leave today or tomorrow?"

"Preferably."

She sat up in bed, her hair messy from the way my fingers had run through it. "Well, I need to put my two weeks' in first. I signed a six-month lease, so I need to take care of that too. To pack and ship everything will take a while…"

I was already an impatient man, but there was no way I waiting for all of that to get wrapped up. "We can take everything you need on my plane. You've seen it—it's huge."

"My dressers and bed?" she asked incredulously.

"You shouldn't take that stuff anyway. I'll buy you new things."

She stared at me hard.

"What?"

"That's not part of the independence condition. I don't need you to buy me anything."

We hadn't even had breakfast yet, and she was already annoying me. "I don't want you to move in to a shady place like you had in Edinburgh."

"There was nothing wrong with that place."

"It wasn't a good side of town. There's a lot of criminal activity in that area. I know the area a lot better. Let me choose."

"You're gonna choose a castle or something."

"If I were gonna choose a castle, it'd be my castle. No, there's a nice community in Edinburgh that I approve of. I'll get you situated there."

"A community?" I asked.

"A nest of houses. It's in a gated community."

"Well, I don't have a car, so I wanted to walk everywhere."

"You aren't walking anywhere," I snapped. "I'll get you a car or a driver."

That same look returned to her face.

"That's nonnegotiable. Scotland is a beautiful place, but it's certainly not safe."

She made the smart choice by not pressing it. "So I leave all my stuff behind."

"Except the essentials. I'll help you get settled. And if you ever want to change your mind about moving in to the castle, the offer is always on the table." I missed having a quickie on my desk in the middle of the day. I missed seeing her in the bedroom the second I walked in the door. Her need for independence was irritating, but after keeping her as a prisoner for six months, I would be insensitive not to understand.

"I know, Crewe."

"So, can you leave tomorrow?"

"I still need to put in my two weeks'."

"Why?" I demanded. "Just tell them you're leaving."

"What if one of your employees just got up and left?"

"I'd get over it and hire someone else. Life goes on."

"Well, I don't own a business, so I can't afford that luxury. I need to be a good employee if I want to get a good job later down the road."

"Don't forget who you're sleeping with," I reminded her. "I can get you whatever job you want." Even though I'd prefer it if she had no job at all.

"I'd rather get a job on my own, Crewe."

I hated it when she didn't need me. That clingy act she put on before was probably all for show, but I wish she would behave that way again. "Two weeks is too long."

"You don't have to stay. I can put most of my stuff on your plane then fly out on my own later."

I didn't want to return to Scotland without her. I didn't want to sleep in that big bed alone. I wanted my woman protected in my arms and surrounded by the stone walls of my keep. "You're really going to wait two weeks?"

"Yes." She was just as stubborn as I was. Sometimes I respected it, and sometimes it just annoyed me.

When she didn't leave me any other choice, I caved. All of this could have been avoided if I'd just pulled my head out of my ass sooner. We would already be in Scotland right now. "Fine. But you're staying here with me. Move your stuff out of the apartment and hand over the keys."

"And where do I put my things?"

"I'll arrange for my men to fly it out so it'll be ready when we get there. How does that sound?" That was the best compromise we were going to find.

"Good. And you're going to stay here the whole time?"

I wasn't leaving her again. "I can work from my laptop."

"You said that already but didn't answer my question."

"Yes. I'm staying here." I was going to make up for the past month in the next two weeks. I didn't just want good sex like I had been having with my other lovers. I wanted the incredible passion I only experienced with London. Ever since I'd fallen in love with this woman, the sex had blown my mind. It didn't matter how good Sasha was between the sheets—she couldn't compare to London.

"Then I'll get my stuff and talk to my landlord."

I propped myself up on my elbow. "Great. Now we can talk about breakfast."

"Yes!" She snatched the menu off the nightstand and flipped it open. "What are you getting?"

"Egg whites and a protein shake."

She rolled her eyes. "Still boring as ever…"

"My body isn't boring."

She rolled her eyes again, but this time she smiled. She looked at the menu again. "I'm getting the French toast, bacon, and eggs. And a coffee. Oh, and an orange juice."

"Then call it in."

She lay on her stomach and grabbed the phone off the nightstand, her knees bent and ankles crossed as her feet rested near her ass. Her curves looked amazing in my t-shirt and her underwear.

My eyes honed in on her ass, and I was thinking about pulling her panties down so I could shove my cock into her pussy. I missed how wet it was. I'd been wearing condoms, and condoms sucked. My eyes couldn't turn away as I listened to her call room service. As much as I wanted to fuck her, I hadn't forgotten about the man who stopped by the apartment. I didn't want to know the details, but I needed to hear them anyway. I needed to know that he meant nothing to her.

That she thought about me when she was with him.

Just as I thought of her when I was with Sasha.

And I needed to know there would be no one else besides the two of us—from here on out.

After we picked up her essentials at her apartment, we headed back to the room. She grabbed her scrubs for work, as well as the rest of her clothing and accessories. The second we walked back into the hotel room, I felt more at ease. Now that she was living with me, even if it was temporary, it felt the way it used to. We shared the same space together, the same bed and the same bathroom. The hotel didn't feel like a castle, but it would do.

She put her stuff away in the closet and the drawers, and soon the bathroom counter contained her toothbrush and makeup bag. Her razor was in the shower, as well as the special shampoo she preferred to use on her long hair. Panties were placed in my underwear drawer.

It felt like home.

It was past noon, but I wasn't hungry—at least not for food. I finally had this woman all to myself without any interruptions. If my phone rang, I could ignore it. Ariel thought I was here on business, and I would allow her to think that until I was ready to come clean.

I came behind London as she stood at my dresser, and I ran my finger up her arm. I moved up until I reached her shoulder, feeling her skin prickle under my touch. Her breathing changed slightly, reacting to my sudden proximity. She was an expert at reading my mood, especially at times like this.

My hands circled her waist, and I pressed my mouth against her ear. "I missed you." I let my hot breath enter her ear canal, knowing she liked it. I'd been sleeping with her for six months. I knew all the things she enjoyed.

Her hand moved behind her shoulder and around my neck, her fingers digging into my skin as they moved into my hair. Since I'd confronted her on the street, we still hadn't kissed, probably because we both knew where it would lead. "I missed you too."

I pulled her tightly against me, wanting her to feel how hard I was for her. The second she set her things in my drawers, I was reminded of scorching nights with her within the stone walls of the castle. There's nothing I wouldn't give to go back in time and take advantage of those perfect moments. "When you were with him, did you think of me?"

She tensed in my arms.

I waited for her answer.

"Yes."

I gripped her tighter. "Did he make you come?"

She moved against me, her perky ass against my crotch. "Yes…"

"But did he make you come the way I do?" I hated myself for allowing another man to touch my woman. If I'd just kept her close, this never would have happened. But I would make her forget he was ever between her legs.

"No…no one does."

Good answer.

"Did you think of me when you were with them?" she whispered.

I yanked on the neck of her t-shirt and pulled it to the side so I could kiss her bare skin, sealing my mouth around the area and giving her a gentle nick of my teeth. "Yes. They were nothing compared to you."

She leaned back into me and turned her head my way, her breaths falling over my skin.

"Just you and me from now on." My hand slid down her stomach and into the front of her jeans. My fingers found her underwear, and I slipped them under the lacy material. "Understood?"

She took a deep breath when she felt my fingertips reach her clit. "Yes…"

I rubbed the nub harder, feeling her writhe against my chest. I knew when I slid inside her warm channel it would be as incredible as I remembered. But I was torturing myself, taking my time to make the final moment truly incredible. I loved making her feel good, making her heavy breathing escalate the longer I touched her. I used another finger to rub her, to massage the area aggressively and make her nerve endings go off. Listening to her moan quietly was just as satisfying as if I were deep inside her. My mouth moved over hers, and I kissed her as my hand pleased her, making her want me more with every passing second. I wanted her to beg me to fuck her, beg me to rip her clothes off.

Her hand cupped the back of my hand, and she kissed me back with the same desperation. Her tongue dove into my mouth, and she filled my lungs with air as she breathed through the pleasure.

Kissing her was just as I remembered—powerful, blinding, and sensational.

How did I go so long without kissing her?

She gripped my wrist and steadied my hand just as she moaned into my mouth. "Stop."

My fingers kept going. "I'll stop when I feel like it."

"I want to come when you're inside me…"

My fingers slowly stopped as I kept my face pressed against hers. I wanted to watch her face contort into a look of immense pleasure as she came for me. I could make her come now and again later, but my cock was anxious to feel her tighten around me.

I pulled my fingers out of her pants and placed them in her mouth.

She sucked them immediately, her eyes on me.

My cock twitched in response as I watched her suck her own pleasure off my fingertips. She wasn't kinky or adventurous in bed like some of the women I'd been with, but she had a special touch that made her incredible. I didn't miss the threesomes or the strippers. Why would I want them when I could have London?

I pulled my fingers away and got to work removing her clothes. Her pants were undone and the shirt was gone, and she turned around and did the same to me. With anxious fingers, we peeled away everything until we were both laid bare. I stared at her small and perky tits, missing the way those hard nipples felt in my mouth. I appreciated her perfect hourglass figure, the way her slim waist curved inward with flawless skin. The small muscles of her core could be seen, and they shifted under the surface every time she moved.

I forgot how beautiful she was.

I'd jerked off to her memory countless times, but I could never truly picture her perfection. Seeing her in the flesh reminded me of her incredible qualities, of her stunning beauty that no other woman could match.

I guided her to the bed and got her on her back, exactly where I wanted her. I wanted to see her face, see the way her hair stretched across the pillow and the way her eyes lit up like stars. Rarely did I face a woman during sex. I preferred their face against the comforter and their ass in the air. But I thought London's face was her sexiest feature. Direct eye contact brought me comfort, not unease. I could look into her soul and have her look back into mine without fear.

Her legs circled my waist, and her ankles locked together against my lower back as she prepared to take me. Her fingers hooked under my arms and over my shoulders, gripping me tightly as she positioned herself for the ride ahead.

I rubbed my cock against her folds and felt her lubrication coat the surface of my length. She was ready for me, had been ready since the moment I walked into the room. I pressed my head inside her slit and was greeted by a fold of her moisture.

She was soaked.

"Jesus Christ…" I was used to the uncomfortable dryness of a condom, but I'd never forgotten how incredible she felt. Now I was reliving one of my favorite memories, feeling the pussy I'd become obsessed with. I slid all the way inside her until I was completely sheathed. I held myself steady, feeling my heart race at record-breaking speed.

She dug her nails into me and possessed a fiery expression in her eyes, just as affected by the combination of our bodies as I was. She squeezed her knees against my sides and let out a low moan.

My hands dug into the mattress as I suspended my body on top of hers. I gave my first thrust and slid through her tightness, feeling my entire body shiver in pleasure. She was so slick, wetter than I'd ever felt her.

She craned her neck up and kissed me, her lips gentle despite the tension in both of our bodies. With restrained passion, her lips moved with mine. Her breathing was building into a crescendo, an explosion that would leave her screaming underneath me. Her nails dug into me harder, and her hips worked with mine to meet my thrusts.

I wouldn't last long, but thankfully, she wouldn't either.

"I'm already gonna come…"

I rocked into her harder, pressing her deep into the mattress where she couldn't slip away. I gave her every inch of me over and over, hitting her hard in the perfect spot. I got off on getting her off. She turned me into a real gentleman.

Like I'd hit a button, she ignited. Her sexy legs squeezed my hips as she came around my cock, her moisture oozing down my length all the way to my balls. My name rolled off her tongue in the sexiest way possible. "Crewe…" Her hair was sprawled around her body, her long strands perfect for me to fist.

I wanted to keep going, but my cock couldn't handle the wait. I needed to put my seed inside her now, to claim her as my woman again. After a few more pumps, I released inside her, feeling the most exquisite rush through my body. "Lovely…" Nothing made me feel more like a king than coming inside my queen.

She tightened her legs and pulled me deeper into her, making sure she got every drop I had to give. Her arms hooked around my neck, and she looked into my eyes with a beautiful face and red cheeks. Her eyes were lidded like she was both satisfied and exhausted, but she wanted more the second I was ready to give it. "I missed that so much."

"That makes two of us."

She pulled on her scrubs then placed her hair in a bun. "I need to get to work. I'll see you in a few hours."

I already hated this. "Do you always work the night shift?"

"It's when the ER is the busiest."

Why did she have to choose a career that was so dangerous? "I'll walk you." I grabbed my coat from the coat rack and threw it on.

"You don't need to walk me, Crewe. I'll see you in the morning." Even in baggy scrubs and a jacket, she looked beautiful. No way in hell was I letting her walk around alone.

"I can either walk you or my driver can drop you off and pick you up again."

"Neither is necessary."

I blocked the door with my body and stared her down. "Pick one."

"I've been living in this city my whole life. I'll be fine."

"And my men snatched you without a struggle," I reminded her.

She crossed her arms over her chest, irritated by the comment. "That was totally different, and you know it."

"Anything can happen. That's what I know."

She tried to get to the door, but I didn't move. Like I was a mountain blocking her path, she had no way of getting around me. "Crewe, move."

"Lovely, pick."

London finally saw reason, knowing I wasn't going to change my mind. When I wanted something, I got it. "I guess your driver can take me."

"What time do you get off?"

"Seven."

"I'll ride with you on the way there." I took her hand, and we walked to the lobby together. My driver was at the curb when we walked through the doors, and we got into the back seat and got comfortable for the short drive.

This whole night shift thing was annoying. I was supposed to sleep all night without her. That defeated the purpose of having her in my life. My arm circled her shoulders, and I pressed my face near hers. "Put your two weeks' in?"

"I'll do that tonight."

She didn't do that three days ago? "You couldn't have done that earlier?"

Her green eyes were always a little darker when she was annoyed. "I didn't think a few days would make much of a difference."

"It makes all the difference in the world."

"Well, I'm doing it now. That's all that matters."

The car stopped at the entrance to the hospital, and I got out and walked her to the door. It was cold outside, piles of snow still sprinkled in the gutters. The sky had been overcast all day, and I suspected another storm was coming. "I'll see you in the morning." I gripped her hips and gave her a kiss.

"I might wake you up with a surprise…"

I smiled against her mouth, forgetting about the small argument we'd just had. "I look forward to it."

8

LONDON

I PUT MY TWO WEEKS' in, but since they made the schedule by week, they didn't hold me to the full two weeks. Crewe would be thrilled, but I hadn't told him just yet. I arranged to have all my stuff taken from my apartment, and I put the rest of the stuff on Craig's List. All of my valuables were slowly taken away by college students.

Crewe worked from his office in the hotel room while I was at work. When I came home in the morning, he was usually already awake and on the phone, talking about his thriving scotch business. It didn't seem like he had much to do with his intelligence business anymore, but I'd never really asked him about it—because I didn't want to know.

When I walked into the hotel room, he was sitting at his desk near the floor-to-ceiling windows where the natural light filtered through. Since he wasn't going to be seen by anyone, he didn't wear a suit, sticking to jeans and a t-shirt.

I preferred the casual look, where he could show off his nice arms and his sculpted shoulders. His ass always looked great in his dark jeans, and the dark colors he wore always complemented his brown eyes. He looked great in a suit, of course. But when he didn't wear a suit, I could see more of the man underneath.

I walked inside and gave him a slight wave.

He was on the phone, but his eyes were trained on me. "Yeah, I agree." He scooted the chair back from the desk and patted his thigh, beckoning me toward him even though he was in the middle of a conversation. "Let's increase production. The more visibility we have around the world, the better the marketing."

I sat on his thigh and wrapped my arm around his shoulders.

His arm circled my waist, and he held my gaze as he finished his phone call. "Let me know." He hung up and tossed the phone on the desk.

"Who was that?"

"Pias."

I was surprised it wasn't Ariel.

"He's my ears and eyes in the distillery. Distributor."

"Oh, okay. I think I met him once."

"You probably have. So, how was work?" He didn't take much of an interest in my job, probably because he didn't like the fact that I was gone for twelve hours at a time and in the middle of the night. If he had it his way, I'd stay home all day long and service him like a whore in a brothel.

"Hectic. There was a gang rivalry tonight, so we had a few patients with gunshot wounds."

Crewe nodded, but his jaw tensed. I knew him well enough to understand what he was thinking, that he didn't like me working in an environment he deemed unsafe. But there was nothing he could do about it, so he kept his thoughts bottled up inside. "I had a hard time sleeping without you last night."

"Well, you shouldn't have any more trouble. Today was my last day."

"It was?" His eyes narrowed in interest.

"I put my two weeks in a while ago, but since they make a weekly schedule, they just didn't schedule me."

He didn't smile with his lips, but his eyes showed his relief. "So we can leave whenever we want now?"

"I guess so."

"Good. I'm eager to get home. No offense, but I'm not a big fan of your country."

"You obviously haven't seen much of it, then. Where have you been?"

"New York and LA."

"You prefer nature and the outdoors. No wonder why you didn't like it. When we have time, I'll show you some of the most beautiful places you've ever seen."

A grin stretched across his face. "Consider it a date."

"Great."

His phone rang on the desk, and Ariel's name popped up. He silenced the call and returned his attention to me. "Should I get the plane prepared now, or do you wanna leave tomorrow?"

"How about a red-eye flight? I need to get some sleep."

"Sounds good to me."

"Besides, you have some work to do." I glanced at his phone before I stood up.

"I'm always working. It's okay to take a break now and then." He stood up and walked with me, towering over me with his masculine height and build. He followed me into the bedroom where I shed my scrubs and dropped them onto the floor.

"But I don't want to be a distraction…and it seems like I'm always a distraction." I stepped into the bathroom connected to the bedroom and got into the shower.

Crewe stared at me through the glass then leaned against the wall with his ankles and arms crossed. He watched the water pelt my naked body and drip to the drain in the floor.

"You're just going to stare at me?"

"Yep."

"Think of all the work you could be getting done."

"Don't give a damn about work right now." His eyes roamed over my naked body. "Once you're clean and dry, I'm gonna make my move. I'm just not sure what I'm going to do yet. I'm gonna take my time figuring it out."

"Yeah?" I massaged shampoo into my hair then tilted my head back to rinse it out. "Have any ideas?"

"I think I want your ass in my face. That's always a beautiful view."

"Maybe can we face a mirror—that way you can get both views."

His smile immediately dropped, and his expression hardened.

I liked teasing him. It was always so easy.

I slowed down and took longer than I had before, making the time stretch on indefinitely.

"You're being a pain in the ass, you know that?"

"You tease me all the time. It's my turn to tease you."

"If you tease me any longer, I'm gonna get in there with you."

"Shower sex isn't bad." I preferred lovemaking in the bed, where we had all the room we wanted. We could change positions and not feel guilty for wasting water. Sex in the shower was for a quick fuck before work in the morning.

I finally finished and patted myself dry with a towel. My hair was damp, but I didn't think he would mind.

Crewe watched me the entire time, waiting for me to come out of the shower so he could ambush me. The longer he had to wait, the angrier he seemed. He was the kind of person who never had to wait for anything in life, but with me, his patience was seriously tested.

I finally swung the door open and stepped onto the mat.

The door hadn't even closed yet before he lifted me into his arms and carried me to the bed. He dropped me on the mattress then ripped the towel off so my naked body was revealed. No foreplay was involved, not that I needed it. His pants and boxers were gone, and he was deep inside me an instant later, his throbbing cock soaked in my pool of moisture. "Lovely." He grabbed the back of my neck and pressed my face against the mattress, forcing my ass to stick higher up into the air.

I liked it soft and gentle, but I also liked it rough just like this. I liked it when Crewe fucked me like he just wanted to get off, like he needed to give me his seed as desperately as I wanted to take it. "Crewe."

He pounded into me hard, giving me every inch of his length with speed. "I'm gonna do this to you. Every. Fucking. Day."

I gripped his wrists as he pushed me into a powerful climax. "Please do."

The plane was already spacious with his whole crew on board, but when it was just the two of us and a few of his men, it felt like a palace in the sky. Crewe sat beside me with his tablet out, working on emails as the plane prepared for takeoff.

After flying so much, I figured I would get used to this. But once the engines thrust and we sped down the runway, I gripped Crewe's hand for dear life. The plane lifted off the ground and headed high into the sky, carrying us away from the ground and into the deep blue up above.

Crewe placed the tablet on his lap and gripped my hand tighter. "You wanna know something?"

I knew he was trying to distract me. "Sure."

"I've flown at least two hundred times in my life. On different planes, on airlines, on other people's planes… never had a single problem."

"Because you're a duke."

"Well, you're traveling with one, so I assure you nothing is going to happen to his plane. Alright?"

"I know we aren't gonna crash. It makes me uneasy. I wish I would just get over it…but I never do."

He brought my hand to his lips and gave it a gentle kiss. "We're all afraid of something, Lovely. It's okay."

"What are you afraid of?" The question popped into my mind automatically. The plane was still accelerating into the sky, and it would be a while before it leveled off.

A cloud of annoyance didn't pass over his eyes like it normally would. "Betrayal. Disloyalty."

"Nothing life-threatening?"

"Dying doesn't scare me," he said simply. "Dying is the beginning of peace, if you ask me. The lowest times of my life have always been caused by someone betraying me. First, it was the man who murdered my parents. Second, it was Josephine. And the third…you know what the third is."

I hadn't asked him about Josephine because there was never a right time. But now we were on a plane with twelve hours to kill. The plane finally leveled out, and we began to cruise at the right altitude.

Crewe loosened his grip but didn't drop my hand.

"So…you were engaged?" I didn't know how else to broach the subject.

"Yes." Crewe wasn't talkative on the matter. He wasn't usually talkative about anything other than sex.

"What happened?"

"I told you what happened."

"You know what I mean." Times like these made me miss his honesty. When we were close, he opened up to me a lot more. I probably could have asked him about this if I'd known about it.

"We were introduced by mutual friends. I liked her, and she liked me. She was a good match for me because she has a lot of ties to African businesses. Her own wealth exceeds mine. But when I got to know her, I actually liked her for her. When I told her I loved her, I meant it. When I asked her to marry me, I wasn't just interested in her connections. But six months into the engagement, she decided to leave me for Sir Andrew because he has a greater chance of being king someday if he plays his cards right. So she left."

Damn, she was stupid.

"She came back to me a few months ago and asked if we could work it out. I said that would never happen, but she didn't drop the subject—until she saw you."

She better back off. I'd punch that bitch in the face if she didn't. "Do you still love her?"

He held my gaze without flinching. "I don't believe you can love two women at once."

That was enough to answer my question. "When she wanted you back, did you love her?"

"No. I stopped loving her the instant she left me. All the feelings were sucked out of my soul at the snap of a finger. She left me for a man with more wealth, so she never really loved me anyway. She was using me. I consider myself lucky."

My thumb brushed over his knuckles now that I knew the entire story. No wonder why Crewe was so wounded by what I'd done. He'd been betrayed recently, so I'd ripped open an old wound. "I'm sorry…"

"No reason to be sorry, Lovely. I know it hurts you to know I'm in pain, but I assure you, I'm no longer in pain. At the moment, I'm very happy." He leaned toward me and pressed his forehead to mine. He didn't place a kiss on my forehead or rub his nose against mine. But the affection was still special. It made us connected in a new way.

"For what it's worth, she's an idiot."

He smiled as he pulled way. "Yes, she is an idiot—but for different reasons."

"Does she even like the guy?"

"Doesn't sound like it. And I know he screws other women."

He cheats on her? "And she's okay with it?"

"No much she can do. She can't leave him for someone else. One scandal was bad enough, and any man besides the two of us would just be a step down for her. She has to suck it up and accept the consequences."

I would feel bad for any woman having to marry a man she didn't love, but I felt no pity for her. Crewe's real estate, title, and business weren't enough for her. More importantly, his heart wasn't good enough for her. "You're too good for her anyway, Crewe."

"You think so?" He still wore the slight smile on his face.

"I know so. I'd be the happiest woman in the world if I got to spend the rest of my life with you." It was one of those rare moments when I lived in the present, saying exactly what was on my mind the second it entered my brain. But the words were inappropriate, the meaning immense. It was a future Crewe said we could never have, and I didn't want him to think I was pressuring him into something he didn't want.

Crewe's smile dropped, but he didn't look away or show any sign that he was uncomfortable. He held my gaze with the exact same confidence, never shying away from the tension.

I was the first one to drop my gaze because my words embarrassed me. I'd never say that to any other man, even if I had been dating him for years. All I could do was change the subject and hope that was enough to clear the air. "Are you still doing stuff with intelligence?"

Crewe wore the same expression, so I wasn't sure if he was going to say anything. "Not so much lately. I've been distracted with the second distillery. Why do you ask?"

"Just curious. You never talk about it."

"A lot of people are focused on hostilities in the Middle East. With their heads turned, I'll be able to gain intel on the stuff going on in Western Europe. But that requires me to attend more social functions, or at least send someone in my stead. Lately, I've remained in Scotland."

"I see…are we going back to Fair Isle anytime soon?"

"Do you like it there?"

"It's beautiful. But I love it in Edinburgh too. That castle is something else…"

"I love both places," he said. "Italy as well."

"How are Crow and Cane doing?"

His eyes fell, and all he did was shake his head.

I hoped that didn't mean what I thought it meant. "They couldn't save Vanessa?"

He shook his head again. "She's dead."

"Oh…" Unexpected tears filled my eyes, sorrow for a woman I never knew. I didn't even know what she looked like. There was no face to put to the name. "I'm so sorry…I feel so terrible for them."

"Crow told me what happened but didn't say much else. He got off the phone, and I haven't heard from him. I called him a few weeks ago, and he didn't answer. I'm sure he just wants to be alone right now."

"How can you do business with a monster like that?" Bones raped and killed innocent women for pleasure. "You're better than that, Crewe."

"Business isn't personal," he said simply. "The second you make it about morals is the second you go out of business. I did what I could to help the Barsetti brothers. I'm not responsible for what happened to her."

"But your hands are still dirty."

"Bones gets me a lot of intel about the weapons arena. He's vital."

I couldn't agree with him. "You can't do this forever. One day, you're going to have a wife and children. You can't risk their lives with this secret business of yours."

"When that time comes, I'll rethink a few things. But for now, it's nothing personal. Please don't forget that I never claimed to be anything else but a bad guy. I never gave you any reason to have high expectations."

I tried not to roll my eyes. "But you are a good guy, Crewe. Let's not pretend otherwise."

"Maybe I'm a nice guy to you, but that's it."

I didn't believe that. I'd seen his moral compass, and it pointed straighter than most. "You have more money than you know what to do with. Why do you need this business at all?"

"It's not about money. It's never been about money."

"Then what's it about?"

"Power." My tears stopped falling, so he wiped his thumb across my cheek, catching the last drop that clung to my skin. "Information is the most powerful weapon you can have. I managed to discover there was going to be an assassination attempt on the queen's life. If I'd never uncovered that, she could be dead right now. I use information for leverage, but I also use it appropriately."

"But you're never going to get any good information out of a man like Bones."

"Actually, he was the one who told me about the queen."

Since Crewe had a response to everything I said, my points didn't come across well. "I still think you should walk away from that life now—not later. I'm sure you make enemies that way."

"Life is boring without a few enemies." He smiled in his typically handsome way.

I didn't appreciate his words, but nothing I said would make a difference.

He dropped his smile when he saw my annoyance. "I used to live a boring and mediocre life, but I lost my family anyway. I treated Josephine like a queen, but that wasn't enough to make her stay. I treated you well, and I still got shot in the chest. I don't play it safe because it doesn't guarantee anything."

My hand moved up his arm as the pity rose in my heart. "Just because the world turns dark doesn't mean you have to."

"Yes, it does. Making everyone fear you is the best way to keep people in line. The second I go soft, bad shit happens. In order for a king to rule over his kingdom, his subjects must fear his wrath. That's just how it goes."

That made me feel worse for him. "You know what I think would be nice?"

The only encouragement I got was a stare.

"Living in solitude on Fair Isle. No connection to the outside world, no people. Just the two of us. We don't need power or wealth, just a roof over our heads and Finley to cook for us. There would be no subjects, no reason for power. It would just be quiet…all the time."

His hand loosened on mine, but he didn't pull away. His callused thumb brushed over my soft skin, and his eyes were trained on my face. He glanced at the spot where he wiped a tear away before he looked me in the eye again. "That sounds nice…really nice."

Now that we were together, I kept blurting out things I shouldn't. I said things that I didn't realize I thought about. I talked about a future we could never have together, a future I didn't even know I wanted. I wanted to practice medicine, to fulfill the dream I'd had since I was a little girl. But the longer I stayed with Crewe, the more I sacrificed the things I wanted. Now I was moving to Scotland to enroll in a medical program I couldn't apply to America. I was changing everything around for one man.

But I didn't mind it.

Everything was changing—including me. I wasn't sure if it was a good thing or a bad thing.

He tilted my face toward him and placed a gentle kiss on the corner of my mouth. The scruff from his jaw was always coarse, but I liked the way it felt when it brushed against my skin. He let his mouth linger there, absorbing my attraction through his lips. When he pulled away, his eyes were lidded with disappointment like he wanted to keep kissing me.

But he didn't.

Maybe it was because we were on a plane with some of his men lingering about, or maybe it was for a different reason altogether.

"Can I ask you something? I'm not sure if I want to ask it or not…"

"Ask it. But I'm not sure if I'll want to answer it or not." The corner of his mouth rose.

"It's about my brother. What does he do, exactly?"

"For a living?" Crewe asked.

"Yeah. He's not like Bones, is he?" Joseph had been planning to take Ariel as a prisoner, and I hoped it wasn't to do horrific things to her. Maybe he'd just wanted to keep her as a hostage for ransom or something…at least, I hoped.

"We're all like Bones, honestly."

"No, you aren't." Being with Bones was standing in the presence of evil. I never felt that way about Crewe, even when I was locked in a cage in his basement on Fair Isle.

"You really want to know? I'm not sure you're gonna like it."

"Just tell me he doesn't kill people."

He shook his head. "We all kill people, Lovely."

"But bad people, right?"

He shrugged. "That's subjective. Joseph makes his money by hacking bank accounts. He finds out when there's going to be a large deposit from an Arabian prince or a Chinese CEO. When he figures that out, he intercepts the wire transfer. It's complicated cyber-robbery. He relies on my intel to know when big deals are going down. But he burned that bridge."

While my brother's actions were illegal, I was relieved it wasn't something worse. In his line of work, there were limited casualties. He didn't walk into a bank with guns blazing and shoot innocent clerks behind the desk. He was committing an international crime, but at least it wasn't murder. "I'm so relieved." My hand moved across my chest as the adrenaline faded away and I was left feeling relaxed.

"You're relieved your brother is a thief?" he asked with a chuckle.

"I'm relieved he's not a murderer."

"At least you have a positive outlook on things." Now that the plane was cruising at a constant speed and there was no turbulence, Crewe removed his safety belt. "I'm gonna make some calls in my office. Get some sleep."

"You can call people on the plane?"

"I can do anything on here." He winked. "Even fuck you in the bedroom."

It was a twelve-hour flight, so that might happen. "Can I lie down?"

"Of course. Come with me."

9

CREWE

WHEN THE PLANE landed on the strip, London was noticeably more relaxed. I'd flown with her several times, and her attitude was always the same. She was tense, uncomfortable, and nearly terrified the entire flight.

I found it interesting because she was a strong person in every other regard. When she first became my prisoner, she never showed a single ounce of fear. All of my remarks were met with insults, and even when I grabbed her by the neck, she didn't cower in fear. If she fell, she got back to her feet even stronger than before.

But a plane was enough to make her uneasy.

Didn't make any sense.

We got into the car and drove from the airport to the castle at the edge of Edinburgh. London had slept for most of the plane ride, so she was rested. I'd been on the phone or taking care of emails, so I'd been awake most of the time.

I'd fucked her when she woke up and took a short nap before we landed.

Now I was about to pull up to my house at three in the morning. Ariel wouldn't be there, so I had a few hours before I had to tell her the truth about London. She would be insanely pissed, and our heated argument would last for several days before she finally accepted my choice.

Or maybe she would never accept it.

Ariel was one of the few people I trusted in the world, so a part of me felt guilty for doing something she was so strongly against. She'd been right about London to begin with, but I was still bringing her back.

I knew I looked weak in Ariel's eyes.

When we pulled up to the house, London stared at it like she'd never seen it before. She stepped out of the car and stared at the lights that glowed outside the walls. The fountain in the front splashed with water that echoed in the clearing. A slight breeze moved through her hair, pulling it in front of her face.

The men grabbed the suitcases and carried them into the house, leaving the two of us alone to admire the stone walls of the ancient structure that had been refurbished ten years ago. When I remodeled the place, I preserved as much as I could while maintaining the integrity of the foundation.

I came to her side and stared at the two enormous front doors. "Feels like home?"

She crossed her arms over her chest, her thin jacket not heavy enough to keep her warm. "Actually, it does…"

I let her admire the castle for another moment before I grabbed her hand and took her inside. Since she'd been gone, I hadn't changed much. The only difference was the rug and the walls in the hallway where I'd been shot. Everything had to be changed because of the bloodstains. I purposely took her in a different direction so she wouldn't have to revisit the memory from the past.

We entered the royal chambers, where our suitcases sat inside the walk-in closet. The bedroom was exactly how I'd left it when she left. I hadn't used the bed or anything else in the room. It turned into a storage facility for my clothes and watches.

"It smells different in here."

I stripped off my jacket and placed it on the hanger. The left side of the closet was for the maids to pick up for dry cleaning, so I placed it far to the left and shut the door. "I can have the maids clean it again."

"No, it's not that. It just…doesn't smell like you. A hint of your cologne was always in the air. I remember it always smelling like wood and smoke from the fireplace. Something is just off. I can't explain it."

I unbuttoned my shirt and tossed it in the hamper. "Well, I haven't been living in here for a while."

"I guess that's true. You have been in America for the past week or so."

Ever since she'd left me, I hadn't used the bedroom. I slept in different quarters down the hall. The sheets and bedding had been washed, but she and I were the last people to have enjoyed the bed. Every time I tried to come back, the pain washed over me. Everything reminded me of her, and it was impossible not to think about her when her presence was still heavy in the walls. Sasha and I stayed down the hall because I couldn't fuck her in the bed I used to make love to London in. Just couldn't do it. "I haven't slept in here since you left." I turned my back and unfastened my watch, an excuse to hide my face. My expression remained stoic, but my eyes always gave me away.

"Then where have you been sleeping?"

"Down the hall."

Silence followed my words. London didn't speak again, probably because she didn't know how to respond. I never told her how devastated I was when she left because I wouldn't even admit to myself that I was in pain. That was the biggest confession I ever could have made, that I missed her so much I didn't want to tarnish my last good memory of her.

She came up behind me and rested her face against the area between my shoulder blades. "Why?"

It was a stupid question because she knew the answer. I couldn't fuck another woman on a bed I considered holy. I couldn't brush my teeth and not expect to see her reflection in the mirror. I couldn't open a drawer and be indifferent to her panties and socks sitting on top. But I didn't say any of that. I gave the simplest response. "Because I loved you just as much when you were gone as I did when you were here."

She pressed a kiss against my skin, her soft lips sticking to my body like glue. She left her mouth there for a few seconds before she pulled away, keeping her hands on my triceps. "Crewe…" She rested her forehead against my back, her breathing uneven. "I missed you so much. When you told me we were done…I was devastated."

Initially, her tears had made me happy. I'd wanted to hurt her the way she hurt me. But now I didn't ever want to cause her pain. "I was just angry."

"I know that now." Her arms circled my waist as her face remained against my back. "When I went back to New York, it didn't feel the same. Nothing had changed. The crowds were the same, the buildings were the same, my morning coffee tasted the same…but everything was different. I tried dating, but I never liked anyone. When I touched myself, I thought about you…"

I closed my eyes at her confession, picturing my woman touching herself and thinking about me. I'd witnessed it before, and it was definitely the hottest thing I'd ever seen. I'd touched that clit a hundred times, but I loved watching her do it herself.

"What do we do now?" she whispered.

"About?"

"My living situation, Ariel…everything."

We'd just walked in the door, and I certainly didn't have a plan. "Ariel will know before she gets here tomorrow. The only reason she doesn't know now is because she's asleep. I'll handle her."

"Would it help if I spoke to her?"

It'd just make it worse. "Unlikely."

"Is there anything else I can do?"

I turned around, feeling her arms snake around my body as I moved. My hand moved into her hair, my favorite place to grab her. With a slight tug, I arranged her face exactly where I wanted it, her mouth easily accessible. "Fuck me." One of the things I missed most was waking up to her riding me in the morning. Sometimes I woke up to her mouth around my dick, and that was just as good. She was talented at taking the reins, being in charge of my fantasies. She had a confidence unlike any other.

She held my gaze as her hands moved to my belt and stripped it away. She didn't kiss me, but this was just as intense. I felt the belt slide out of my loops and hit the floor next to my feet. Her hands undid my fly and buttons next, getting me free from the material.

Her hand wrapped around my length, and she stroked it without blinking.

My hand loosened from her strands, but my eyes didn't leave her face.

She finally rose on her tiptoes and pressed a kiss to my mouth, a light one that lacked tongue. She purposely kept her distance, wanting to keep our eyes focused on each other instead of our mouths.

She pivoted me toward the bed then pushed me, making my body fall back and land on the bed.

The only reason why I moved was because I fell before she even touched me. I wanted that beautiful body on top of mine, to feel her take me as roughly as I took her.

She didn't give me a chance to remove my shoes and the clothes around my ankles before she shed her jeans and panties and straddled me. She didn't bother with her top, assuming it would take too much time.

She pointed my cock at her entrance and slid all the way down, her pussy soaking wet. She didn't need much time to get ready, which made me wonder if she was ready anytime I was in her presence. Her attraction matched mine.

I held myself up on my elbows and watched her move up and down on top of me, taking my length with even strokes. Her hair flowed with her movements, and my feet pushed against the ground when I thrust back. I yanked up her shirt and bra so the bottom half of her tits were visible. They were one of my favorite features, so I needed to see them. I needed to grab them whenever I felt like it.

"How this?" she said through her heavy breathing.

I already wanted to come. She was taking me all the way to the hilt before she rose up again. My dick was smeared with her arousal, and her pussy was tight around me even though she hadn't come just yet. "Fucking perfect." I wanted to do this until morning, but when she fucked me this well, I knew I wouldn't last. It wasn't the end of the world—I loved coming inside her anyway.

All I could do was move my hips up and down while she did the rest. Of course, she looked absolutely stunning while she did it. Every woman that had ever ridden me looked breathtaking, but there was something different about London. It must have been the look in her eyes—because she loved me.

I closed my eyes every now and then as I suppressed the urge to dump all my seed inside her. I'd fucked her less than twelve hours ago, but it felt like days. I could feel all the come in my balls, all the essence I wanted to give her.

She gripped my shoulders as she rode me harder. "Trying not to come?"

"Yeah…"

"I want you to come. I love feeling you inside me."

Jesus Christ. I used one hand to adjust her body, to tilt her forward so her clit rubbed against my pelvic bone. I didn't need clit stimulation to make a woman come, just when I was in a hurry.

And I was in a big hurry now.

I sucked two fingers into my mouth then placed them at her back entrance. I'd fucked her in the ass and knew she liked it. My fingers weren't as thick as my length, but they would do. I pushed inside and fingered her from behind, activating all her nerve endings to make her come hard.

Her breathing sped up, and she dug her hips into me harder, rubbing her clit against my body. She increased her pace and nearly cut my skin with her nails. Once her hips began to jerk on their own, I knew she'd reached her climax. She let out a scream as her movements slowed down, and she took my hard cock slowly. "Oh god…"

My fingers pulsed inside her ass, and my cock felt her tightness. I was in heaven, watching this beautiful woman get off to me. She was my fantasy, and I loved being hers. My cock throbbed until it was nearly painful, and I knew I couldn't keep my orgasm back. "Here it comes, Lovely…"

She increased her pace again, taking my cock hard.

I fingered her ass harder, moving with her as she bounced on my dick. "Fuck…"

Her hands dragged down my chest and cut into my pecs.

The slight amount of pain pushed me over the edge. I came violently, moaning as I filled her small pussy with all of my seed. I loved claiming her as mine again, giving her so much come it wouldn't fit inside her.

I was disappointed it was over, but too satisfied to really regret it.

She leaned down and kissed me, a long and sensual embrace that involved a lot of tongue. My fingers pulled away from her ass and gripped her cheek, and I felt aroused by the kiss she just gave me.

She pulled away then lifted herself, pulling my length out of her. My cock slapped against my stomach once he was free, still slightly hard. That's when the come oozed out of her body, white globs dripping down her thighs.

Now I had to fuck her again.

I'd only been asleep for a few hours when my alarm went off.

London was dead asleep and didn't even stir at the sound ringing from my nightstand. I turned it off then got into the shower to start my day. I'd worked while I was in New York, but I still had a lot of catching up to do. I shaved the scruff off my face and put on a crisp suit before I headed out the door.

Ariel knew London was there with me. That woman knew everything about the business, and since my personal life involved the business, she knew about that too. I rubbed the back of my head and sighed as I took the stairs to the main floor. My office faced the courtyard, and she would undoubtedly be there waiting for me.

And she was.

With arms crossed over her chest, slender glasses on her face, and an attitude that reached every corner of the room, Ariel projected her anger directly into my skin. Without saying a single word, she told me off.

Which was pretty impressive, if you asked me.

"Morning." I walked past her and sat behind my desk, refusing to absorb her ferocity. She was waiting for me to make the first statement. That was how she always played this game. I opened my folder and looked through my checklist of things I needed to complete. "I have a meeting with Pias in fifteen minutes. You can sit in if you want. Afterward, I'm gonna stop by the distillery in Edinburgh. Are you coming or do you have other matters to attend to?"

All she did was stare—coldly.

I met her gaze and waited for a response. When I didn't get one, I moved on. "I'm going to take that as a yes, then." I opened my laptop and ignored her altogether.

"Goddammit, Crewe." She slammed her fist down on my desk, making everything shake.

"Here we go…" I shut my laptop and leaned back in my chair, getting comfortable for the long conversation ahead.

Her hand moved to her hip, where her gold bracelet hung on her petite wrist. "I've already made my feelings perfectly clear, and I don't want to repeat myself—"

"Then don't." I respected Ariel's opinion, but she needed to back off. This was my life—I was gonna fuck whomever I wanted.

Her eyes widened immediately. "We lost four men because of her."

"She told Joseph not to come, but he did anyway."

"And you believe her?" she asked incredulously. "The woman who staged a coup behind your back?"

"She didn't stage a coup—"

"She fucked your brains out until you trusted her—"

"Don't. Fucking. Interrupt. Me." I rose to my full height, provoked and angry. There was nothing I hated more than disrespect. While Ariel was vital to my success, she worked for me—not the other way around. The scotch was mine. The royalty was mine. She was just a partner—an employee. "I'm aware of all the ramifications surrounding London. I'm aware she lied to me. I'm aware of everything she's done." I worked my jaw to control my anger, feeling the need to spit fire at her. "But I want to be with her. She loves me, and I love her. She has no other motive to be with me other than love, so I trust her. She won't interfere with our business. And she would never be disloyal to me ever again." I watched Ariel's face darken in more anger as she held her tongue. "That's how it's going to be, Ariel. You may as well accept it."

"I don't accept it, Crewe. How can I do business with someone who thinks with their dick and not their brain?"

My hands gripped the edge of the desk. I was much gentler on her than I was on other employees because she was a woman, but if she wanted to play rough, we would play rough. "Then maybe you should leave."

"I think I will."

I continued to wear my poker face, but the statement was like a punch to the gut. She and I were a perfect team. She was just as ruthless, determined, and ambitious as I was. I'd never met a more intelligent businessperson in my life.

"I could've dealt with that little whore being your wife, even if she ruined my chances of capitalizing on our business. But after what she did, I can't tolerate it. I can't work in the garden every day when there's a snake slithering around."

"Don't call her that again."

Ariel held her ground, unflinching. "What's it going to be, Crewe? Her or me."

"There's no choice. She's my lover, and you're my partner. I don't have to choose."

"Yes, you do. I can't work under these conditions. I don't trust you, Crewe Donoghue. I no longer trust your judgment. It's completely impaired. The second a hot piece of ass walks by, you can't think straight. I need a partner more focused than that."

"I'm still not going to choose." I kept my voice steady even though I wanted to scream at her. "If you want to leave, that's your decision. I'll pay back your investment in the company as well as a severance. What's it going to be?" She believed in my scotch and in my intelligence organization. She knew I was an exemplary business partner, London excluded. She was walking away from both wealth and security.

"I'll be back tomorrow with my lawyer." She turned around and walked to the door, her hips swaying.

I called her bluff and realized it wasn't a bluff at all. My eyes watched her walk away, but I kept a straight face. "London did nothing wrong."

Ariel stopped at the door and turned around. "How can you say that?"

"She did what she had to do to survive. Neither one of us can judge her for that."

"But I judge you for allowing her to survive. You should have sold her to Bones because she fucked with all of us."

"If I remember correctly, you were in handcuffs and London freed you." London didn't owe Ariel anything, but she helped her when Ariel had been nothing but cold to her. That kind of compassion was nearly nonexistent.

"And if I remember correctly, she was the reason I was in handcuffs in the first place."

"She took me to the hospital. She could have just left me to die, but she didn't."

"But she let you get shot in the first place."

All of her responses were black and white. "She asked Joseph not to hurt me or any of my men. It's not her fault he didn't listen."

She released a cold laugh. "No, Crewe. Everything is her fault." She threw the door open and stormed out.

I slowly sank into my chair and stared at the open doorway. Her heels clicked against the tile of the grand entryway, and I listened to the sound until she walked out the front doors. When she was gone, I knew she wasn't coming back.

My best employee just quit on me.

I'd been a businessman long before she came around, and I would still be a great one with her gone. But that didn't erase the scar her departure left. Her words sank into me like bullets in the flesh. My life was uneventful before London got off that helicopter. But the second she was a part of me, everything began to change. I lost my judgment, and now I lost someone close to me.

It made me question everything.

10

LONDON

CREWE DIDN'T COME BACK to the room at his regular time. Even when dinner was served, he still didn't show up. I knew he had a lot of work to catch up on, but I was surprised he hadn't popped in for at least a visit.

I started to get worried.

I hadn't shown my face to the rest of the castle because I knew everyone hated me. If I ran into Ariel in the hallway, nothing good would come from it. None of the men would touch me, but Dunbar would strangle me with just his eyes.

But the later it got, the more concerned I became.

I didn't have a cell phone to call him. My only option was to search for him in the castle. If I didn't find him, one of his men would know where he'd disappeared to. I put on a pair of jeans and a sweater and walked downstairs. The first person I came across was Dimitri, the man who took Dunbar's place when he'd been put on guard duty. He gave me a quiet scowl but didn't say anything. His hands were held together at his waist, his gun on his hip. He didn't draw his weapon or insult me, but his eyes did enough damage on their own.

I walked into Crewe's office and found it vacant. His laptop was closed and everything was neat and tidy, like he hadn't used it at all. I took a look around to see if he left any clues behind, but there was nothing.

I walked back outside and saw another guard in the hallway. He gave me the same derisive look as Dimitri and kept walking.

At least they wouldn't touch me.

I walked to the front door where Dunbar stood. In dark jeans and a black jacket, he looked as deadly as Dimitri. He kept his arms over his chest like he had no intention of hurting me, but I wouldn't push my luck. "I'm looking for Crewe. Do you know where he is?"

He stared at me in silence.

I knew I wasn't going to get an answer out of him. "When I do see Crewe, I'll let him know how accommodating you were." I turned around and retreated, knowing Crewe would turn up sooner or later.

"He left a few hours ago."

I turned around. "Where did he go?"

"He took the Jaguar and left on his own. I'm not sure where he went."

He and Ariel must have gotten into a fight. "Can I call him from your phone?"

"Unlikely that he would answer."

"Can I at least try?"

He sighed before he pulled his phone out of his pocket and handed it over.

I found his name in the address book and hit send. I listened to it ring four times before Crewe finally answered.

"Yes?" The single word told me exactly how he was feeling. He was in a particularly bad mood. Something must have happened with Ariel today.

"It's me."

He sighed into the phone like my voice was displeasing to him.

"When are you going to be home?"

"Stop acting like my wife. I'll be home when I feel like being home."

He was definitely drunk. "A heads-up would have been nice."

"Don't owe you a damn thing."

I could actually hear the sound of his glass hitting the hardwood table at the bar where he sat. Or maybe it was just part of my imagination. I didn't want to start our new relationship like this, but I couldn't let him talk to me that way. "We can do this in two different ways. You can be a real man and come home to me. You can tell me what you're so pissed off about, and I can help you through it. Or you can keep acting like the biggest asshole on the planet and sleep alone tonight. Which path do you want to take?"

Silence.

"I'm hanging up, then."

"I'll be home in twenty minutes," he said with a growl.

"Can you drive? I'll have Dunbar pick you up."

"I'm fine."

I wasn't buying it. "Dunbar is picking you up. Tell him where you are." I handed the phone back to Dunbar. "Get him home in one piece."

Crewe got home after midnight. His suit was no longer crisp because he'd been slouching in it all night at the bar. He tossed his expensive watch on the table like it wasn't worth more than a car. When he took off his jacket, he threw it on the floor like he didn't give a damn.

I was sitting up in bed reading when he walked inside. I hoped he'd had a chance to sober up on the drive home, but my expectations weren't high. The fact that he was happy last night and took such an unexpected turn told me something significant happened. He didn't just have a fight with Ariel. Something serious went down.

He didn't look at me as he undressed. He made a pile of his clothes on the floor and kicked his shoes off like he was a child. He stripped all the way down until he was naked, and in all his glory, he looked nothing like a child. He was over six feet of man vertically, and nine inches of man horizontally.

He pulled the sheets back and got into bed like nothing happened. He lay on his back and immediately closed his eyes.

I didn't say a word because I assumed he was so drunk he was about to pass out. Maybe it was best to let him sleep it off before I interrogated him in the morning.

He suddenly turned over and got on top of me, pinning me to the mattress and sticking his tongue down my throat. He didn't give any warning before he kissed me and separated my thighs with his knees.

For a moment, I just went with it because that's what my body was used to. But when I remembered he was being a dick all night, I shoved him off. "Crewe, what the hell are you doing?"

"Fucking you. Was that not clear?"

"Well, I'm not in the mood to be fucked right now."

"I've never heard you say that before," he said with a dead serious expression.

I pushed my hand against his solid chest and forced him on his back. "Just go to bed, Crewe."

"You expect me to sleep with this thing?" He nodded to his hard cock that lay against his stomach.

"You can do whatever you want with it. But I'm going to bed." I set the book on my nightstand and turned off the lamp.

He lay back and sighed, his hands finally off me.

I'd never seen Crewe this drunk before. That meant he'd exceeded his personal record in scotch drinking—which was a lot. I wouldn't be surprised if he didn't even go to work tomorrow. Having a deep conversation about his problems simply wasn't possible right now.

"Lovely?" His hand moved for mine in the darkness.

"Hmm?"

His fingers wrapped around mine, his fingertips warm. "I apologize."

"For?"

"For earlier," he whispered. "The way I spoke to you. I can't remember what I said, but I know it wasn't good."

He wasn't the kind of man to apologize for anything, so when he showed his remorse, I knew it was heartfelt. "We can talk about it in the morning."

"Just accept my apology."

"I will later." When we could have a completely coherent conversation.

"I just…need to know you'll be here when I wake up. So please accept my apology." His heavy words surrounded us even though he didn't raise his voice. They contained more emotion than I was used to hearing from him. Crewe was an aggressive drunk, but he was also honest.

"I'm not going anywhere, okay?"

"When you were gone…I was so fucking miserable. I had all the money in the world but still felt like shit."

I turned to look at him in the darkness. His eyes were closed and he faced the ceiling, and his eyebrows moved as he spoke to me.

"So…don't leave."

"I won't."

"Promise me." He'd never expressed any hint of need. He showed his affection but always kept me at a distance. But now all his walls were down.

"I promise, Crewe."

He finally dropped the argument and relaxed, his hand still in mine.

I was still angry with him, but I couldn't resist his vulnerability. Crewe didn't show his true colors to anyone, including me, but he let me see his heart on his sleeve. I moved to his side of the bed and wrapped my arm around his waist and rested my head on his shoulder.

His arm immediately moved across mine, and he turned his face into me, his lips resting against my hairline. His smell washed over me, along with the overpowering scent of gin. Maybe it wasn't gin, but I was so used to smelling scotch on him that I could tell he hadn't been drinking it.

He fell asleep almost immediately, his breathing changing.

I stayed that way for another few minutes and listened to his heart beat against my palm. Crewe could be cold and cruel, but he was just a man underneath that exterior. He had a heart of gold that he couldn't hide as much as he tried.

That's why I forgave him so easily.

Crewe's alarm went off at the same time as it did every other morning, and this time, he smashed his fist against it, shattering it into pieces across the nightstand.

Damn.

He didn't open his eyelids as he rubbed the sleep from his eyes, his mood already black like it was last night.

I assumed he wouldn't go to work at all today.

He dragged one hand down his face and finally opened his eyes, squinting as he took in the early morning light. He turned to me and focused on my face, taking a few seconds to recognize my features.

"I'm pretty sure your alarm is busted."

He released a quiet growl before he sat up. "Jesus Christ, my head hurts."

"Already got you covered." I grabbed the two tablets off my nightstand along with the glass of water.

He swallowed the pills dry before he downed the water.

"You should just go back to sleep. You're gonna feel like shit all day."

"I can't." He kicked off the sheets and got out of bed. He was in a pissy mood like he was last night, before he apologized to me. He obviously didn't remember that conversation at all.

"Why not?"

"I'm meeting with Ariel."

I hoped it wouldn't lead to another fight that would send him to the bar. "You guys work it out?"

"No." He ran his fingers through his hair as he stood upright, looking sexy completely nude and with an impressive morning wood. "She's leaving my company."

I stopped thinking about how hot he looked. "What? She quit?"

"Yeah. Now I have to buy her out for her portion. It's really a meeting between lawyers."

I hopped out of bed. "She's quitting because of me?"

"She's not your biggest fan." He walked into the bathroom and got the shower running.

I followed him inside. "Do you realize how stupid that sounds? I have nothing to do with your partnership."

"I agree. But she doesn't trust my judgment anymore." Crewe acted like he didn't give a damn, like we were talking about what color we should paint the bedroom, but I knew that was just a front. They'd been working together for nearly ten years. They were more than just business partners—they were family. He grabbed a towel and hung it on the rack outside the shower door.

"That's not fair."

He shrugged before he stepped inside. "I did just fine without her once. I'll do fine without her again." He shut the door and stood under the water, his ass muscles thick and tight.

I didn't have much time to think about my actions before I did them. I threw on jeans and a t-shirt before I left the room, knowing Crewe wouldn't realize I was gone for at least ten minutes. She might not be there yet, but since she was so punctual all the time, she probably would be early.

I walked into Crewe's office and saw her sitting on one of the sofas, accompanied by a man in a black suit.

When she looked at me, it was like she saw right through me. She was indifferent to my appearance, as if I was a cloud of air she couldn't see. She turned away as soon as she saw me, examining the bookshelf stored with old classics.

I shut the door and took a seat on the opposite sofa, not backing down despite her attempt to ignore me. "Ariel."

She turned her gaze back on me, giving me a look colder than winter. "Will Crewe be in shortly?"

"He's in the shower and doesn't know I'm here."

"Oh, good," she said sarcastically. "This should be fun."

I didn't have time to be sensitive to her insults. I had an objective. "Ariel, I don't think this is a good idea—for either of you."

"I'll be fine. Thanks for the concern." Her lawyer sat there in silence, watching our interaction with little interest.

"Are you really leaving because of me?"

"Yes." She adjusted her glasses before she looked down at her folder. "I can't trust a man who behaves this stupidly."

She could insult me, but not the man I loved. "He's not stupid, Ariel."

"How does that saying go? Stupid is as stupid does? That describes him pretty well."

"That's not true, and you know it. Things didn't work out the way I wanted them to. I didn't mean for Joseph to come here. I didn't mean for Crewe to get shot. I didn't mean for anyone to get involved in this. I was going to speak to Crewe about our situation and ask him if I could have my freedom. But I never got the chance."

"But you had the chance to call Joseph?"

I gritted my teeth. "To tell him he didn't need to ambush Crewe, that I had a better plan to get out of here."

Ariel stared at me without blinking.

"Joseph and his men came to the distillery opening in Edinburgh."

Her eyes narrowed.

"He was waiting until Crewe left me alone before he could snatch me. I didn't want that to happen, so I stuck to Crewe's side like glue. When I saw Joseph in the hallway, I pulled Crewe inside another room so he wouldn't get shot. I could have betrayed you before, but I didn't. I always tried to protect Crewe and Joseph at the same time, while trying to get myself out of harm's way."

"Crewe isn't harm's way."

It was like she didn't listen to anything else I said. "Ariel, I don't have any ill will toward Crewe or anyone else he interacts with. Joseph won't be a problem ever again. I told him how I felt about Crewe, so he'll never touch a hair on his head. I wish Crewe and I started out differently, but it doesn't change the way we ended up. When I say I love him, I mean it. Why else would I be here?"

"I don't give a damn how much you think you love him. That man has been to hell and back, and he doesn't deserve any kind of disloyalty. You betrayed him—stabbed him in the back."

"Uh, he kidnapped me. Why is that important fact never included in the conversation? What would you do if you were kidnapped? Would you ever give up, Ariel? I sure hope not."

Her gaze remained steady, her eyes unflinching. "And that would be fine. I expected you to try to escape. But you chose to manipulate him to do it, and the idiot actually fell for it."

"I fell for it too," I snapped. "While I was trying to get him to fall in love with me, I fell in love with him instead. I wanted to talk to Crewe about having a different kind of relationship, one where I had independence. If I'd really wanted to betray Crewe, I would have let Joseph kill him at the distillery. I would have stabbed him in the neck while he was sleeping. I would have bashed a vase against the base of his skull while he was in the shower. But I didn't."

She rolled her eyes and looked away. "If you're done, I'd like to wait for Crewe—alone."

Geez, she was a bitch. "You can't leave, Ariel. He needs you."

"Not as much as he needs what's between your legs."

I chewed on the inside of my lip as I swallowed the insult. "What can I do to prove myself to you?"

She grabbed the glass of water from the coffee table and took a long drink. "You want to know what you can do?"

"Yeah," I snapped. "I just asked."

"Leave. Leave him and never come back. Then I'll stay."

That was impossible. "Then he'll be miserable. He'll be miserable if he loses you too. He needs both of us, Ariel."

"Leave," she repeated. "Let him get his life back on track."

"Back on track? I'm the one who's gotten him to cut back on drinking. I'm the one who gets him to crack a smile once in a while. I understand business is important to both of you, but it's not everything. He needs more than that."

"He didn't before."

"It's a good thing he does now."

She glanced at the lawyer then returned to ignoring me.

"Ariel, come on. We can work this out. You're like family to Crewe."

"I was—until he picked you."

"Why does he have to pick at all? Ariel, why am I such a threat to you? I would never hurt Crewe."

"Oh, really?" She raised an eyebrow. "Crewe is supposed to marry someone of his station, and not just for business. He needs to carry on his bloodline through someone of noble birth. That's how it works. And you're telling me you're just gonna step aside and let that happen?"

The idea of Crewe spending his life with someone else made me sick to my stomach. Watching him walk off with a princess or a duchess while I slowly faded into the background would make me hurt worse than anything else in my life. I didn't know what the future held for us, but I knew letting him go would break my heart.

She cocked her head to the side when I didn't answer. "That's what I thought. You've done nothing but ruin Crewe's life. You're a fucking cockroach that just won't die. You're selfish and inconsiderate. I can't stand by and watch Crewe throw away his legacy like this—because he's family."

"If he's family—"

Crewe walked inside in a gray suit and black tie. With a look of consternation and professionalism, he didn't seem hungover at all. Maybe a hot shower and a few painkillers had been enough to straighten him out. "London." He walked to the couch and looked down at me, his hands in his pockets.

I didn't appreciate the cold way he spoke to me, so I spoke just as coldly. "Crewe."

He didn't give a smartass comment like he normally would. "Give us the room."

My eyes narrowed even more. I didn't appreciate being bossed around when I was only trying to help him.

He picked up on the tension. "Please, Lovely."

I stood up and ignored Ariel as I walked around the couch. Before I passed Crewe, he grabbed me by the elbow and leaned into me, pressing a gentle kiss to my cheek.

I knew it was the only form of apology he could express.

He let me go then walked to the couch.

I left the room and shut the door behind me. I lingered outside the doorway in the hope I could catch a word or two, but his door was so thick and the room was so big that I couldn't make out a single word.

All I could think about was what Ariel said to me. The only way I could make her stay was if I walked away. I had to let Crewe move on and marry someone who was more worthy of his affection. I was okay with not knowing what would happen between Crewe and me, but I didn't like the idea of knowing nothing ever could happen. But if that was the case, why did I move all the way here?

Crewe returned to the bedroom a few hours later. He was still stiff in his suit, his mood black and palpable. He looked the same as he did last night, pissed off and drunk. Except he hadn't been drinking—at least to my knowledge. "What did you say to her?"

"She didn't tell you?" I asked in surprise.

"She's not my partner anymore." He immediately moved for the liquor cabinet, needing booze the second he walked into a room. He couldn't even carry on a conversation without having a glass in his hand.

"Crewe."

He held the bottle as he looked at me.

"We can't erase all the progress you've made."

He turned around and poured a glass. "I erased all my progress when you left." He took a drink and faced me. "So, we're back to square one."

"Whether I'm here or not, you should take it easy."

"We both know you're the key to both my health and happiness." He took another long drink before he set the glass down. "What did you say to her?"

"I asked her to stay."

"That obviously didn't work…"

"I told her she was overreacting, that my feelings for you are genuine and I would never hurt you…again. But that wasn't enough for her. She said I already betrayed you." I left out the part about marriage, knowing that put unnecessary stress on our relationship. "It's frustrating because I explained my side of the story, but she just won't listen. I know she's not stupid. She's just…"

"Stubborn," Crewe finished. "Yeah, I know." He chuckled. "I've known her for a long time. She hasn't changed since I first met her."

"You didn't fight for her?"

"No." He fell back into one of the high-backed armchairs in the living room. "She made her decision. I'm not going to chase her. The money has been handled. I don't owe her anything, and she doesn't owe me anything." He finished his glass then set the empty cup on the table.

"There's more to your relationship than business."

His eyes fixated on my gaze. "What are you implying?"

"That you love her."

He shook his head slightly. "I've never had feelings for her. You know she's gay, right?"

"That's not what I mean, Crewe. I know you love her like family."

He looked away, as if admitting it was too difficult. "She's one of the few people I trust…"

"You can't just let her go, Crewe. Maybe you can give her some space then talk to her."

"It won't do any good. She gave me an ultimatum, and I made my decision."

Me. "There shouldn't be an ultimatum at all."

"I understand her point of view. I've made some unusual decisions, so she questions my judgment."

"Your personal life has nothing to do with your work."

"That's not completely true. If you have a DUI, it's a lot more difficult to get a job. That has nothing to do with a position you're applying for, but it's relevant. If you make bad decisions off the clock, will you make good decisions on the clock?"

"First of all, a DUI is a traffic offense. Not the same thing. And second of all, are you implying I'm a bad decision?"

"If you were, would I still be here?"

"You never answered the question." I crossed my arms over my chest.

"Objectively, yes. You are a bad decision. You aren't a suitable partner, and we started off in a complicated situation. But you shouldn't take that personally."

"Yeah, that's easy to do…"

"You asked me a question, and I answered honestly." He crossed his legs, resting his ankle on the opposite knee. He ran his palm up the side of his face, feeling his five o'clock shadow that had already started to come in. "Forget about Ariel. She's gone, and we need to move on."

"I just don't think it's fair that you're losing her because of me."

"I don't either. But that was her choice."

"And you're really okay with this?"

"Okay with what?" He looked at me, his fingertips resting under his chin.

"Losing her so you can be with me." She was far more valuable than I ever was. I was the reason he had a scar over his chest at that very moment. I didn't help him with his business or anything else. I was easily replaceable; Ariel wasn't.

He shrugged. "I'm not happy with the way things turned out, but I know I can't live without you. Been there, done that." He avoided my gaze, his fingertips moving over his chin.

When I walked toward him, he finally looked up, his gaze intense and vulnerable at the same time. It was a look I'd been seeing more of, particularly last night. Sometimes it seemed like he wanted to be more open with me but was afraid of doing it.

I stood at his side and ran my fingers over his forearm as it rested on the armchair. "Why did you go out last night?"

"I don't know."

"Why didn't you just come to me upstairs?"

He looked away again. "I don't know that answer either."

"I think you do, Crewe." My fingers slid underneath his sleeve so I could feel his bare skin. His corded veins were prominent across his forearm. I traced one with my fingertip.

He didn't give me an answer.

I lowered myself to my knees in front of him, sitting between his knees.

His gaze shifted to me instantly, his jaw hardening.

My hands started at his knees and moved up, pressing over his thighs all the way to his waist. When I creased the fabric of his slacks, I defined the outline of his hard cock as it sat over his left thigh. "Why didn't you come to me last night?"

He watched my hands. "I was angry."

"And when have I ever not helped you with your anger?" My hand slid over his hard cock on the way to his fly. I undid his belt and popped the button.

His eyes moved to my face.

"Why didn't you come to me, Crewe?"

His eyes darkened with arousal. "Because I was afraid Ariel was right."

I unzipped his fly and pulled the front of his pants down so I could see his black boxers underneath. "Right about what?"

"About my judgment. About my leadership. About you."

I grabbed his boxers and pulled them down, his nine-inch length coming free. "Why couldn't you confide this to me?"

"It's hard for me to let you in."

"Why?" I pulled his slacks and boxers down to his ankles, letting his cock lie against his stomach and his balls hang over the edge of the chair.

"Because you betrayed me." His eyes were mixed with both sadness and arousal, two very conflicting emotions.

"I would never betray you again, Crewe. I promise." I pulled my shirt over my head and unclasped my bra. "No more going out whenever you're upset. I want you to come to me."

His eyes moved to my tits.

I grabbed his length and ran my tongue from the base to the tip. When I got to his head, I tasted the arousal that had already begun to seep out. I positioned myself closer to the chair so I could press his dick between my tits. "Okay?"

He moaned quietly as he felt his dick slide through my tits. "Okay."

I pressed my tits together so there was a smaller gap to slide through. My tits weren't impressive, but I had enough cushion to make this work. He had a long enough dick that I could straighten my back and be eye level with him. I pressed my mouth against his and gave him a slow kiss as I moved up and down, sliding his dick between my tits.

His mouth trembled against mine slightly before his hand dug into my hair. His tongue moved against mine, and he deepened the kiss until he possessed me. A moan entered my mouth, but I couldn't tell if it came from him or me. I got more of his tongue than I had before, and I liked feeling it in my mouth. I liked feeling his arousal through him and not just his dick.

"I want to be what we were before I left…" I knew I was asking for the impossible. The kind of trust we had was built on a six-month relationship. Now we had to start over, come back from a tragedy. The only thing keeping us together was the fact that we loved one another, but everything else was working against us.

He kissed me harder then sucked my bottom lip into his mouth. "I do too. But I need more time."

"Time for what?"

He breathed hard against my mouth as he rubbed through my soft flesh. "It's hard for me to trust people. You know that."

"You can trust me."

He pressed his forehead to mine and squeezed my tits in his strong hands. "I know, Lovely."

"Then do it."

He looked into my eyes as he thrust his cock through the valley between my breasts. When he was aroused at this magnitude, he was even more handsome than usual. His jaw was tighter because his mouth was slightly parted. "Alright." He grabbed the back of my neck and guided my face down to his lap, telling me exactly what he wanted.

I opened my mouth wide and gave it to him.

11

CREWE

Pias entered my office then glanced at the seat where Ariel usually sat. He came with his folder stuffed with supply reports and took a seat, a glass of scotch already sitting there. "I have everything you asked for."

"Great." I eyed my own glass and knew I needed to slow things down. When I had cut down on my alcohol intake, I was less moody and much happier. I had more energy, and I didn't snap so easily. But it was hard to go back to that because the initial stages of quitting were always difficult. Being drunk all the time made me more indifferent—and I liked not giving a damn.

We discussed the last quarter's numbers, and we had to use Ariel's paperwork for data. Everything was neatly organized, and I knew it would be difficult to replace her. She'd never made a mistake in the ten years I'd known her.

When we were finished, Pias closed his folder. "Would you like me to begin the process of finding a replacement for Ariel?"

No one could ever replace her. Not just because she was a phenomenal worker, but because she was loyal and trustworthy. Her shoes were simply too big to be filled. "I'm not sure. Don't even know where to begin."

"We can start by encouraging people to apply for the position."

The only reason why Ariel had been made a partner to begin with was because she was the best at what she did. I would never give that position to anyone else. What I needed now was just an assistant who could handle all the tedious and annoying things. "I could use the help, but I'm not looking for another partner."

"I'll get on that, sir."

"Thanks, Pias."

"Of course." Pias left the room.

I sat at my desk and dragged my hands down my face, feeling a migraine approach. Instead of taking painkillers, I usually just drank more scotch. But now that I shared my life with the queen sitting upstairs, I had to make some changes.

Losing Ariel was a lot more difficult than I thought it would be. I felt like someone had ripped out one of my kidneys so my body was required to function with one instead of two. It wasn't life-threatening, but it was still uncomfortable.

But I couldn't give up London.

She was the only woman I'd ever had these kinds of feelings for. I thought I'd loved Josephine, but my love for her was nothing compared to what I felt for London. I'd been shot because of her, and I still protected her. When Josephine betrayed me, I stopped giving a damn about her.

London was definitely different.

But Ariel was important to me. She was a family member I assumed would always be there. She and I had a good friendship as well as a business relationship. I couldn't ask for anything more.

I felt like shit.

But I couldn't allow Ariel to tell me how to run my business and my personal life. I couldn't allow her to insult me like that. If I did, she would have more power than I allowed anyone to have.

There was no other option. She had to go.

Now I would have to work longer and harder to make up for Ariel's absence, but it wouldn't be too difficult. Once I hired one or two people, everything would slowly return to normal. Ariel couldn't be replaced, but her necessity could be erased.

Dunbar knocked before he stepped into my office. "Sir, Ariel is here to see you. Should I let her in?"

I stared at him blankly as I processed what he said. "What does she want?"

"Said she forgot a few things."

"Such as?"

He shrugged. "She didn't say, and I didn't think it was my place to ask."

I shut my laptop and gave a slight nod. "Send her in."

Dunbar shut the door and disappeared.

My heart began to race, and my fingertips felt numb. No one ever made me feel nervous. Even when Joseph pointed that gun at my chest, I wasn't nervous. When I lay on the ground with my blood soaking into the rug, my pulse rate didn't increase.

The door opened again, and Ariel stepped inside. She was in dark jeans and a black t-shirt, casual for the first time ever. Her hair was pulled back into a rigid ponytail, and her glasses were gone. She seemed to be taking her unemployment well.

I rose to my feet and placed my hands in my pockets. "Ariel, how are you?"

"Good." She stood in front of my desk with her hands held together at her waist. "You?"

"Good," I lied. "What can I help you with?"

"I left a few things behind. I was wondering if someone could fetch them for me."

I was stupid for hoping she wanted her job back. Ariel was far more stubborn than I was. I was more likely to fold than she was, and that was never going to happen. We both cared about image, about pride. "Of course. What are they?"

"I left fifteen thousand in your grand safe. I left it there for traveling expenses."

I'd forgotten about that. "Anything else?"

"Yes. I have some sentimental jewelry in Fair Isle. I'd let Finley mail it back, but I don't feel comfortable with that arrangement. If you can fly me out there, I can retrieve it myself. Or you could have one of your men escort it here."

"I'll arrange for Dimitri to fetch it for you."

"Thank you."

I walked around the desk, keeping my shoulders straight. "I'll be right back with the cash. You can take a seat if you'd like."

Ariel remained in place.

I left the office and walked upstairs to the bedroom. I had safes in various places around the castle, dispersing important items in separate locations so it would be difficult to rob me. Ariel's cash was in this safe, along with some of my family heirlooms.

When I walked inside, London had just finished drying her hair with a towel wrapped around her waist. "What a nice surprise." She walked up to me and kissed me, dropping the towel at the same time.

My hands slid up her back and to her shoulders as I kissed her, my body automatically reacting to hers. Her perky tits were pressed against my body, and my hands slid down to her ass and gave both cheeks a squeeze. For a second, I forgot the reason why I came up here to begin with. I pulled away and ignored the hard-on that formed in my slacks. "Ariel is waiting for me downstairs. I just came to grab something from the safe."

"There's a safe up here?"

"Yeah." I walked around her and entered the private living room. The safe was behind one of the picture frames. No one knew where it was besides myself. I didn't even share that knowledge with my employees. I was about to ask London to go into the other room so I could have some privacy, but I knew that wasn't how I wanted our relationship to be. I trusted her, and I needed to prove it.

I pulled the picture off the wall then spun the dial left and right until I got the code right. Then I opened the door and saw the heirlooms inside. My great-great-grandfather's crown sat on the top shelf, the material rusty and some of the gems missing. There were a few other things passed down from my ancestors, including a brush that had most of the bristles missing.

London stood beside me and peered inside. "Oh my god… are those real?"

"Yeah." No matter how many times I looked at them, I never forgot how significant they were. These were relics that had lasted hundreds of years. There was a time when civilization didn't rely on the internet, mass production, or even automobiles. My ancestors survived long enough to have me, and now I lived a life of luxury that my relatives never dreamed.

"That's incredible…" She stared at them for a long time and didn't try to touch anything.

I didn't put my hands on any of the relics because the oils from my fingertips were damaging. They weren't exposed to sunlight and stayed at a constant temperature at all times. I pulled out the bag of cash and left the door open. "Make sure you close it when you're finished."

"You're gonna leave it open like that?" she asked incredulously.

I wanted to prove that I trusted her so we could be the way we used to be. I knew she didn't want me for my wealth or my connections. If anything, she loved me in spite of those things. "I know you'll take care of it."

A slight smile crept into her lips. "Ariel stopped by for money?"

"Yeah. She has some stuff at Fair Isle as well. I'll have to have someone fly out and bring it to her."

She nodded slightly. "You aren't gonna try to talk to her again?"

"No." Ariel wouldn't change her mind unless I gave her what she wanted. I walked out so I wouldn't have to listen to London convince me to fight for a woman who didn't want to work with me anymore.

I returned to my office and set the cloth bag stuffed with money on the desk. "I haven't touched it since I put it in the safe. You can count it if you want." I sat in the leather chair and crossed my legs.

She opened her purse and placed the money inside. "I know you're good for it. So, you'll let me know when my jewelry is back?"

"Of course."

"Thank you." She wasn't just civil, but slightly cold.

"Where are you living?" It was strange not knowing about Ariel's life. It'd only been a short time since she left me, but it felt like an eternity.

"I'm moving to London—with Cassandra."

"That's great. I'm happy for you." Maybe she was taking this opportunity to settle down and have a life that wasn't centered around work. "She seems like a nice woman."

"She's incredible. I'm looking forward to living with her."

I suddenly felt a pain in my chest, missing her before she even walked out the door. "You know, you can always call me if you need anything. I'm more than happy to write you an incredible recommendation."

Her coldness finally dropped, replaced by a soft expression I'd hardly ever witnessed. "I know, Crewe. I appreciate that."

I came around the desk and extended my arms to hug her. At our previous interaction when we were closing our partnership, it wasn't the right time for a real goodbye. We got down to business, and she got her check and walked out the door. I was too angry to say how I really felt.

She smiled before she hugged me back, moving into my chest for a real embrace.

I held her for the first time since I met her. We were never affectionate, hardly giving each other a handshake. This was a big deal—for both of us. "Please invite me to your wedding."

"Of course, Crewe." She was the first one to pull away, that softness in her eyes. "Good luck with everything."

"Good luck to you too."

She smiled and finally turned around and walked out the door.

The second she couldn't see my face, I let my smile fall. I let the pain enter my chest, the paramount loss crippling me. Most of the people I was close to had passed away. There were a few people I considered family, like Finley. He'd been in my life for a long time. I saw Ariel in that same regard, and watching her walk away was more difficult than I expected it to be.

I tried to swallow the pain and pretend I didn't care.

But I did care.

I hoped it would get easier in time, but I suspected it never would.

I'd just have to make my peace with it.

———

Work wasn't enough to block out my thoughts. But I did manage to cut down on the scotch since London would smell it on my breath the second I walked through the door. I was in the mood to be alone, but I knew I couldn't push her away—not like I did the other night.

She was finally back in my life, and I couldn't take her for granted again. When I was with her, the pain didn't seem so bad. At least I had someone to carry the burden with me rather than suffering alone.

It was a cold evening and the sun was gone, but I asked Dunbar to get the fire pit going so I could sit outside and watch the flames with a cup of hot tea.

Yes, I was drinking tea now. Tasted like shit.

I instructed Dimitri to fetch London for me—and to tell her to dress warmly.

She came out to the courtyard fifteen minutes later in jeans and a thick snow jacket. She took the seat beside me on the couch and pulled a blanket over both of us. "The fire looks nice." Her tone suggested she recognized I was in a particularly bad mood. She treaded carefully, talking about things that had no real meaning.

"It does."

"Are we gonna make some s'mores?"

"Some what?" I asked.

"S'mores," she repeated. "You know, you roast the marshmallows over the fire and then put them between two graham crackers with a piece of chocolate."

I'd visited America enough times to know most of their customs, but this one was lost on me. "Can't say I do."

"We'll have to do it sometime. You'll love it."

I didn't have a big sweet tooth, so I doubted it. But I didn't mind doing something she enjoyed.

"So…something else happen with Ariel?"

"No." I stared at the fire. "We ended on great terms."

She continued to watch me, her face turned in my direction. "Then why do you seem so devastated?"

I rested my hands together on my lap, feeling the wool blanket underneath me. "Because I am devastated. We had a little exchange before she left…we hugged. She told me she was moving in with Cassandra. I asked her to invite me to her wedding…it was nice."

Her hand moved to mine where she intertwined our fingers. "I'm sorry, Crewe. I really wish the two of you could have worked it out."

"Yeah, me too."

"There's nothing I can do?"

I squeezed her hand. "No. It's difficult to lose her, but losing you would be far worse." I brought her hand to my mouth and gently kissed her knuckles. I didn't think it was fair that I had to choose between the two women to begin with, but I knew I made the right decision. London was essential for my happiness.

She gave my hand a squeeze. "You're sweet…"

I lowered her hand to my lap and watched the fire in the stone fire pit. "It'll take me a while to get over it, but one day I will. People come and go. That's just how it is."

"Unfortunately."

I sank back into the chair and watched the flames with lazy eyes. The pain in my chest was constant, but it would disappear in time. After a full night of rest, I already feel better. I just needed to give it some time. And with London with me, things would get easier.

"Thanks for coming to me…and not going to a bar." She moved into my side and rested her head on my shoulder.

"You're much better company."

She wrapped her arm around my waist then pressed a kiss to my cheek. "Only because I'm with you."

12

LONDON

I was crushed.

I hadn't seen Crewe wear that expression too often. He downplayed his sadness over losing Ariel, but I could see the devastation in his eyes. His mood wasn't just dark like it was when he was angry about something.

He was lifeless.

I didn't like it at all.

After a few days, he lightened up a bit. When he came to the bedroom after work, he was the worst. After spending an hour with me, he usually came back around, probably because he wasn't thinking about the mess she left behind.

I knew all too well what it was like to lose someone. I was young when my parents died, but I was never the same after they were gone. I don't have a foundation, with the exception of Joseph. Ariel wasn't a mother to him, but she was inside his circle deep enough that she was definitely family.

I didn't want him to lose that. He already lost so much as it was.

But I didn't know how to fix it. I'd already tried talking to her once, and she was so disgusted by me that she could hardly look at me. How would I persuade someone that didn't trust me?

Crewe was in a particularly bad mood that morning. He was silent, and his shoulders were tighter than usual. He showered in less than five minutes then brushed his teeth with an irritated expression. He didn't bother to shave, which told me he was either too stressed to remember or he just didn't give a damn.

"Everything alright?"

Crewe looked at my reflection in the mirror as he finished securing his tie around the collar of his shirt. He didn't dance around the topic like he used to. If something was on his mind, he didn't beat around the brush. "Ariel is coming by to pick up her things."

"Ooh…" Now it all made sense.

He folded down his collar then pulled on his jacket.

I didn't feed him empty lines to make him feel better. He didn't bullshit with me, and I didn't bullshit with him. "Anything I can do?"

He held up his forefinger before he turned to the stand-up dresser against the wall. It reminded me of something out of a fairy tale because I'd never seen a dresser like it anywhere else. Men usually just had closets. But Crewe had so many clothes and accessories that he needed every nook and cranny. He opened the door and pulled out a black ensemble, a lacy bustier and a matching thong. "Yes. Be ready for me when I walk through that door." He tossed the racy outfit on the bed then gave me a quick kiss before he walked out.

My mind wasn't on the lingerie or his expectations of what I would do when he finished work. I was thinking about Ariel, the root of his sadness. I could fuck him as many times as he wanted, but that wouldn't put him back together.

He needed both of us to be happy.

"What are you doing?" Dimitri asked when I stepped out of the front doors.

"I'm a free woman. I can do whatever I want." I saw Ariel's car pulled up to the steps in the gravel roundabout. A black Audi with tinted windows, it perfectly matched her infuriating personality. "I'm just waiting for Ariel."

Dimitri narrowed his eyes in suspicion.

I couldn't expect any of Crewe's men ever to trust me again. "I want to convince her not to leave, that's all."

Dimitri continued to stand with his hands in front of his waist, but he didn't take his eyes off me. "I'm watching you."

I rolled my eyes and stood near her car, knowing she would leave soon. Crewe never walked his guests to the door, so I didn't expect him to do it today. Knowing him, he would stay in his office and down a glass of scotch. He wouldn't want to interact with anyone, not even me. So my chances of getting caught were slim unless Dimitri wanted to piss me off.

Ariel walked through the front doors minutes later, a small duffel bag over her shoulder. Her sunglasses were already on, and she wore a black dress with matching heels. For no longer having a job, she looked awfully professional.

When she noticed me, she halted in her steps. Her glasses hid her expression from view, but I pictured how threatening her eyes must have looked. She started moving again, taking the stairs until we were level with one another. "Get away from my car."

I ignored the insult. "Ariel, I need you to stay."

"Now you have him all to yourself, wrapped around your finger. No, you don't need me for a damn thing." She opened the passenger door and placed her stuff on the leather seat. She shut the door then turned back to me, her expression still grim.

"Ariel, he's devastated. He acts like he's fine with it, but trust me, he's not."

"I'm not happy about the arrangement either, but that's how it has to be."

"But it doesn't have to be that way. Look, I'll do anything to make this work. Please stay for Crewe. Don't punish him because of me."

"This has nothing to do with punishment," she said coldly. "I'm an opportunist. I no longer see an opportunity here."

"Crewe is a brilliant man. You can't downplay that."

"How would you know? All you ever do is suck his cock and manipulate him."

I narrowed my eyes, feeling my skin prickle at the insult. "I love him. And you know that, Ariel."

I couldn't see her eyes, but I imagined she just rolled them.

"Meet me halfway here, Ariel. What can I do to get you to stay?"

"Disappear. I already told you that."

"Well, that's the one thing I can't do. Anything else?"

"Nope."

"Ariel," I said through gritted teeth. "I wouldn't be putting this much effort in if I didn't love Crewe so much. I could just turn my head the other way so you'll leave. It's not like I like you or you like me. I'm only doing this for him. So that right there should be enough to make you consider everything."

She took off her glasses and hooked them on the front of her blouse. With a cold and calculating expression, she stared me down like an enemy about to attack. "I'll make a deal with you, London. You want to prove yourself to me? Here's your chance."

I held my breath, hoping she wouldn't ask for anything ridiculous.

"You can stay with him until this relationship runs its course. But Crewe needs to marry someone else, someone royal, and you're going to make sure that happens. You need to give me your word that you'll never marry him, that you'll encourage him to find someone else, and if he asks you to marry him, you'll say no."

My heart stopped beating, not from adrenaline, but from depression.

"Give me your word, and we have a deal."

I could spend a year with him, maybe longer. But now our relationship had a deadline. I could love him every night for now, but one day, I'd have to give him up. I'd have to step aside and watch him spend the rest of his life with someone else. I didn't realize how much I wanted to grow old with him until the option was taken away from me.

"London?" she pressed.

Could I really do that? I asked Crewe to trust me. By doing this, I was lying to him. But I didn't want him to lose Ariel. Maybe Crewe and I would never get married anyway.

Maybe our relationship would grow old and stale. Anything could happen. This was the only compromise I could think of that allowed Crewe to have both of us. "Okay…"

"Yes?" Ariel asked.

"Yeah. I give you my word."

She couldn't keep the surprise from flooding her features. "Maybe you do really love him."

"Of course, I do."

She crossed her arms over her chest and looked at the front door.

"When are you going to talk to him?"

"It'd be too obvious if I did it now. I'll wait a few days." She turned away and walked to the driver's door like our conversation was finished.

"Okay."

"If you ever tell Crewe we had this conversation, I'll deny it."

"Have a good night, Ariel." I walked away before she got into the car and shut the door. I heard the door shut and the engine start as I walked up to the front doors.

Dimitri watched me like a hawk. "What was that about?"

"Just wanted to say goodbye."

I spent the afternoon reflecting on my conversation with Ariel.

More formally known as the devil.

I made a deal I never wanted to make, but I knew it was best for Crewe. He couldn't marry someone like me anyway. I wanted to have my own life, my own ambitions. Being his wife would involve a lot of etiquette and social decorum. I would be a full-time wife, not a physician or anything else. People would stick their noses in my business around the clock.

So maybe it was better this way.

Joseph hated him, and I couldn't have my brother hate my spouse. And I couldn't have my spouse hate my brother either.

And I brought nothing to the table except for piles of student loans.

When Crewe came to the bedroom after five, I was dressed in the bustier with my hair big and my makeup heavy. I pushed my conversation with Ariel from my mind and tried to concentrate on the fact that I had Crewe right now—and for the foreseeable future. I wanted to soak up every moment, not think about the day when we would part ways.

He walked inside and immediately looked me up and down, the shadow on his face nearly a full beard. His brown eyes were fixed with colors of amber and gold, and the intensity was enough to make the sun melt. He slowly removed his jacket and tossed it on the ground before he slipped his shoes off.

I stood near the foot of the bed, my hand propped on my hip and my feet aching in the five-inch heels I wore. I would be lying if I said I didn't love it when Crewe looked at me that way. I loved every second of it, seeing the fiery desire in his eyes that was going to explode like hot molten lava.

He unbuttoned his shirt as he walked up to me, taking his time with each button until he yanked his tie loose. His hand moved to my hip, and his fingers traced over my smooth skin, causing my body to prickle naturally in response.

He felt the lace in his fingertips and wrapped up the strap of my thong in his index finger.

My breathing was heavy in my ears while his was so calm I could barely hear it.

He gripped both of my tits in the push-up and squeezed them hard with his strong hands. His eyes watched his movements, watching the swell of my breasts change as he massaged me.

My hand went to his cock in his slacks and felt the nine inches of definition.

He craned his neck and pressed his mouth to mine, giving me a slow and sensual kiss that made my knees weak. Heat flushed my body even though we barely touched. The explosive reaction this man caused was supernatural.

My fingers undid his belt and pants until I could push down everything, including his boxers. When his cock was out, I wrapped my fingers around him and stroked him as I continued to kiss him, our tongues moving together harshly. The slow sensuality died away, and only carnal need remained behind. I kissed him harder as my hand jerked his long length, moving from tip to base.

His breathing hitched when a restrained moan escaped his lips. His hand dug into my hair just the way I liked, and he kissed me with the kind of passion no man ever had before. Crewe made me feel beautiful, sexy, and incredible all at the same time.

He guided me backward until the backs of my legs hit the foot of the bed. "On all fours," he said through our kiss. "Ass in the air."

I turned around and obeyed, my back arched to make my waist look smaller and my ass bigger.

Crewe pulled my thong down to my knees then positioned himself at my entrance. With perfect ease, he slipped inside me, stretching my channel for the millionth time. I was soaking wet, and I coated his entire length, my moisture lubing his balls.

A quiet moan escaped his lips. "That pussy…goddamn." He gripped the back of my neck as he moved into me slowly, giving me long and even strokes. His head hit my back wall every time he thrust, and I felt an orgasm already beginning.

He pushed my head into the mattress then propped one leg on the bed, deepening the angle. He gave me more of his length every time, my fluid making audible noises each time he pushed inside me.

My mouth was open against the comforter. "Crewe…"

"Lovely." He pressed his hand to my lower back and fucked me harder, giving me his big cock over and over. His fingers dug into my skin, and as his grip tightened, I could feel his cock thickening with overwhelming arousal.

I loved it when he came inside me. I didn't care if he went before me. It always felt so incredible to have his seed buried deep inside.

He suddenly pulled out of me, his cock shiny from my arousal. "Turn over."

I didn't want him to stop, but if I argued, it would take longer for him to be inside me. I flipped onto my back and looked up at him, my bustier still squeezing me like a corset. My waist appeared slimmer than it really was, and my tits were pressed higher and tighter than ever before.

He kicked his pants and boxers away before he crawled on top of me, his knees moving behind my legs as he positioned me into the mattress. With a clenched jaw, he pushed himself inside me again, hitting me hard.

I moaned when I felt him stretch me again, bringing me back to how I was just a moment before. My nails dug into his skin, and I widened my legs so he could take all of me.

He fucked me harder than he did before, ramming me into the bed and making my entire body shake. With eyes locked to mine, he watched every single expression form on my face. When I bit my bottom lip, his eyes narrowed in intensity.

My hands moved up his chest, feeling this powerful man conquer me on his bed. I loved feeling his heart pound, feeling the sweat form on his beautiful skin. I loved watching him exert himself to please me.

I knew I wanted to do this for the rest of my life.

I didn't want another man to be my husband. I wanted it to be Crewe. I wanted him to be the father of my children.

But that could never happen. It was just a dream.

My fingers slid into his damp hair. "I love you…"

When he thrust inside me, he didn't pull out again. He left himself inside my channel, and he closed his eyes as he stopped himself from exploding then and there. He released a loud sigh before he rocked into me again.

My hand moved to his face, and I kissed him as he made love to me. "I love you." I didn't say it again because I wanted to hear him say it back. Now I wanted to take advantage of every opportunity that I had to tell him how I really felt, that he was the only man in the world I adored. When he was deep inside me like this, taking me like it was the first time he'd ever had me, I was out of my mind and in the moment.

He hooked my leg over his shoulder and deepened the angle, my other leg opening to the side so he had greater access to fuck me as hard as he wanted. He thrust hard inside me. "I." He did it again, his eyes locked on mine. "Love." He gave me a kiss before he thrust again. "You."

13

CREWE

I WAS PLANNING on taking a trip back to Fair Isle, to have some quiet time on an island in the middle of the sea, but due to the extra work Ariel's absence had caused, I didn't have that luxury. Her presence in the company was vital because it allowed me to have the freedom to do what I wanted, when I wanted.

But now that freedom had been taken away.

I could pay someone else a ton of money to do it for me, but I was meticulous when it came to my business, and everything needed to be done correctly. I couldn't trust a stranger to care about the details between the lines, the image I was trying to maintain.

My legacy was on the line.

I was sitting in my office when London walked inside, looking beautiful in a deep blue dress that Dimitri had recently bought for her. He took a picture to my designer in

London, and she handpicked all the clothes that would complement London's figure.

She was worth every cent.

Her hair was pulled back in an elegant updo, and she looked like she was born in this castle the way I was. "Ready for lunch?"

I eyed my watch. "It's ten."

She welcomed herself into my lap, straddling my hips and sitting right on my crotch. I wasn't hard at the moment, but that was about to change. "You caught me. I just wanted an excuse to see you." Her arms circled my neck, and she looked at me with that playful expression I'd come to worship.

If I didn't have a ton of work to do, I'd blow off the workday and take her into the city to do something fun. But I had meetings and paperwork…the nightmare never ended. I never would have opened that second distillery if I'd known Ariel was going to leave. If I didn't want to work all the time, I might have to sell it.

But instead of saying any of that to London, I shut my laptop. "We can get a second breakfast."

"I'm actually pretty full. Maybe we can take a walk or something? Make love against a tree."

I smiled. "You have a thing for public places?"

"No." She smiled back. "I just have a thing for you."

Now my cock was rock-hard. I could see the love in her eyes without searching to find it. It was a look I got from some women, but not to the same degree. The look I got from London was special, something she probably hadn't given to anyone else. "Good answer." I pulled her harder into me and kissed her, wanting a quick embrace before I stood up. But like usual, the kiss developed into something more. She ground her hips and rocked against me, stroking my cock against her clit. We breathed into each other's mouths as she ground against me, the friction feeling great for both of us.

Now I wasn't leaving this office. I was gonna fuck her on my lap right then and there, not giving a damn about all the work that was piling up at that very moment. All I would need to do was pull her thong over and undo my slacks. Then I would slide into home plate, feeling that warm and wet channel.

A knock sounded on my door. "Sir?" Dunbar's voice entered the room.

I growled against London's mouth then pulled away. "What is it?" London moved her lips to my neck and kissed me anyway, dragging that sexy tongue across my skin to the corner of my mouth.

"Ariel is here to see you."

She was? Why?

London stilled against me, her breaths landing on my neck.

"What does she want?"

"Didn't say," Dunbar replied.

Did she forget something else? Or did she realize this whole thing was idiotic? "Lovely, we'll pick this up later."

She got off my lap and straightened her dress. "Okay." She walked out the door, Dunbar's wide frame appearing in view. He normally opened the door when he wanted to speak to me, but he probably second-guessed it when London was inside with me.

"Send her in," I commanded.

Dunbar shut the door and disappeared again.

I didn't know what to expect from Ariel, but I tried not to get my hopes up too high. Chances were, she just forgot something or had a financial document that needed to be signed. She wouldn't change her mind unless she had a very good reason to.

Ariel entered my office in the dark clothing she always wore. Her glasses were back on the brim of her nose, and she carried herself with more class than the Queen of England. She strode toward me and took a seat in the armchair facing my enormous desk.

I couldn't get a good reading on her. "How can I help you, Ariel?"

"I've done some thinking."

I rested my hands together in my lap, my cock soft the second London walked out the door.

"I've loved working with you for the past ten years. I've always seen you as something more than a business partner, more like a friend."

Hope surged in my heart. "As have I."

"And I don't want to walk away from this business. I can learn to accept London in time. All I ask is that you be more astute this time around."

As insulting as it was, that statement was fair. "She won't be a problem."

"If that's the case, do you still want me?"

I couldn't suppress the smile on my lips, feeling the relief wash over me like a tide. It was a stupid question, and we both knew it. "You already know the answer."

She rose from her chair then extended her hand. "It's good to be back."

I shook her hand. "It is. Work has been shitty since the second you walked away."

She chuckled. "Nothing you couldn't handle."

"I could handle it—just didn't enjoy it." I dropped my hand and slid both palms into my pockets. "So, you want to start fresh tomorrow? Take the rest of the day off to enjoy your last bit of freedom."

"Sounds fair. I'll bring my lawyer so we can reinstate everything."

"Okay."

She gave me a slight wave before she walked out. "Until tomorrow."

"Until tomorrow," I repeated.

Once the door was shut and I was alone with my thoughts, overwhelming relief washed through me. Ariel wasn't just important to me because she ran my businesses like a boss, but because of the comfortable friendship we had formed. Getting that back made me realize I couldn't take her for granted ever again.

Dimitri rapped his knuckles on the door before he poked his head inside. "Can I speak to you for a second, sir?"

"Certainly." I was in such a good mood I'd probably give him a raise if he asked for it. "What's up?"

He approached my desk then lowered his voice, not that anyone could overhear us talking. "Ariel has returned?"

I nodded. "Things will go back to normal."

He rubbed the back of his head then stared at the floor.

"Anything else?"

"Uh…I'm not sure how to say this…not even sure what I'm reporting."

"Okay…" I narrowed my eyes, my mood taking a serious dive with his odd behavior. "Just spit it out, then."

"The other day when Ariel left, London met her outside and they talked for a while. I don't know what was said, but the conversation went on for a while."

My interest immediately picked up. "What day was this?"

"When Ariel came to pick up her jewelry."

"Interesting."

"And then Ariel comes back a few days later…I find it suspicious."

I found it suspicious too. "Thanks for letting me know, Dimitri."

"Of course, sir." He walked out and shut the door behind him.

I took a seat and crossed my legs, my fingertips rubbing against my jawline. The fact that London hadn't mentioned any of this to me told me something significant happened, and it was peculiar for Ariel to change her mind.

And that meant London said something to make Ariel reconsider.

In that moment, I felt like a very lucky man. The woman I loved did whatever she could to keep my business partner in my life, even though she personally hated the woman. Despite our shaky beginning, she really proved her loyalty to me. She cared about my happiness, even if it sabotaged her own.

That was real love.

I wouldn't take it for granted.

London immediately questioned me when I returned to the royal chambers. "What happened?"

I adjusted my cuff links and did my best to keep a stoic expression. "Ariel changed her mind. She starts again tomorrow."

London did such a remarkable job with her performance. Even though I knew she had something to do with it, she nearly fooled me into believing her innocence. "Wow. That's incredible. I'm relieved."

I inserted my hands in my pockets as I walked closer to her. "I'm glad to have her back. She makes my life a lot less complicated."

"I know. You've been working a lot…"

A smile formed on my lips as I looked at her, seeing the genuine happiness in her eyes. "It's too bad you two don't get along. Looks like you'll be seeing a lot more of her."

"She's not so bad," she whispered. "When she's around, I see you more. So, this is a win for me."

"Yeah." I could have told her I knew everything. I was tempted. I wanted her to know I appreciated the gesture she made for me, that she pressured Ariel into staying, whatever her argument was. I wanted London to know it meant a lot to me that she cared about my happiness so much. But not saying anything at all made it just as special. She proved she loved me without getting anything in return. So I kept it to myself and chose to stare at her instead. "I love you."

Her eyes softened at the unexpected words. When she was emotionally moved, she looked even more beautiful. She looked even more gorgeous than she did when she said she loved me when we made love. She looked perfect. "I love you too."

Like nothing happened, Ariel came to work the following day and picked up where she left off. She caught up on everything she had missed, rearranged the data sheets, and managed to pick up another client all within the first hour.

She was definitely a hustler.

In the afternoon, we had a meeting with a client in Edinburg. He owned a branch of high-end restaurants in Greece, and he was interested in making a large order of scotch on a regular basis. Since he was considered a VIP, we met him in person—and even I tagged along.

We got through the meal and signed the papers at the end. He had to leave to catch his flight, so he left us with the bill

—not that it made a difference to us. It gave us more time to enjoy the bottle of wine we hadn't finished.

"That was easy," Ariel said. "Now he's in our top ten."

"Easy money." I checked my phone for emails before I drank my wine again. Having Ariel at my side made everything smooth. I enjoyed her company as well as her brilliance. "Where did you find him anyway?"

"Cassandra," she explained. "She's friends with his brother-in-law."

"I'll have to thank her next time I see her."

"I'll thank her for you." She winked then drank her wine.

I didn't know much about Cassandra, other than the fact that Ariel adored her. "What does Cassandra do for a living?"

"She's a lawyer."

That didn't surprise me. Ariel seemed like someone who would be drawn to another successful person. "What kind of law does she practice?"

"Mainly divorce cases. But she enjoys it."

"That's great. The four of us should have dinner together sometime. I'd love to get to know her better."

"Sounds like a plan." Her nails were painted black, and she wore a gold bracelet that contrasted against her olive skin. Ariel was a natural beauty who accessorized minimally. Less was always more with her.

"Dimitri told me he saw you and London having a private conversation."

Ariel swirled her wine like I said nothing of consequence.

She didn't respond, so I pressed forward. "I don't know what London said to you, but I'm glad she said it. I was pretty miserable when you left."

She finally set down her wine and looked me in the eye. "I still don't like her. I'll never trust her. I'll never forgive her. But I will say that she genuinely cares for you, and that's the only thing I tolerate about her."

My assumption had been confirmed, and it only made me fall for London harder. The scar over my chest was just a bad dream now. We had our differences, a difficult beginning, but everything had been worth it. Now I was happy again. "Maybe your tolerance can grow to fondness someday."

"Unlikely, but possibly." She poured herself another glass of wine. "But you know me. I always keep an open mind."

"You do." I tapped my glass against hers. "To new beginnings."

She smiled. "To new beginnings."

14

LONDON

THE SECOND ARIEL walked back into his life, Crewe was in a much better mood.

And he worshiped the ground I walked on. When we weren't making love, he was still fiercely affectionate. And if he wasn't touching me with his hands, his eyes still explored me with their usual intensity.

I made a deal with the devil, but right now, I didn't regret it.

One day I would. But that day was not today.

He walked into the bedroom just before lunch, our usual daily routine. He used to have working lunches when Ariel wasn't around, but now he had plenty of free time. "Would you like to join me for lunch?"

"Definitely." I was dressed and ready to go, knowing he would walk in the door between 12:00 and 12:15. "Where are we eating?"

"The sun is out today, so I thought we'd eat in the courtyard. How does that sound?"

We could eat in the bathroom and I wouldn't care. As long as I got to be with Crewe, it didn't matter to me. "Perfect."

He circled my waist with his arms and pressed a quick kiss to my mouth. If he didn't have time for a rendezvous, he usually avoided giving me too much affection. When he did, it always led to other things. And if that happened, neither one of us would be eating lunch. He took my hand and walked with me to the courtyard. The second he appeared in the midst of the stone, flowers, and neatly trimmed bushes, the maids walked out with platters of sandwiches, salad, and assorted fruit. They set everything on the table underneath the umbrella then disappeared. Even though Crewe said thank you, they didn't say much back. It was as if they were afraid to anger him in some way.

I knew Crewe could be intimidating, but he wasn't *that* intimidating.

"How's your day?" Crewe had a cup of coffee with his lunch instead of a glass of scotch. He'd had to quit drinking all over again, but at least he was sticking to it.

"Pretty good. Did some reading." I hadn't even begun the process of applying to a school. Now that I knew Crewe and I wouldn't last much longer than a year, I didn't see the point. It would be a waste of time and money since the credits weren't transferrable. "How's yours?"

"Ariel brought a new client to the table. He owns over two dozen restaurants in Greece, Turkey, and Austria, so he's brought big business. Apparently, Cassandra had a connection to him."

"That's nice."

"We're gonna have dinner with Ariel and Cassandra soon. They seem serious, so I'd like to get to know her."

I wasn't sure why a sweet woman like Cassandra was with Ariel in the first place. That woman didn't have a heart. "Let me know when."

Crewe set his napkin in his lap and ate like we had visitors. His manners were an integral part of his demeanor, so he never ate like a normal person. I, on the other hand, always made a mess—one way or another.

"There's something I wanted to ask you."

"I'm listening." He popped a strawberry in his mouth and focused his expression on me. He always gave me his entire focus whenever I asked for it. I'd dated a lot of guys who only partially listened to what I had to say.

"Can you help me get a phone?"

"A phone?" he asked, his eyebrows raised.

"Yes, like a cell phone." I made it clear I was an independent human being this time around. "I'd also like a laptop and a car."

Crewe didn't shut me down. He took a bite of his salad and slowly chewed, considering my request. "I can arrange that."

"I can pay for my own car. I just need help getting a license. I can pay for my own laptop too, but since I don't have a license, I can't just go out and get one."

"I can have one of the men take care of that for you."

"I'd like to pay for it, Crewe." I didn't want him to buy everything for me. His wealth didn't matter to me, and I needed to prove that.

When his eyes darkened in intensity, I knew he wanted to shut me down and say he would pay for it anyway. But he knew how important it was for me to be respected as a real person, not a prisoner. "If you transfer the money into my account, I can have them pick up everything you need. Is that fair?"

That was the best compromise I was going to get. "Yes."

"We'll work on the license. I can arrange for you to take the exam here and get your license immediately."

"Okay."

He drank his coffee then took another bite of his food.

"I was also wondering if I could use your phone to call my brother." I knew this would be a difficult subject. When I called Joseph before, I planned my escape so I could get away from Crewe. Crewe would carry that scar on his chest until the day he died. There was no way Crewe could just brush that off like it was no big deal.

He didn't hesitate before he pulled his phone out of his pocket and slid it across the table from me. "Of course, Lovely. You don't need to ask."

I got a much better reaction than I hoped for. "Thanks…"

Crewe looked across the courtyard as he chewed his food, his hard jaw masculine and his features sharp and beautiful. It didn't matter what he was doing, he always looked sexy doing it.

He took my request a lot better than I expected, and I wasn't sure if his positivity came from Ariel's return or something else altogether. I was just grateful the conversation went so well.

When he finished his food, he left his dirty dishes for the maids to clear. "I'll be in my office. Return my phone when you're ready. I'll arrange for one of the men to pick up the things you asked for."

"Great. Thanks."

He came around the table and kissed me before he left. "See you later."

It was the kind of quick embrace that existed between a husband and a wife, or between two partners who were used to saying goodbye for a short period of time every day. I liked how natural it felt. I liked the fact that I could picture myself doing it every single day.

But I also hated that fact too.

When he was gone, I called my brother.

"London?" Joseph immediately assumed it was me, knowing Crewe had no reason to call him ever again.

"Yep, it's me. How's it going?"

"Good. I'm guessing things are going well with you since I haven't heard from you in nearly a month." His voice was heavy with accusation, but not enough to make me feel guilty.

"Yeah, I'm happy."

"Well, that's good. I'm in London right now."

"So you aren't too far away."

"But far enough that I wouldn't be able to help you if you needed it," he said. "You don't need it, right?"

"No. He takes good care of me."

"Good," he said with a sigh. "I'm relieved. So, what's your plan? You're gonna stay there forever?"

"I was going to go back to school and get my own apartment...but I don't think that's going to happen anymore."

"Are you pregnant?" he blurted.

"No." I rolled my eyes. "My time with Crewe is limited. I want to enjoy it the best I can."

"Why is it limited?"

I told him the story about Ariel.

"Man, she's a freak. I hate that bitch. You should have let me take her."

"Joseph," I said coldly. "That's not funny."

"Wasn't trying to be. But she's a bitch, and you know it."

"I do know it. But she's important to Crewe."

"Is he in love with her or something?"

"I sure hope not," I said. "Since she's gay."

"She is?" he asked in surprise. "Oh. Well, I guess you don't have to worry about that…"

"Yeah."

"So, you're really going to leave him when the time comes? I thought you loved this guy?"

"I do. I really do. That's why it has to be this way."

"Doesn't make any sense to me."

Joseph had never been in love, so he would never understand. "Even though my time with him will be short, it's still worth it. I'd much rather spend a little amount of time with him than none at all. Life is short. Live in the moment."

Joseph sighed over the line. "Whatever you say. Do you have a number where I can reach you?"

"Crewe is getting me a phone today."

"Well, let me know when you have those digits."

"Okay."

"I'll talk to you later. Bye."

"Bye."

He hung up, and I set the phone on the table. I was supposed to return it to Crewe, but I didn't feel like getting up just yet. Telling the truth to another person made it feel more real, that I agreed to hurt both Crewe and myself at the end of the road. When I asked Crewe about marriage in the past, he didn't have a real answer to give me. Maybe he never wanted to marry me.

But I knew he loved me.

As soon as Crewe walked through the door after work, he set a bag on the table and stripped his jacket off. "I got the stuff you asked for. Your driving exam is next week."

"Damn, that was fast."

"That's what I pay my men for." He unclasped his watch and slid it off his wrist. "And you know I'm fast too." He winked then leaned down and kissed me where I sat on the couch.

"I do, actually." I set my book on the table and rose to my feet so I could give him a hug. "So, I have a number and everything?"

"Expect a lot of inappropriate texts throughout the day."

"Oh, I will."

He grabbed the bag and pulled out the phone and a MacBook. "You're set. I added the Wi-Fi information for you."

"Thank you."

"No problem." He slid his arms around my waist and looked down at me. It was rare for him not to kiss me, but he seemed content with just a stare. He slightly swayed from side to side with me, almost as if we were slow dancing at a junior high dance.

"What is it?"

"Nothing," he whispered. "I just like to look at you."

"Good thing I like to look at you too."

"Well, how can you not? I'm a very handsome man." He smiled like he was teasing me.

"Very true."

He pulled me tighter against his chest, his powerful physique feeling like concrete. "So, are you going to apply for classes with that laptop?"

"No. I just need something to do during the day while you're at work."

He gave me a quizzical expression. "Are you saying you won't be taking classes again?"

"Probably not."

He couldn't hide the happiness on his face. He didn't smile, but the joy was in his eyes. "Why is that?"

"I don't know. Just not sure if I want to go to class while I'm here. Seems like a hassle."

"Well, you're more than welcome to live here—with me." He cupped my face and brushed his thumb across my bottom lip. "Pleasing me is a full-time job. It comes with great benefits."

"So I hear."

"It comes with anything you could ever need. And it comes with a personal heater too."

"You do keep the sheets warm."

His happiness dimmed. "Don't tease me, Lovely. Are you going to stay with me? You know there's nothing I want more."

It was easy to give up everything for him, at least when he looked at me like that. There was no sacrifice I wouldn't make to feel this good, to be this happy. I wanted this man to love me just like this for the rest of my life. I would never forget the way I felt the first time I laid eyes on him. There was so much hatred I couldn't bottle it all inside. But now when I looked at him, I saw the greatest man I'd ever met. "I'd like to stay with you."

His happiness immediately returned. "You've made me a very happy man."

That made everything worth it. When I packed my bags and left, I would remember this moment to give me the strength to walk away. "There's something I want from you…and you aren't going to be happy about it."

"You know I'll do anything for you."

"My brother can't hate my boyfriend, and my boyfriend can't hate my brother."

He stared at me without blinking.

"So I need you guys to get along. He's the only family I've got left."

"Lovely, you know he shot me."

"I know. And you kidnapped me. You're both guilty of terrible things."

"But I never tried to murder you. And when you were in my captivity, I always treated you with respect."

"Except when you stripped me naked and forced me to have dinner with Bones." I didn't remind him of the incident to make him feel terrible, just to prove my point.

His gaze darkened.

"I need you guys to get along. I've done my best with Ariel. You can do this for me."

"Totally different. Ariel has never done anything to you except make a few insults."

And force me to give up the love of my life. "You said you would do anything for me, Crewe. This is what I want."

He sighed as his fingertips loosened on my waist. "Goddammit."

"What's it going to be?"

"Has he agreed to this?"

I hadn't even mentioned it to him. "No…but he will."

"I highly doubt that."

"Crewe." I was giving up a lot just to be with him. He could do this.

He sighed again before he pressed his forehead against mine. "Fine. I'll do one dinner. One time."

"Not one time. I want to spend time with my brother."

"You'll have a car soon. You can leave the castle and see him whenever you want."

"I still need him to be welcome in your home."

He dropped his hands and stepped back. "Don't push it. That man killed some of my men. You think he can just walk onto this property and insult all my employees?"

"He wouldn't insult them—"

"His presence is insulting. I've agreed to dinner, and that's all I'm willing to do, London. Be grateful, and let's move on."

We would have to take this in baby steps. "Okay, that's fine."

Crewe stepped away and unbuttoned his collared shirt. He turned his back to me, hiding the irritation on his face. His jaw was probably clenched tightly in annoyance.

The only solution to this problem was sex. And it usually worked every time. I undressed behind him, stripping off my dress and bra until I was just in my white thong. My heels were on my feet, but I left them on because I thought it would only enhance the ensemble.

He turned around with his shirt open and his tie uneven. He looked me up and down, his eyes focusing on my bare tits. Instantly, the anger was gone as his mind appeared to swim with heavy thoughts of sex. His hands moved to his belt on their own, and he loosened his slacks until they fell to his ankles.

"How do you want me?" There was nothing Crewe wanted more than power. When I freely gave it to him, it made him feel aroused in a whole new way. My hands moved up to my tits, and I squeezed them hard.

He watched my movements, his gaze darkening with every passing second. "Edge of the bed. Ass in the air."

I said the magic words to make everything better. "Yes, sir."

"Are you free for dinner tonight?" I asked Joseph over the phone. Last time we spoke, he was in London, but he seemed to move around a lot.

"I'm in Edinburgh, actually. Just went golfing with some buddies."

"Is that a yes, then?"

"Depends. Are you buying?"

I couldn't suppress the smile that formed on my lips. "Sure. Just don't order the most expensive thing on the menu."

"You know I'm an expensive date."

"Which is strange considering you're such poor company."

"Ha," he said sarcastically. "Now I'm getting two beers instead of one."

"Fine by me. Is seven okay?"

"Sure. There's this great steakhouse in Edinburgh. I'll text you the name."

"That sounds great."

"Alright, see you then."

Before he could hang up, I slipped in an extra detail I didn't mention before. "Perfect. Crewe and I will see you then." I hung up before I could hear him make an argument. Crewe was pissed about spending time with Joseph, but Joseph would be even angrier about it.

He called back—like a pain in the ass. "Hey, what's up?" I answered casually.

"Did you say Crewe was coming?" He spoke with suppressed rage, completely the opposite of how he sounded before.

"Yeah. What's the big deal?"

"The big deal?" he asked incredulously. "If you wanna fuck him, that's your choice. But I'm not having a meal with that asshole."

"Joseph," I said calmly. "I need you two to get along."

"Why? You made it clear you aren't gonna marry the guy. I don't introduce you to all the women I bed."

Too much information. "But he's really important to me. For as long as we're together, I need you two to get along."

"Not gonna happen. The fucker kidnapped you."

"And I fell in love with him, so he obviously treated me well."

"Which makes me hate him even more. If he'd just left you alone, you'd still be in school and living a normal life. You might be dating a normal guy and having a normal relationship. That asshole took that away from you."

"I'm here willingly."

"But he screwed up your path. You expect me to forgive him for that?"

"I never said anything about forgiving each other. I just need you two to tolerate one another. You're both very important to me."

"Does Crewe know about this? Or were you gonna tell him when you pulled up to the restaurant."

"Yes, he knows."

"Bullshit."

"I told him a few days ago. He's fine with it."

He scoffed into the phone. "You expect me to buy that?"

"Okay…he's not thrilled about it, but he at least agreed to do it, which is a lot more than I can say for you."

He sighed.

"Come on, Joseph. One dinner."

"One dinner will lead to two dinners."

"I'm not choosing sides, but what you've done to him is far worse than what he did to you."

"You've got to be kidding me."

"Joseph, you tried to steal four million dollars from him. Don't forget why this mess happened in the first place. And then you killed his men, tried to take his partner as a prisoner, and you shot the guy. You can't be so self-involved not to see the big picture here."

"You know what? I think he's a shithead. I'm not gonna change my mind."

I rolled my eyes. "Don't be annoying, Joseph."

"Too bad."

"You're doing this for me, not for him. Don't forget that. And we both know you'd do anything for me. You're the only family I've got in the world." I knew that would hit him in the right spot. My brother wasn't emotional, but that subject got him every single time.

"Ugh…"

"Is that a yes?"

"I said ugh."

"And in Joseph's world, what does that mean?"

He was quiet over the phone, taking his time before he answered. "Fine…I'll go."

"No men. No guns."

"Be reasonable, London."

"I mean it. No guns or men. Just the three of us."

"How do I know he'll keep his end of the bargain?"

"Because I'll be with him. If you think I'd ever let him hurt you, you're out of your mind."

"That's how it better be. And since Crewe is the one buying, you bet your ass I'm gonna order the most expensive thing on the goddamn menu."

We sat in the back seat as Dunbar drove us to the restaurant. The windows were tinted black so no one could see inside, and that was the reason Crewe and I had screwed in the back seat so many times.

He was dressed in jeans, a gray t-shirt, and a brown leather jacket that made him look yummy. His shoulders looked nice, along with the rest of his body. He shaved before we left, so his jaw was clean, which was something I only saw in the morning before he left for work. He didn't say much, annoyed about this dinner the way Joseph was.

"Any ground rules?" he finally asked.

"No guns."

"You already said that. Anything else?"

"Like?" I wore jeans and a black leather jacket, something Crewe's stylist in London had picked out for me. We never met in person, but she always selected clothes that perfectly fit my shape.

"Topics of conversation."

"Just don't be explicit about screwing me and we should be good."

"Not something I would talk about with anyone…let alone your brother."

"Well, you asked." He looked out the window with his hand resting on my thigh. He didn't seem nervous about the dinner, just annoyed. He preferred to spend his evenings alone with me in the castle, making love in the enormous bed we slept in every night and eating dinner on the balcony that overlooked the courtyard.

"Just because I didn't bring a gun doesn't mean I can't kill him with my bare fists."

I did my best not to roll my eyes at his ridiculous display of machismo. "If either of you does anything, I'll kick both of your asses."

He chuckled at the thought. "Sure, Lovely."

"Hey, I have an awesome right hook."

"You'll have to show me sometime. I'd love to see it."

"I need a punching bag too. Are you volunteering?"

The corner of his mouth rose in a smile. "I miss that…"

"Miss what?" I asked, not following his logic.

"That fiery attitude. You used to talk shit to me all the time when we first met. Now you're just sweet and affectionate."

"Are you saying you want me to be mean and sarcastic?"

"No," he said with a chuckle. "Well, maybe when we're fucking."

"Duly noted."

Dunbar pulled up to the curb and opened the back door so we could exit the car. Crewe took my hand and walked me inside, approaching the hostess desk in the dimly lit room. Tables were packed, but the noise level was low, everyone speaking quietly. A low-burning candle sat on each table.

Joseph already had a table against the back wall, and instead of waving us over, he just stared at us as he drank his beer.

"My brother is in the back."

Crewe looked up and spotted him before he pulled me with him. As we approached one another, my pulse pounded in my ears. The last thing I wanted was for these two men to murder each other over dinner.

"Hey." I wrapped my arms around my brother and hugged him.

"Hey." He hugged me back.

Crewe took a seat, not bothering to shake Joseph's hand.

Joseph probably wouldn't have shaken his anyway.

I sat beside Crewe, and Joseph was careful to choose the seat directly across from me.

Super awkward.

Joseph took another drink of his beer, finishing the rest and leaving a foam moustache on his mouth.

Crewe scanned the restaurant discreetly, probably making sure Joseph didn't have backup lurking around.

There was so much distrust and hatred I could feel it pressing into my skin. "Let's see what the menu looks like…" I picked up the black menu and read through the selections. "The rib eye looks pretty good. What are you having, Crewe?"

"Scotch," he replied.

I didn't dare give him any attitude right now. "Joseph?"

"Beer," he said. "And the lobster."

I eyed the two men, wondering if this was a terrible idea after all. "Thanks for coming out…both of you."

"Didn't give me much of a choice," Joseph said.

"Me neither," Crewe said in agreement.

"Come on, guys," I said. "We're here. Let's just make this work."

"Honestly, what were you expecting?" Joseph asked. "For Crewe and me to apologize to each other then go golfing?"

"That asshole shot me," Crewe said. "Let's not forget."

I held up my hand. "There will be no insults tonight. When we go our separate ways tonight, the two of you can't be enemies. I want there to be peace. Not friendship, loyalty, or respect. Just peace." I wasn't asking for much, just for the two men to be civil to one another.

Neither one of them disagreed with that.

I tried to strike up a conversation that both of them could participate in. "So, Crewe's second distillery is doing well. He opened it a few months ago, and the orders are pouring in. Do you like scotch, Joseph?"

He pressed his lips tightly together like he didn't want to respond. "I do, actually. His is pretty damn good."

I looked to Crewe, silently commanding him to accept the compliment.

Crewe looked annoyed, but he cooperated. "Thank you."

It was a rough start, but at least it was a start. "Crewe is helping me get my license so I can start driving."

"Why don't you just have his men drive you around?" Joseph asked.

"I wish she would," Crewe whispered.

"Because I want my own independence," I answered.

Joseph didn't hide his thoughts on the matter. "Independence is so overrated. You have a team of men who will cater to your every need. Anyone would do anything to have that. Just enjoy it."

"I wish she felt that way," Crewe said. "But she wants to pay for her own things too…"

"This guy is loaded." He pointed to Crewe. "And he kept you as a prisoner for six months. Let him buy you whatever you want."

"I don't need him to buy me anything," I said harshly. "Crewe is my boyfriend, not my sugar daddy."

"I don't mind being your sugar daddy," Crewe said.

"Well, I do," I argued. I waved the waiter over so we could get off the subject. I ordered a glass of wine and my entrée, and the two men ordered afterward. When he was gone, we were back to our bubble of awkwardness.

Crewe didn't strike up a conversation, and neither did Joseph.

I shouldn't have expected them to do anything.

"Where have you traveled recently?" I asked Joseph.

"Russia," Joseph answered. "I was in Moscow."

"For what?" Crewe asked.

"Business," Joseph said vaguely.

I knew Russia was a sore subject for Crewe. Any time it was mentioned, his mood got noticeably darker. "Anywhere else?"

"What kind of business?" Crewe pressed.

Joseph wore an expression that said he didn't want to answer. "There's a big deal going on among the Russia mafia with forty million on the line. I'm going to intercept it."

"How do you know this?" Crewe pressed.

I didn't get these men together to discuss work, but that's exactly what happened.

"Bones," Joseph replied. "Said he met with a Russian representative, but he didn't give me any details."

"Hmm…" Crewe's jaw was tense like he was thinking. "Who's exchanging the money?"

"I can't say," Joseph said.

That wasn't the kind of answer Crewe accepted. "I'm not after cash. If it's someone I'm interested in, I can help you."

"You think I need help?" Joseph asked incredulously.

"Seeing how you pissed me off, yeah," Crewe snapped.

"Hey, guys." I raised both hands. "Let's just take it down a notch."

Crewe ignored me. "Write it down." He pulled a pen from his pocket and pushed the napkin toward him. "Now."

Joseph snatched the pen out of his hand then scribbled the names in tiny print. He folded it and pushed it back to Crewe.

Crewe glanced at it, narrowed his eyes, and then tore it up into pieces. "I want in."

"I don't need help," Joseph said. "And I'm not giving you a cut."

"I don't want a cut," Crewe said coldly. "I just want in."

"Why?" Joseph asked.

"Because one of these fuckers crossed me," Crewe whispered under his breath. "And I want to take something that means the world to him. The only thing he seems to give a damn about is money and pride. I'd like to destroy both of those things."

Joseph watched him with suspicion, his eyes narrowed.

I wanted Joseph and Crewe to get along, but not in this way. But if this brought them closer together, I couldn't object. Crewe was still haunted by what happened to his family. If this gave him closure, I couldn't ask him not to do it. "Joseph, you can trust Crewe."

"None of this makes sense," Joseph asked. "Even if it is about revenge."

"You don't need to know details, Joseph," I said quickly. "Crewe wants in, and I think he can help you."

Crewe looked at me, and deep in his eyes was a look of gratitude that Joseph would never notice. His expression was difficult to read, probably on purpose, but I'd cracked the code a long time ago.

Joseph watched us both with hesitance. "I work with a particular team…"

"Which I don't have a lot of faith in, considering the fact that you tried to fool me with counterfeit. Come on, Joseph." When Crewe took the lead, he had more authority than all the world leaders put together. "I want this mission to be successful."

Joseph looked at me as if he expected me to say something.

"I think it's a good idea," I said. "You have mutual interests. It's perfect."

Joseph shrugged in response. "Okay, fine. But if you cross me, I'll kill you."

Crewe smiled. "Ditto."

"There will be no killing of any kind," I said. "If you both love me, you'll never lay a hand on each other."

"I don't love you that much," Joseph said.

Crewe chuckled. "Like I'd ever believe that. You fucking shot me."

"Well, you had it coming," Joseph said. "If you thought I wasn't going to do anything to save my sister, you're an idiot."

"If I had a sister, I would have done the same," Crewe said.

Maybe this would work out, after all. It wasn't perfect by any means, but it wasn't horrendous either. Guns weren't drawn, and bullets weren't flying through the air. "So you forgive Joseph for shooting you?"

"I never apologized," Joseph said quickly.

"Nor was I looking for an apology," Crewe said. "The best we can do is leave the past where it belongs and move forward. That's the best I can offer."

"Agreed," Joseph said. "Now where the hell is our food?"

It wasn't perfect, but I would take it.

15

CREWE

When we walked into the bedroom, I was relieved the dinner with Joseph was over. It went better than I expected it to, and he was directly involved in conning one of the men I despised.

Of course, I wanted in.

London slipped her jacket off her shoulders and hung it on the armchair. "Thank you for tonight. It meant a lot to me." She turned around and tucked her hair behind her ear, looking like the sexiest thing in the world without even trying.

When she looked at me like that, I would do anything for her—without question. "Looks like we can be civil to one another."

"I know. You guys both really tried." She pulled her shirt over her head, revealing the black bra underneath that pushed her tits together. Slowly, she peeled away the remainder of her clothes, getting her jeans off last until she stood in just her matching bra and panties. "I'd like to show my appreciation."

My throat went dry, so I automatically swallowed, feeling the muscles shift as I pushed the saliva down. Every day, I got to live out my fantasy because I woke up beside her then came home to her after work. She satisfied my sexuality but also fueled it even more. It was a cycle that continued to repeat itself, not that I minded.

She sauntered toward me, her beautiful brown hair framed around her shoulders. She had a slim waistline, the small muscles of her body visible just underneath her bra. She had incredible legs too, the long and slender kind that could hook around my waist while I pinned her to the mattress. When she reached me, she ran her hands down my chest as she lowered herself to her knees on the red rug of my bedroom. Her eyes were glued to mine as she unzipped my jeans and pulled my boxers down, letting my throbbing cock pop out. Her mouth immediately went to my balls, and she licked them with enthusiasm, dragging her tongue across the rough texture of my sac.

I inhaled a sharp breath and closed my eyes.

She dragged her tongue up my length, right over the thick vein on the surface. When she got to the top, she licked away the drop that formed there. It stuck to the tip of her tongue and the tip of my cock, making a sticky line before it broke.

Jesus Christ.

"Tell me what you want, sir. Tell me what you want me to do."

Fuck. "I want to fuck your mouth and watch you swallow my come."

She wrapped her hand around my length and looked up at me, her expression sex-crazed. "Yes, sir." She craned her neck and took my length as far as she could go without gagging. Then she pulled back again, her tongue flat and cushioning my cock so he wouldn't be nicked by her teeth. Saliva pooled at the base of my length then dripped down to the floor. She didn't need to go fast or use her hand to blow my mind. The combination of her on her knees with her soft mouth wrapped around my length was a fantasy I could hardly handle. She was just so goddamn beautiful.

My hand moved into her hair and fisted it, tangling the soft strands she worked so hard to perfect every morning. I got a good grip on her, guiding her up and down at the speed I preferred. I liked giving her the reins, but a part of me would always want some control. I could have fucked her instead, but this satisfied my need to dominate her. The dinner with her brother was unpleasant, but it was totally worth it to have this moment.

Her eyes shifted up to me as she wrapped her fingers around my base and jerked me off. She widened her mouth so she could move up and down with her hand, making sure to catch anything I might release unexpectedly.

I stood still and let her do all the work, taking my length harder and faster. I wanted this to last forever, but I knew my cock was large for her small mouth. I knew her knees must ache from sitting on the wool rug. I didn't care about the comfort of other women when they were getting me off, but I certainly cared about London's. Besides, I just wanted to come. "Here it comes, Lovely."

Her other hand cupped my balls while she jerked me harder and shoved her throat across my length. She worked hard and fast, panting as she gave it to me as best she could.

I stepped closer to her, giving her all of my length just before I exploded. I knew she couldn't take every inch for very long before I hit her gag reflex, so I waited until the last minute.

You know, because I was a gentleman.

My hand rested against the side of her face, and I watched the tears pool in the corners of her eyes. My cock became so thick, and a burst of pleasure started deep in my groin. My core burned from the fire, and a scorching sensation emerged over my body, making me feel cold and hot at the exact same time.

With a moan, I filled her mouth with all of my seed, dropping it on her tongue and down the back of her throat. My hand gripped the back of her head, keeping her in position until I was completely finished.

Tears streamed from her eyes and down her cheeks, but she didn't gag. She kept the natural response of her body under control.

My cock began to soften once I was finished, so I slowly pulled out of her mouth with my eyes glued to her face. "Swallow."

She closed her mouth and did as I asked, her throat shifting with the movement.

This woman made me feel more like a king than anyone else. My fingers gently touched her hair, almost in apology for the aggressive way I fucked her mouth, before I grabbed my boxers and pulled them to my hips. "Get on the bed. I'm not done yet."

Ariel and I worked together in my office, everything falling back into perfect normalcy like she'd never left in the first place. We went over the weekly schedule and discussed the social events I would be attending.

Now that London was in my life, I didn't spend much time gathering intelligence or putting my men on the job. I stuck to my scotch business, taking the less stressful route. So that made me stationary for the first time in my life.

"The Duke of Romania is having a celebration in Manchester. You've been invited, of course."

Leaving the house was less tempting now that I had a pet I loved to play with. I didn't care about fancy parties and famous people. I'd just seen him in London not too long ago, and I vaguely remembered him mentioning it.

"His daughter, the Duchess of Romania, has returned from university in America. I suspect he wants to show her off to the world."

And marry her off. That's what all the royals did. "I'll pass."

Ariel spun her pen in her fingertips. "Well, you already told him you were going."

"I did?"

"When you were in London."

I was so busy thinking about the woman who left me that I hadn't noticed anything around me. I had been speaking to a fellow duke but tuning him out at the exact same time.

"You can't back out now. The dinner is on Saturday."

Damn. "Alright. I'll let London know."

"You're going to bring her?" Ariel looked down and made notes in her folder.

"Why wouldn't I?" Ariel made her feelings for London perfectly clear, but I hoped we had moved on from that by now.

"It's a big event, that's all."

"London did fine during Holyrood."

"True," Ariel said with a sigh. "It's your decision, Crewe."

Where I went, London went with me. It was as simple as that. I didn't give Ariel as much attitude as I would to someone else since we had just been reunited. My temper remained under control for the time being.

"Shall I make arrangements for London's gown, hair, and makeup?"

"Yes, please." I always delegated that sort of thing to someone else. "Thank you."

"Sure."

"Will you be joining us?"

She smiled. "As much as I would like to, I wasn't the one invited."

"I can still bring you along."

"It's okay, Crewe."

"When are the four of us going to have that dinner?"

"Cassandra and I have an open availability. We both work the same hours."

"Then how about Friday night?"

"I'll check with her," she said. "But that should be fine."

"Great."

Dimitri walked inside without knocking. His cheeks were red, and he was clearly flustered since he forgot his protocol. "Sir, we have a situation. Joseph Ingram is outside. We have him surrounded, but he's unarmed. What would you like us to do?"

Shit. "Don't shoot." I tossed my folder aside. "I'm coming."

Ariel watched me through her thick glasses. "Can I help?"

"Stay here." I walked outside with Dimitri and found Joseph standing in front of his car with his arms crossed over his chest. A dozen of my men surrounded him, all holding pistols or AK-47s. Joseph didn't seem the least bit worried about all the bullets sitting inside the barrels.

Joseph leaned against the front of his car. "Beautiful day, huh?"

I raised my hand then lowered it. "He's fine, guys."

Dunbar was the last one to drop his gun. His hand shook before he finally cooperated.

"Search him," I ordered.

"Oh, come on," Joseph said. "If I were packing, I would have shot these fuckers for pointing their guns at me."

"It's not for my sake," I said. "But theirs."

Dunbar did a quick pat-down, feeling Joseph's arms and thighs to make sure there wasn't a Glock or a knife hidden anywhere. He finally stepped away. "All clear."

Joseph adjusted his jacket then walked up to me. "Is this how you greet all your guests?"

"Just the ones who shoot me." I walked to the front door and heard him trail behind. Whatever he wanted to discuss shouldn't take place in front of my men. It either had something to do with London or the heist he was about to pull off.

Joseph chuckled behind me. "Alright, that's fair."

We walked into my office where Ariel was still waiting. "Can you give us the room, please?"

Ariel stared at Joseph with a look colder than ice. She'd nearly been taken hostage, but she didn't show an ounce of fear. She sized him up like he was an easy opponent she could take down in a heartbeat.

Joseph whistled under his breath. "You're looking fine this morning—"

"Speak to her again, and I'll slit your throat." I stared him down, no longer hospitable now that he had the nerve to insult one of my closest friends. If he thought I would let him objectify her, he was stupid. If he weren't London's brother, I would have already shot him by now.

Joseph shut his mouth but didn't hide the annoyance in his eyes.

Ariel shut her folder then rose from her chair. She clicked her pen as she stared at Joseph, threatening him with a single movement. She was slender and lacked strength, but she would stab someone in the eye if she had to—I'd seen her do it before. "Don't take too long. We have work to do." She walked out and left us alone together.

"You're awfully protective of her…" He dropped into the armchair she'd been occupying just a second ago.

I recognized the accusation immediately, knowing exactly what his suspicion was. "She's gay. And yes, I'm very protective of her, so don't try anything."

"Ooh…gotcha." He gripped the armrests with his large hands, his knuckles protruding with corded veins. His green eyes reminded me of London's, along with the fair complexion of his skin. Their bone structures weren't comparable, but I think I would have figured out they were related if I didn't know they were siblings.

"What can I do for you, Joseph?"

"I wanted to talk about the plans you were so interested in."

I leaned back in my chair, spinning a pen in my fingertips. "I'm listening."

"How did you want to be involved?"

"In whatever way you need help. I have men, money, and weapons if you need it."

"I have all of those things. But you do have something I don't have."

"What?"

"Intelligence."

"I can get that for you too."

"Because I'm wiping his bank account clean, but I know he's got a lot more than that. His house has so many relics, jewels, and cash that it nearly doubles his fiscal worth."

"Not surprised."

"So I want everything. But I need specific information about his whereabouts, his guards, codes to the property…"

It could cost me a lot of money to get all that information, at least if I didn't want to get caught, but it would be worth it. "I can get that to you in exchange for something."

"I told you I wouldn't be giving you a cut."

"Not that. I want you to kill him."

Joseph rubbed his fingers across his chin. "Wow. He really pissed you off."

"Don't touch his family. But I want him dead."

"That's not just murder. That's the assassination of the century. I'm not really in the killing business."

"You are now."

"I need to know why you hate this guy so much. I don't get mixed up in personal vendettas."

"He killed my parents and my older brother, Alec. It happened when I was six. He courted my mother, but she didn't reciprocate and ended up marrying my father. He never let it go and couldn't take the damage to his pride. So, he killed all of them."

Joseph watched my expression without blinking, taking it all in.

I'd told this story a million times, but it always caused a pain in my chest. I hardly remembered my parents and fictionalized what they were like, but it still bothered me that they were gone. And having a brother would be nice. He could have taken over the house name, and I could disappear on Fair Isle…with London.

"Sorry, man," he finally said. "I don't know what to say."

"You don't need to say anything. But I need this guy dead."

Joseph rubbed his palm up his cheek. "Like I said, killing isn't really my thing."

"You had no problem shooting me."

"You know that was different. You took my little sister hostage."

"And treated her better than the goddamn Queen of England."

He brushed off my words. "I don't know this guy, so it's still weird."

"You're gonna walk away from this with eighty million dollars. That's more money than Greece has. You're really going to turn that down?"

Joseph didn't hesitate. "No."

"Then we have a deal?"

"What if I get caught?"

"That's your problem, not mine."

"You told me not to hurt his family. But if we clean him out, they'll be left with nothing."

"No, that's not true." Men like that diversified their assets. Their money wasn't hiding in one specific place. As a member of the Russian mafia, he had more money put away somewhere. "I wouldn't worry about that. I know he owns most of the rental properties in Moscow. They'll be fine."

"Okay. Then I'm going to need men and information."

"And I have no problem giving that to you. When do you think this is going to go down?"

"Simultaneously. He'll need to transfer the money, and once that happens, we'll loot his place and take him out. We'll need to be in three places at once."

"Sounds good."

"We can't tell London about this. If she knows how dangerous this is, she'll freak."

"I know." I hated to lie to her, but the less she knew, the better. "I won't say a thing."

He stood up then extended his hand. "Then we have a deal."

I stood up and shook his hand. "We do."

"So…" He placed his hands in his pocket. "She's gay, huh? That's a shame."

"Even if she weren't, she's out of your league."

"Ouch," he said with a chuckle. "Got any other sexy ladies working around here? Maybe set me up with a princess or something?"

I wasn't even going to respond to that. "Get out, Joseph."

"Can I at least say hello to my sister?"

"No. I'd rather her not know you were ever here. You should get going. She stops by throughout the day pretty often."

"Roger that." He finally walked to the door. "I'm not gonna get shot on the way to my car, right?"

I never walked anyone to the entrance, and I wasn't going to make an exception now. "I can't promise anything."

———

London walked into the office in skintight jeans and a light sweater that hung off one shoulder. Her hair was in a braid, and she rocked the girl-next-door look. With a natural looking face with a hint of makeup, she looked beautiful.

I couldn't recall a time she walked into the room and I didn't think that.

"You wanna blow off work today?" she asked as she sauntered to my desk.

"You know I want to blow off work every day." My arm circled her waist when she arrived at my chair. I looked up at her, forgetting about the email I was writing—and everything else in the world.

"I think retirement would suit you."

I chuckled. "Actually, I think I'd go crazy if I were retired. Boredom and I don't mix together."

She ran her hand along my shoulder and gave the muscle a gentle squeeze. "Like I'd ever let you be bored." She slid into my lap and hooked her arm around my neck.

"True. You are a full-time job." My hand moved to her slender thigh, feeling the structure of the muscle through her thick jeans.

"No. Pleasing me is a full-time job. The way you said it makes me sound like a nuisance."

"Definitely not a nuisance."

She leaned forward and shut my laptop. "So…can you spare an hour for lunch?"

"I suppose. That seems a lot more reasonable than retiring."

She scooted off my lap, her curvy ass nearly in my face. She had the perfect figure from any angle. I loved the way her waist narrowed then flared out into womanly hips. She had the right kind of cushion on her, perfect for grabbing.

I ignored my hard cock and walked with her to the courtyard. It was a cold day, but the fire pit was burning and there wasn't any sign of rain. The sky was overcast, but it was always overcast this time of year.

We had a light lunch and tea. I wasn't a big fan of the beverage, but it was growing on me. I tried to have a few glasses of scotch with dinner—a normal-person habit. London noticed my effort but didn't say anything, probably because she knew I didn't want any extra attention.

There was a slight breeze in the air, so it blew one loose strand that was too short to fit inside her braid. When the wind passed through, the strand lifted. When the wind died away, the hair fell against her cheek. With eyes downcast, she enjoyed her meal. But her attention was still on me because her leg rubbed against mine under the table, touching me whenever possible.

I loved it when she touched me. "I have a dinner this Saturday. You're coming with me."

She stopped eating, all of her focus shifting from her meal to me. When one of her eyebrows was raised and her lips were pressed tightly together, that meant she was pissed. "I'm coming with you? How about you ask me if I want to go?"

Old habits died hard. I hadn't officially gotten out of the mind-set that she wasn't my prisoner anymore. She was a free woman who voluntarily wanted to spend every waking hour with me. "You know that's not how I meant it."

She narrowed her eyes further.

Okay, it was how I meant it. "I'm sorry, Lovely. Will you accompany me?"

"What is this dinner for?"

"The Duke of Romania is having a celebration for his daughter. She just graduated from Harvard, a university in the United States."

She rolled her eyes. "I know what Harvard is. I live pretty close to it."

"My mistake. Anyway, you'll come with me?"

"Will there be food and wine?"

I nodded.

"Dessert?"

"Definitely."

"Will you wear a yummy suit?"

"Yummy?" I asked, finding the word cute when it came out of her mouth.

"Yeah. You know, super handsome."

"I look super handsome in everything."

"Very good point."

"But I'll be wearing a suit and tie...like usual."

"Then count me in." She smiled before returning to her meal.

"If you want to go, what was the big fuss before?"

"Don't play stupid with me, Crewe. You're smarter than that."

"Debatable."

"A woman always wants to be asked, not told."

I tried not to smile. "Hmm…that's not my experience with women."

She tried to keep an angry face, but it didn't last long. She grabbed a piece of bread and threw it at my forehead. "Don't be arrogant."

"I'm not arrogant. I'm cocky."

She threw another piece of bread at my shoulder. "Get over yourself."

"How about you get under myself?"

She rolled her eyes but couldn't suppress the smile that formed on her lips. "If you weren't so hot, I wouldn't put up with this."

"But I am hot—so I'm safe." When I spent quiet afternoons with her like this, it gave me a new appreciation for life. I could be myself completely, saying whatever came to mind without thinking twice about it. When I was in the presence of other royals, I had to carefully articulate every single word. But with her, it was just easy. She made me laugh and feel good about myself. She brought me peace when I'd only known war.

She brought everything.

"What are you thinking about?"

"Hmm?" I lifted my gaze, realizing I'd been staring at my plate without eating.

"We were laughing one moment, and then you spaced out on me."

I'd never been very good with words. I said the bare minimum and got to the point. It was easier that way. But to explain the complicated thoughts I'd just experienced…was pretty difficult. "I can't explain it."

"You can't explain what you were thinking about?" she asked incredulously. "You could try."

"Well…I was thinking about you and how much I love you. I guess that's my best description."

Instead of smiling, her eyes started to glow on their own. The sun wasn't out today, so she wasn't reflecting the light. The brightness came from deep inside her, from a place I couldn't see. "I hated you so much when I first met you… but now I can't picture my life without you."

The words went straight to my heart because I knew how much she meant them. She lied to me when she first told me she loved me, but now there wasn't a doubt in my mind that

I was her entire world. She gave up all of her dreams for me. She gave up her entire life. "I can't picture my life without you either."

———————

I pulled London's hand away from mine and hooked it around my arm instead. We walked up to the old palace in Manchester, the lawn ornaments glowing with celebration. The nighttime sky was deep blue instead of black, but the lack of stars didn't dim the brightness of the party. The windows were lit up, and silhouettes could be seen through the tapestries. "This is the proper mannerism."

"Proper, huh?" she asked. "Is it proper to fuck your woman in the ass just before leaving for a dinner party?"

I halted before the stone stairs and looked into her face, both aroused and impressed by her attitude. "Keep running that mouth, and I'll do it again in one of the guest rooms."

"Is that supposed to make me stop?"

Man, she was perfect. "You can hold my hand if you want. I'm just explaining the customs. It's always so important to you to fit in."

"Eh." She shrugged. "I guess I don't care that much anymore."

"Just don't spit on anybody, and you should be okay." I started walking again.

"What's the dude's name again?"

"Dude?"

"Bro, whatever."

I'd never get used to her American slang. "Duke Vasile of Romania."

"Oh, okay. What's his wife's name? I mean, the duchess?"

"She's dead. Passed away ten years ago."

"Oh…"

"His daughter is Anna."

"So she's Princess Anna? Like in the *Princess Diaries*?"

"Huh?"

"It's a movie in America. Never mind…"

I wasn't going to bother learning about that piece of culture. "You refer to her as the Lady Anna."

"Lady Anna?"

"Yes."

"She's not a duchess?"

"No. She only becomes a duchess if she marries a duke. If she marries a commoner, then she loses her title."

She raised an eyebrow. "How do you know all of this?"

"Born into it."

"So, if she married you, she would be a duchess?"

Now I raised both eyebrows, startled by the hypothetical question. "Yes."

"So no matter who you marry, you never lose your title?"

"Correct."

"Gotcha." She nodded slowly.

We walked inside and joined the party. A symphony played in the corner, accompanied by a large grand piano that looked as ancient as the rest of the house. The manor had been restored, but most of the original work had been left alone. The walls had been touched up, but the moldings along the ceiling were original. Spending a lifetime among the nobility gave me a keen eye for this sort of thing.

I made my rounds and spoke to acquaintances and friends. London was quiet, but she was always polite and participated, even if she wasn't entirely certain of the subject we were discussing. Her gold gown perfectly complemented the maroon colors of the manor, and I knew my designer was worth every penny. She knew how to make London look superior to every royal person in the room.

The duke was busy speaking to all the other guests of the party, so I took my time before I bombarded him. At least three hundred people were there. Even if we had a good conversation, he probably wouldn't remember it.

"How do you know him?" London asked when we were alone together. Just like when we were alone at home, she was close to me, a part of her body always touching mine. She drank her wine as her arm brushed against the fabric of my suit.

"Honestly, I can't remember the first time we met. But he's a big fan of my scotch. Has it at dinner parties and the hotels he operates around the world."

"Are all of your friends clients?"

I shrugged. "I guess so. I didn't push the scotch on them. They just happen to like it."

"It is pretty good. Strong as hell, but good." She glanced to the other side of the room then turned back to me. "Is that whore gonna be here?"

I did a double take when I heard what she said. I hoped no one overheard it. "What whore are you referring to? Dunbar?"

She didn't crack a smile. "Josephine."

Hadn't even thought of her. "Not sure. But probably."

"Maybe I'll spill some wine on her. You know, by mistake."

"Is this out of jealousy or loyalty?"

"A little bit of both," she said before she sipped her wine.

"I never think about her, so you shouldn't concern yourself with it." It was like the engagement had never happened. I couldn't even remember what it was like to love the woman. I met London, and my entire life changed. It seemed like she'd always been in my life, that no other woman ever mattered.

"I still hate that bitch."

I pressed my forefinger over my lips. "Shh...you can say that when we're alone together, but not here."

She rolled her eyes. "You're no fun." She finished her glass of wine and set it on an empty tray a waiter was carrying. "I'm going to use the restroom. I'm not opposed to the idea of you joining me." She winked then walked away.

I couldn't tell if she was teasing me or not, but that's why I loved her.

"Crewe Donoghue." Vasile appeared at my side in a midnight black tux. He was in his late sixties but had a youthful appearance. A life of exercise and veganism had served him well. "A pleasure, always." He shook my hand.

"The pleasure is mine, sir. Your party is lovely."

"Thank you. I wish I could take credit for it but I can't. I just get to show up." He laughed.

I laughed too.

"I hope you didn't come alone, Crewe. You're too handsome not to have a woman on your arm."

It was ironic that London had walked away at the worst possible time. "Thank you, sir. I—" I spotted Ariel coming toward me, Cassandra trailing behind her. They weren't showing any display of affection, probably because Ariel was all business—all the time. "Allow me to introduce you to my business partner, Ariel."

"Oh yes, we've spoken on the phone." Vasile kissed her on each cheek. "You're much easier to work with than this one." He nodded his head in my direction. "He's all drink and no talk."

Ariel smiled. "Trust me, I know. Let me introduce you to another business associate of mine…" She turned to Cassandra.

"And girlfriend," I added.

Ariel narrowed her eyes at me, caught off guard by my honesty.

I knew Ariel wasn't ashamed of who she was, and I didn't want her to be ashamed just because we were at a royal dinner. If she was protecting me, she didn't need to. Anyone who had a problem with that could buy their scotch somewhere else.

Cassandra covered for Ariel and shook his hand. "It's so beautiful here. I love the lawn ornaments."

"Why, thank you," Vasile replied. "They're nice, aren't they? Lighten up the place." If he was uncomfortable by the turn of events, he didn't show it.

Ariel glared at me when he wasn't looking.

I shrugged in response. "Sir, I haven't had a chance to meet your daughter yet. Is she here?"

"Oh yes." He tapped one of the waiters on the arm and whispered for them to retrieve Anna before he turned back to me. "She's spent the week settling in. You know, getting used to the time change by sleeping all day. I sincerely hope she wasn't this lazy while she was at university."

"She just graduated college," I reminded him. "She deserves a break."

He chuckled. "You're a lot more understanding than I am. My father taught me to work around the clock as if someone else is working around the clock to take your job away from you. Wise man."

"Very."

His daughter joined our group a moment later, wearing a sweetheart neckline gown that was boldly gold with a subtle sequence of red. When it trailed past her hips, the red color became more prominent and took up the gown nearly to the bottom, where the gold color returned. She had dark brown hair like her father and blue eyes. She looked royal but also possessed a hint of mellowness. I could imagine her at a coffee shop with her laptop on a Sunday morning. When she smiled, it seemed genuine. "Father, you called?"

"Yes." He introduced me. "I want you to meet Crewe Donoghue, informally known as the Scotch King."

"Pleasure to meet you." I grabbed her hand and kissed her on each cheek. "Your father told me you've been catching up on sleep."

She pressed her lips tightly together and sighed like she was trying not to roll her eyes. "Did he also tell you I haven't done the laundry since I've been home?"

"Not yet," Vasile said. "But I was getting there."

I chuckled. "Congratulations on your graduation. That's a worthy accomplishment."

"Thank you. I'm relieved my education is over, but I also miss it."

"Did you like America?"

"Very much. Their hot dogs are out of this world."

I laughed, picturing a lady like her eating a chili dog at a ball game. "I'll have to try one next time I'm around." I introduced her to Ariel and Cassandra. Anna didn't seem bothered by the situation either, which made me like both her and her father even more.

"So, you make scotch?" she asked. "I understand how wine works, but scotch sounds complicated."

Vasile got pulled away by another guest, and Ariel and Cassandra drifted away to grab a glass of wine.

I wasn't sure where London was. She was taking a long time, but there could have been a line at the bathroom. If this were six months ago, I would have assumed she'd shattered the bathroom window and jumped. "It's not too complicated. I have a few distilleries in Scotland. I opened my second warehouse not too long ago."

"Fascinating," she said. "I drink a lot of scotch, so that's probably why I'm so interested."

"You do?" I asked in surprise.

"Don't get me wrong, I enjoy wine as well. But scotch has a great kick to it that you can't find anywhere else."

There was no way I could dislike a fellow scotch drinker. Not possible. "Looks like we have something in common."

"We do," she said. "My father told me about your parents. I know it's not the same thing, but I was pretty devastated when Mom died. I loved her very much—still do. It's just not the same when they're gone. And I never really got the chance to appreciate her. I was too young." She said everything with obvious sincerity, but she didn't get choked up about it.

Reminded me of myself. "It's hard. I told myself it would get easier as time went on, but it never really does."

"I know exactly what you mean."

I liked that she was easy to talk to, not stuffy like everyone else. It was smart of her to move away to college, to a place where no one knew about her noble background. That was probably why she was so laid-back. "Your father never remarried?"

She shook her head. "I don't think he's even dated anyone. My parents were really in love…"

I nodded, unsure how else to respond.

"What part of Scotland do you live in?"

While she was nice to talk to, I started to worry about London. She went to the bathroom nearly fifteen minutes ago, and she didn't have her phone on her to communicate anything to me. I didn't want to be rude and walk away from Anna, who turned out to be pretty good company, but if London didn't show up in three minutes, I was going to look for her.

Even if it made me look rude.

16

LONDON

I THOUGHT I would have more time with Crewe.

But the second I walked out of the bathroom and overheard him talking to Anna, I knew it was over.

I thought I had a year. Maybe more.

But I had just months, if that.

I wasn't sure why I stood there and subjected myself to the torture. Not only was Anna beautiful, but she was cool. She didn't remind me of the other stuffy noble people Crewe introduced me to. I could even see myself being her friend —if she weren't going to take Crewe away.

I was smitten with her—so there was no way he wasn't.

I could just break my promise to Ariel and not leave, but then she would walk away and Crewe would be miserable again. As tempting as that sounded, I knew it wouldn't work anyway. Seeing him interact with Anna told me I was a terrible partner. With Anna, he would have everything he wanted—and he might even fall in love.

I wanted to cry—right there in the middle of the room.

Ariel swooped in out of the shadows, clinging to my sadness like she fed off it. "Crewe looks like he's having a good time, huh?" She sipped her wine as she stood beside me, her shoulder touching mine.

I couldn't speak.

"I've never met Anna before, but I've always heard good things. They have a great chemistry."

I'd never hated someone so much in my life.

When I didn't say anything, Ariel stared at me.

I ignored her look as best as I could.

"We have a deal. Remember?"

"Like you would ever let me forget…"

"I'll find reasons to put them in the same room together. You work on your exit strategy."

The idea of walking away made me want to hurl. "I just got him back…I thought I had more time."

"I thought you did too. But she's lovely. With exceptional business ties and a great title, she's perfect for Crewe. Plus, she's a few years younger than him so he doesn't need to have kids right away."

Now I really was going to throw up.

"Do we have a problem?"

"No…" I turned away, feeling the tears pool in my eyes. "If you had a heart, you would show some compassion."

"I only show compassion to people who don't get my business partner shot. If you need a moment, go outside. Don't want Crewe to see you."

I didn't bother arguing with her. I just wanted to get away, get some fresh air under the blue sky. I pushed through the crowd before I made it out to the stone steps that led to the turnaround driveway. An enormous fountain spilled water into the pool, making a constant melodic sound. It was refreshing but only for an instant. I walked to the fountain and crossed my arms over my chest, grateful the sound would drown out my tears to anyone who walked by. Right now, everyone was inside enjoying the party, so no one would notice I was gone.

Crewe would eventually.

I didn't have much time, fifteen minutes max. I had to pull myself together and accept the horrifying end to my relationship with Crewe. It was stupid of me to come here in the first place, to give up what I had in New York. He and I were from different worlds, and we should stay in different worlds.

I would never be a duchess.

I would never be anything.

He was meant for greater things. I was meant for an average life with an average husband. When I returned home, it would be painful. But one day, it wouldn't be so bad. Maybe I'd meet a nice guy and find love. Not the passionate love I had with Crewe, but something that resembled close companionship.

Maybe I would survive this.

I just had to be strong, swallow my tears, and accept the inevitable. Nothing lasted forever, and my relationship with Crewe was no different. I should be grateful we got to spend time together at all. We went from being enemies to passionate lovers. It was a story nobody would ever believe.

I closed my eyes and cleared my thoughts, meditating just as if I were in yoga. I thought of nothing at all, letting all the heartbreaking feelings inside my chest dissipate. When I went back into that hall, I would wear a smile and nothing else.

"Lovely?" Crewe's concerned voice reached my ears from the bottom of the stone steps.

I had less time to recover than I hoped. I had to bounce back and pretend everything was perfectly fine. After a final deep breath, I turned to him. "It was a little warm in there. I need to cool off." Now that I knew we'd reached the end of our relationship, he looked even more handsome. With strong shoulders and a cleanly shaven jaw, he looked more like a king than a duke. His exterior was dark, but if you looked beneath the skin, you would see a man who had a heart that was brilliant like gold. He was more complicated than he appeared, hiding his good nature like a bad secret. His entire life was fueled by revenge, but that anger was caused by fierce loyalty to his deceased family. He was a man perfect in every way.

And I couldn't have him.

Crewe came to my side and moved his arm around my waist, surrounding me with his protective touch. His strong fingers dug into the thick fabric of my dress, and his cologne surrounded me with a heavenly smell. "You've been gone for a long time. I got worried."

"I went to the bathroom, and there was a long line. Then all the perfume and the body heat…I just needed some fresh air." Crewe could read me pretty well so I wasn't sure if he would believe my lie, but I had to try.

He moved closer into me and pressed a kiss against my hairline. "It's a beautiful night…even if we can't see the stars."

"Yes, it is."

"Unfortunately, the duke and his daughter started talking to me right after you stepped away. We'll hunt them down because I'd like them to meet you."

There was nothing I wanted less. "We'll see."

He surveyed the enormous lawn in front of the manor, looking at the lawn ornaments and perfectly manicured bushes that resembled safari animals. It seemed like everything was calm, like he believed my lie, until he turned back to me. "Are you sure everything is alright?"

"Of course it is." I looked past his shoulder and saw Ariel emerge from the entrance, a glass of wine in her hand. She watched me with her pointed expression, and even from this distance, I could see the disapproval in her eyes. After a haughty look, she walked back inside. "Just needed to cool off, that's all. You're used to these social events, but I'm not."

"Give it some time. You'll be a pro."

But we didn't have time.

"Come on, let's head back inside." He grabbed my hand and gently pulled him with him.

I didn't want to speak to Anna, to smile and pretend she didn't just change everything. But I had no other choice unless I pretended I was seriously sick. As tempting as that sounded, I couldn't do that. "Okay."

Luck was on my side, and I didn't have to interact with Vasile or Anna. Five hundred guests attended his party, and we didn't cross paths with him again in the throng of people. I couldn't imagine having a party like this because I didn't even know five hundred people.

Had I even met that many people in my lifetime?

At the end of the night, Dunbar drove us home. I propped my head against the window and closed my eyes, drowning out the painful truth as best as I could. I could think about it all day, but it didn't change anything.

I needed to stay positive.

Crewe's hand entered my hair as he ran his fingers down the strands. "Tired?"

"What gave me away?" I whispered.

He chuckled and continued to run his fingers through my hair. "Come here." He guided me down until I rested across his lap, the safety belt tight against me in an uncomfortable position. I pushed it farther down to my waist and rested my head on his muscular thigh. His fingers moved through my hair again. "You look beautiful tonight. I meant to say that earlier, but it slipped my mind."

I kept my eyes closed, but my lips pulled into a smile. "Thank you…"

"Did you have fun tonight?"

Not at all. "Yeah. The food was great."

"I'm glad Ariel came—and brought Cassandra."

"I really like Cassandra…" I wasn't sure what she saw in Ariel, though. The woman was pure evil.

"I do too." Crewe halted the conversation, probably wanting to let me sleep.

I kept my eyes closed and tried to think of nothing, to appreciate the quiet companionship we shared. It didn't seem like Crewe was interested in Anna, but he wasn't immune. He must know she was a great catch. He would be stupid not to.

It took forever to get home. By the time we arrived, I wasn't tired. I hadn't been tired to begin with because all I could think about was the heartbreak—and he hadn't even left yet. I was anticipating the end before it even arrived. I prepared myself for the devastation even though there wasn't a single thing I could do to soften the blow.

There was no cure for a broken heart.

We walked upstairs to the royal chambers where the bed was already turned down for the evening. Fresh washcloths were placed in the bathroom, and the drapes were shut over the windows so the morning light wouldn't peek through and wake us up.

I didn't bother removing my makeup because I didn't care enough. I'd probably have a breakout because of it, but whatever. I unzipped the back of my dress and let it fall to my feet, my tits immediately exposed to the air.

Crewe's hands moved to my shoulders, and he pressed a kiss against the back of my neck. His lips were soft but rugged at the same time, definitively masculine despite their elegance. He dragged his tongue across my skin, his warm breath drafting over the tiny hair I didn't know I had. His hands automatically gave me a gentle squeeze as he inhaled a breath, smelling my perfume that had mostly faded by now.

I knew exactly what that touch meant—what that kiss meant. We did the same thing every night before we went to bed, sensual lovemaking that made up for the aggressive way he took me during the afternoon. When the sun disappeared and it was just the two of us in the bedroom, he softened in a way the rest of the world never got to see.

All I could think about were his hands. Soon, they would caress someone else. They would grip Anna and never let her go. They would hold his children when they were born. They would fill out paperwork with his elegant handwriting. They would touch and feel a world I would never know about.

But I had to block that out. Because his hands were still mine—for now.

His arm hooked over my chest, and he gripped my left tit, his thumb causing my nipples to pebble. His mouth moved to my neck, and he kissed me more aggressively, holding me tighter against him as his affection deepened.

I gripped his arm, using his stance for balance.

He kissed me everywhere, and when he brushed his mouth over my ear, he whispered something that I could barely make out. "I love you, Lovely…" A gust of warm followed, and he tightened me against his chest, his hard cock pressed right against my back.

Tears formed in response, and I shut my eyes so they would stop. But it was too late because they fell and dripped down my cheeks. His affection never ceased, and he showered me with his love, his body moving with mine in the dance we performed.

He guided me to the bed and quickly undressed at the same time. Piles of clothes trailed like breadcrumbs to the bed, and soon he was behind me and naked. My heels were still on, but he didn't bother sliding them away.

He bent me over the foot of the bed then moved to his knees.

I knew exactly what would come next, and I took a deep breath in anticipation. The only thing I loved more than his body was his gorgeous mouth. It could do incredible things to me, and it was about to do even greater things.

He kissed me on my sweet spot, sliding his tongue across my throbbing clit. He was just as aggressive as he was when he kissed me, his powerful hands gripping both of my ass cheeks.

My face was pressed against the comforter, and I released a moan that probably disturbed the rest of the castle. I dug my fingers into the sheets and writhed as he played me. When the scruff from his jaw rubbed against my soft thighs, I adored the coarse friction. Thoughts of Anna disappeared when we were together like this. No one else existed except the two of us.

He rose to his feet again and wrapped his fingers around my neck. He hadn't grabbed me like this in a way, and when he did it now, it felt different. He wasn't as aggressive as he used to be, just possessive. He lifted up my upper body, deepening the arch in my back as he kept my lower body in place. He pointed his cock at my slit and slid inside, moving through my soft flesh and the arousal that met him. He released a satisfied growl, pleased with my pussy's reaction.

I gripped one of his hips and used my free hand to suspend myself up. The second he was inside me, my body was ready to explode. It didn't take much for Crewe to make me come, and as time went by, it took even less time.

He thrust into me hard, giving me his entire length every time. "Tell me you love me."

My nails dug into his flesh, and my nipples became so hard, they ached. When I swallowed, I felt my muscles shift underneath his grip as he continued to hold me. I turned my head slightly so I could see him in the corner of my eye, his powerful body working hard to hit me in the right spot with every thrust. "I love you…" I rolled my hips and took him over and over, feeling his thick cock stretch me. "You're the love of my life."

He stilled while he was inside me for a moment before he thrust again. A moan accompanied his movements, distinctly masculine and sexy. "Lovely…" He fucked me harder and tightened his grip around my throat, taking me so roughly that I was forced to combust, to explode around his dick with my come surrounding him. I gripped the sheet underneath me as I screamed loudly, my eyes rolling in the back of my head and stars appearing in my vision. "Crewe…"

He gave it to me hard until the orgasm finally passed through me, leaving a tender sensation behind.

Crewe let me go and turned me onto my back before he positioned himself inside me again. He dragged my ass to the very edge of the bed and widened my legs with his arms. Eyes locked on mine, he thrust into me, all the muscles of his body tightening as he moved. There was nothing but lines of muscular strength on his body, a strong physicality that only severe dedication to exercise would allow.

He leaned far over me so we were eye-to-eye, rocking together as his cock slid through my drenched pussy. His hair was slightly damp from the sweat, and the moisture glistened on his body. When we made love, his jaw was always sterner than it usually was, hard and defined through his arousal.

My hands snaked up his chest, and my right palm could feel his pounding heartbeat, the mutual passion we felt in that moment. His cock was thick inside me, ready to burst at any moment. He pressed his lips against mine just before release, his breathing deep and rugged. He came inside me with a loud moan, filling my cavity with everything he had.

My arms hooked around his shoulders, and I pulled him deeper into me, wanting all of him—as much as I could get.

He gave a few more pumps even though he was softening, and his eyes were still dark with sexual ferocity. When he looked at me like that, it didn't seem like there was anyone else in the world besides the two of us. His look was hard, but it was also soft. It was a look he never showed to anyone else—only me.

"I know you're tired so I should let you go to bed…but I don't want to."

Now that the clock was ticking, I didn't have a moment to spare. I had to enjoy every second before the pendulum stopped swinging. Sleep was negligible. Even food was irrelevant—which was saying a lot. "I'm not tired…I want you."

17

CREWE

ARIEL WAS WAITING in my office when I walked inside.

"I'm glad you showed up."

"To work?" she asked with a smile.

I chuckled. "To Duke Vasile's party."

She shrugged. "Cassandra wanted to go. She's obsessed with all that royalty bullshit. I wanted to impress her so I would get laid."

"You'd probably get laid anyway."

"True. But I like it when she goes the extra mile."

I sat at my desk and looked through the messages Ariel piled on my desk. My inbox was relatively empty, but that would change as the day passed. We had a new client interested in a bulk deal, and we were currently breaking into Canadian businesses.

"Did you have a good time?"

"I did." When London slipped from my arms, I wasn't pleased. But I eventually tracked her down again, and everything felt right. It seemed like something was wrong, but she assured me everything was fine. The only reason why I believed her was because there was no reason to lie. If something was on her mind, she usually told me.

"Duke Vasile was very generous. Thanks for putting me on the spot, by the way."

"Stop hiding who you are. I'm just giving you a nudge."

"I don't hide who I am." She made a note in her notebook. "In my personal time, I do exactly what I want. But when I'm at work or a work function, that's totally different. Wouldn't want to offend anyone."

"If they're offended, that's their problem." I looked out the window and saw the heavy fog roll in. In waves, it blanketed the countryside and blocked out the sight of the hills in the distance. Winter was approaching fast.

"I enjoyed Lady Anna's company."

"Yeah, she was nice." She had a personality, unlike most members of the nobility. Spending four years in America suited her well. "Her father is nice too, so that's probably where she gets it from."

"That kind of loveliness comes from a whole new place."

My eyes moved to her face. "Have a thing for her?"

"No," she said quickly. "It's very obvious she's straight."

Honestly, I couldn't tell. I didn't know Ariel was gay, and I'd known her for ten years. I grabbed my phone and called Dunbar, asking him to bring us coffee. Then I hung up and tossed the phone back on the desk.

"What did you think of her?"

"Think of whom?"

"Ana."

I raised an eyebrow. "I said she was nice." I'd talked to her for ten minutes. It's not like I knew her well enough to know her life story. "Why?"

"I think she's smart, refined, and more important, fun. She'd make a great partner."

Like a business partner? "What do you mean, Ariel?"

"I mean in marriage. She's the daughter of a duke, and you are a duke." She spoke with simplicity, like everything she said was perfectly normal.

I didn't let my anger get to me because I didn't want to make assumptions. "You think I should marry her?"

She shrugged. "We've always talked about finding you a good partner. She clearly fits the bill."

"She's not my type." I thought she was beautiful, but my thoughts didn't exceed that quality. When she walked away from me, I didn't think about her again. I hadn't put a lot of thought into marriage, but I knew Anna wasn't the one for me. There was only one woman I could picture myself with.

"Not your type?" she asked incredulously. "She's perfect. And I think she was smitten with you."

"Didn't notice."

"I thought it was obvious. I could always contact her and see if she'd like to have dinner with you."

Now she was pushing it too far. "Ariel, I'm not interested. You can stop playing cupid."

"I thought we established you wanted someone with her exact qualities?"

When the time came for me to do it, I couldn't go through with it. I was certain Anna was capable of being everything I wanted in a partner, but when I spoke to her, I didn't feel anything. All I could think about was the woman who left my side. I could barely participate in the conversation with Anna because I was distracted about London's well-being. In my heart, I knew I would never be happy with anyone else but the woman currently sharing my bed.

That's when everything hit me.

London was never meant to be anything more than a pawn in a game, but now she was the center of my world. She made me a better man, far happier and far less bitter. She tested my strengths and erased my weakness. That void that was created when my family was taken had been completely filled by her spirit, something Josephine had never accomplished.

London didn't satisfy my political and financial goals, but she made me happy in categories I'd never considered to be important. In turn, she made those previous goals seem negligible. I felt like an idiot for even considering marrying someone else. Seemed stupid to let a woman like London slip away. "I don't want anyone else but London." I didn't care about Ariel's reaction. I broke my promise to her, something I never did, but if she was a loyal friend she would let that go. This woman made me happy, and happiness was something I had never experienced before.

Ariel looked at me with an unreadable expression, a purposeful poker face so she could hide her thoughts underneath her skin.

London asked me what our future included, and at the time, I didn't really have an answer. But if I offered her my commitment, wealth, and fidelity for the rest of my life, she would undoubtedly make the lifelong sacrifice to be my dutiful wife. She'd probably give up her career to be a mother to my children. "I intend to marry her, so we can forget Anna."

Ariel gripped her pen and pressed her lips tightly together. With a look of consternation, she sighed quietly and avoided my look. When she looked up again, she couldn't hide the annoyance deep in her eyes. "Are you planning to propose soon?"

I hadn't thought about it until this moment. As time progressed, I began to understand what London meant to me. And now that everything hit me at once, I began to understand what I wanted for the rest of my life. There was no reason to wait. I didn't need more time to know how well she completed me. "Yeah...I think so."

Ariel spun the pen with her fingertips.

"I know you aren't happy about this, but it would mean a lot to me if you could be supportive. Maybe the two of you could spend some time together and find a way to coexist." London had enough influence to make Ariel stay in the first place, so there was hope they could reconcile.

Ariel held my gaze in silence. Her annoyance was palpable, like heat rising to the ceiling. "I'm sure she and I could work something out." She looked down at her folder, dismissing the conversation because that was the best support she could offer.

And that was more than enough.

When London was in the shower, I opened the safe behind the portrait and looked through the relics that had lasted hundreds of years. My ancestors had touched the prized possessions, their DNA possibly still on the metal from their oil secretions. Timeless and elegant, the ancient crown reminded me of where I'd come from. I knew the noble thing was to marry someone of equal status.

But I wanted to be happy.

I'd tried to do it the right way by choosing Josephine. She was the best woman at the time, and I'd managed to love her. But that love was never real, so neither was her loyalty. Didn't it make sense to choose someone for deeper reasons than political gain? I never really knew my mother, but based on stories I heard about her, she would want me to be happy.

I think she'd want me to marry for love.

With the handkerchief, I pulled the artifacts out of the cabinet until I found the ring that had been passed down through every duchess until my mother received it. My father had given it to my mother, and she wore it every single day until she died. She probably would have been buried with it if the custom didn't dictate it.

Now it was my turn to give it to someone.

I never gave it to Josephine because I intended to give it to her on our wedding day. I proposed with a slender band infused with rare diamonds as a placeholder. Now I was grateful for my decision in the past.

Because this belonged to London.

I dropped it in my pocket and returned everything to the safe before I locked it up again. I corrected the picture then left the room as the water still ran in the shower. Dunbar was downstairs at his post, so I walked up to him and handed the ring over. "Could you call Eleanor to come and clean this? I just want it to shine a bit more."

He took it in his large hand, examining the diamond before he closed his fist around it. "Of course, sir. When do you need it by?"

"As soon as possible."

18

LONDON

CREWE WENT to lunch with a client in town, so I spent the afternoon alone. Even though I was with him every morning and every night, any missed opportunity to spend time with him felt like a waste. I liked having lunch with him in his office or on the terrace. Sometimes we didn't have anything to talk about, but that was perfectly okay.

I changed into my active gear and walked downstairs to go for a run. I was restless and bored, and exercise was usually the only thing that could cure my jitters. Besides, sitting around all day was making me gain weight. I found myself eating less and less just to prevent that.

I got to the bottom of the stairs when Ariel appeared. "Hello, London."

Yuck. That's what I wanted to say. "Hey, Ariel. Is Crewe back?"

"No. He'll be out for another hour, at least." She held her folder to her chest and walked me to the office. "Can I talk to you for a second?"

I knew exactly what she wanted to discuss. It was only a matter of time before Ariel pounced. "Sure."

We walked into his office, surrounded by the masculine power that existed even when he was absent. The brown and black tones echoed his personality perfectly. I was happy to see there wasn't a bottle of scotch anywhere in sight. He was back to drinking a reasonable amount, the kind that wouldn't give him cirrhosis of the liver.

I took a seat on one of the leather sofas and crossed my legs.

Ariel sat opposite of me and set her folder on the coffee table. She crossed her legs too, her calf muscle hard and defined below her dress.

I waited for her to execute me.

"I talked to Crewe."

"You talk to him a lot. What's that supposed to mean?"

She ignored my attitude. "He's not interested in Anna."

He's not? I expected him to be attracted to her the way everyone else in the room was.

"Said he only wants to be with you."

My eyes automatically wanted to soften and my lungs to suck in a delightful breath.

"I think if you weren't corrupting his thoughts, he'd be able to think more clearly. Anna is perfect in more ways than one. Also, Crewe told me he's going to propose to you."

Now I couldn't hide my reaction at all. My hand moved up my chest, and the tears welled in my eyes. I had asked him about marriage once before, but he never gave me a concrete answer. Instead of caring for Anna, he was only interested in being with me. It gave me the kind of high I'd never felt before. But the higher I soared, the further I crashed.

"So you need to leave now before he asks you."

She couldn't be serious. "Are you crazy? Crewe told you he wants to spend his life with me. You really can't just be happy for him and keep your pettiness to yourself?"

She narrowed her eyes. "We made a deal, London."

"I'm aware. But you really haven't changed your mind?"

"No."

Cold bitch. "If I leave, Crewe will be miserable."

"He'll get over it."

"Didn't seem like he got over it last time."

"It'll take time, but he'll bounce back. He's experienced far worse."

This woman was seriously evil. "I'm not sure if I can do it…"

"If you do, I walk. That's our arrangement."

Now I was back to square one. I had to do the right thing for Crewe or the right thing for myself. What would it be? "He'll be devastated if he loses either one of us."

"I've known him for ten years. I'm family to him. You're a woman he'll forget in six months."

I couldn't believe how terrible she was. It was unbelievable.

"London, we made a deal. You can't back out now. I don't respect you, but I thought you were someone who kept her word."

"I do keep my word…"

"Then you know what you need to do, and you need to do it soon."

I refused to cry in front of Ariel. I refused to appear weak. But in that moment, I wanted to sob on his couch until my chest couldn't heave anymore. I wanted to drown in my own sorrow and never recover. The warm tears burned behind my eyes, but I never let them streak down my face.

Ariel must have sensed my depression because she silently excused herself from the room. "I know you'll do the right thing, London. If you really love him, you'll let him go. We both know you don't deserve him."

Thankfully, Crewe went straight back to work when he came home, so I had a few hours to collect myself. I argued with myself continuously, wondering if I should keep or break my promise to Ariel. I loved him so much that I was willing to let Ariel walk away. But when I remembered how upset Crewe was the first time she left, I reconsidered.

And I was the reason he had a scar on his chest.

I was the reason he lost his men.

I was the reason Ariel had almost been taken.

After the way things turned out, I knew I didn't deserve him. I had nothing to offer besides my love. Apparently, Crewe thought that was enough. But after a few years, the resentment would begin to sink in.

Letting him go was my only option.

I hated the idea of returning to America and starting over— for the second time. I hated picturing my wedding to a faceless man in a suit. I hated imagining my children, who looked nothing like Crewe.

But I had to do it.

I procrastinated for several days, much to Ariel's displeasure. Every time I thought I could do it, I chickened out. I kept wanting to soak in every second that I had left with him. Our relationship had returned to the way it used to be—full of trust and affection. I would miss that when I slept alone.

By the third day, I still hadn't done it. I slept well with his muscular arms wrapped around me. I melted every morning when he kissed me goodbye. When we made love during his lunch hour, I was a woman in love. There were so many reasons to stay that sometimes I forgot why I was leaving in the first place.

When Ariel had enough, she confronted me while Crewe was in his office. "London." That's all she said to me when she walked into my bedroom. In black heels and a black dress, she looked stuffy and sophisticated. Her appearance almost never changed.

"I know." I didn't need to hear her pressure me again.

"You obviously don't know because you're still sharing this bedroom with him." She wasn't nearly as calm as she was before. Now her attitude had fired up like a revved engine. "You're playing a dangerous game with time right now."

Subconsciously, I hoped I could wait long enough to see him get down on one knee. I wanted to experience that moment even if it ended badly, as selfish as that was. "Get off my case, alright? You're asking me to do the hardest thing I've ever had to do."

"And if you can't do it, I'm leaving now."

"Seriously, how does Cassandra put up with you?"

Her eyes narrowed the second her girlfriend was mentioned. "That's a road you definitely don't want to take."

"How would you feel if you couldn't marry the one person you loved?" I asked incredulously. "If Crewe didn't accept your sexuality and made you choose? I distinctly remember him wanting you to be yourself. I distinctly remember him not giving a damn what anyone thought of you and supporting you. This is how you repay him?"

She placed both hands on her hips. "Cassandra didn't shoot me—"

"I didn't shoot Crewe."

"But you pretty much pulled the trigger. You lied and deceived him. Just because the two of you worked things out doesn't erase the past."

"Maybe you should get over the past. Seems like everyone else has."

"The men haven't killed you because Crewe ordered them not. Only reason why you're safe. But they'll hate you for as long as they live."

"You all sound pretty petty to me. I'm a good person with good intentions. You need to forgive me and let it go."

"Forgive you?" she asked. "I don't forgive anyone who fucks with Crewe like that."

We'd already had this argument before, and I didn't want to have it again. She was too cold even to understand what forgiveness was. I would always be condemned here. Even if I became his wife, I would never be welcome here. I couldn't allow my children to witness them disrespect me.

Maybe Crewe and I wouldn't have worked out anyway. "I'll leave, alright?"

"When?"

"Tomorrow."

"Actually tomorrow?" she asked. "Or are you just saying that?"

"Tomorrow. I'll call my brother and arrange for him to pick me up. Is that better?"

She dropped her arms to her sides. "It'll never be better until you're truly gone. When he gets off work tomorrow, I want you to say your goodbyes and leave. Alright?"

She punched me in the face when I tried to get Crewe to the hospital. I would love to return the favor, but I couldn't sink to her level. She may look elegant in her clothes and glasses, but I was still the better woman—if you asked me. "Alright."

I wasn't sure if I could make it through the night.

It was my last evening with Crewe in the beautiful castle. We'd made so many memories here, infecting the halls with our laughter and kisses. I was the only woman who had slept on these sheets, and I wondered how long it would be before he replaced me with someone else, probably Anna.

Crewe got undressed before he came to bed. In the nude, he slid under the sheets until we were close together. Immediately, his heat filled the sheets like a personalized heater. He kissed my shoulder and my hairline before he rested against me, his powerful body rising with every breath he took.

As much as I loved to lie with him, I wanted more. We usually made love before we went to sleep, but we'd been having a lot of sex so he was more tired than usual. Based on the way he lay beside me, he didn't have any intention of making a move.

That wasn't how I would spend my last night with him.

I rolled him onto his back and straddled his hips, feeling his soft cock underneath me. I ran my hands up his chest, feeling the powerful slabs of muscle on either side of his spine. With no fat and smooth skin, he was beautiful. Even the scar over his left nipple was beautiful.

Crewe's cock hardened in response. "Figured you were tired."

I wouldn't get any sleep tonight. "I'm never too tired for you."

His hands moved to my hips, and he rocked his cock through my folds. "You always know what to say, Lovely."

I groped my own tits as I stared into his eyes, my thumbs causing my nipples to pebble in response. I trailed one hand down my stomach and between my legs, rubbing my clit as my other hand remained on my chest. I never did these scandalous actions with other men because I was far too self-conscious. But the arousal in his eyes gave me the courage to do anything.

His hands moved to my waist, and he gripped my sides aggressively, his eyes exploring my body even though he'd seen me a hundred times. His cock thickened as the seconds passed, reaching a combustive level. "Lovely." His thumbs swiped across my nipples, and then he gripped my tits in his strong hands.

I rubbed my clit harder, feeling his hard cock underneath me.

He moved to my shoulders and pulled me down, forcing my lips to lock with his. He pulled my hand away from my clit and rubbed his cock right against my nub, giving me the perfect friction to make my body shake.

He sucked my bottom lip into my mouth as he ground against me harder, trying to make me come without even being inside me.

I always wanted an orgasm, but I wanted one with him buried inside me. I pulled away before my senses could be overly stimulated, and I slipped him inside my slit. The second I felt his massive length, I rolled my head back and moaned.

His hands returned to my waist, and he guided me up and down, wanting me to bounce on his cock just the way he liked. He loved to see my tits shake and my eyes roll to the back of my head. "Fuck…"

My hands returned to my tits, and I touched myself for his benefit, doing all the things I knew he loved. I wasn't a sexy person, but being sexy with him was easy. He was the kind of guy who made it easy.

I reached behind me and cupped his balls with my hand, my fingers massaging his sac as I continued to rock him.

His fingers dug into me harder, and he closed his eyes as he fought the urge to explode.

The sight gave me an extra push that shoved me over the edge. As if I were on fire, my entire body burned white-hot. I screamed through the pleasure and clung to the sensation for as long as I possibly could, knowing I would miss it once I couldn't have it again. "Give me your come. I want it."

"Yeah?" He rolled me onto my back and positioned himself on top of me, one of my legs over his shoulder while the other stretched out to accommodate him. He pounded into me harder, stretching my clit into a circle with every thrust he made.

I gripped his arms and prepared for his load, knowing he was going to give me a ton of it—like usual. "Please, sir."

"Jesus Christ." Three thrusts later, he hit his threshold and filled me. He shoved himself completely inside me so he could give me every drop. His need to pump all of his seed inside me always turned me on all over again.

"Yes…" I ran my fingers through his damp hair and felt his cock start to soften when he was completely finished. I watched the tightness soften in his jaw and the satisfaction enter his eyes. He rarely pulled out of me to come on my body rather than deep inside me, and I knew it was his ultimate way to possess me.

Not that I minded.

His hand slid into my hair, and he kissed me hard even though we were finished. His tongue moved with mine before his kiss suddenly turned soft, nearly apologetic.

My fingers wrapped around his wrist, and I felt his pulse, my favorite lullaby.

When he finished kissing me, he kept his forehead pressed against mine. "I love you more than anything in this world."

Instead of feeling happiness, I felt a surge of heartbreak. I was broken in two, and I hadn't even left yet. Despair washed over me, but I was forced to ignore it, to pretend it never happened at all. "I love you too."

He kissed my forehead before he gently pulled out of me, taking his time so he could secure his deposit inside my slit. He liked knowing his come was sitting inside me all night long while we both slept. That was the kind of possession he liked to take.

He finally pulled out of me then got comfortable in bed, his powerful body next to mine. He draped his arm over my waist and nuzzled his face into my neck, the coarse hair rubbing against my soft skin.

I didn't think I could sleep tonight since I was going to leave tomorrow, but my eyes grew heavy and I fell asleep almost immediately.

"Everything okay?" Crewe checked his black tie as he watched me.

"Yeah…why?" He was about to leave for work, and I was doing my best to pretend everything was fine. Since he was so in tune with my mannerisms and expressions, he probably knew I wasn't behaving like I normally did.

"Seem a little off." He grabbed his watch and secured it around his wrist before he walked up to me and kissed me on the mouth.

"Just tired."

"Alright." Crewe didn't press me further and kissed my hairline. "I'll see you later."

"See you later." He walked through the door.

"I love you," I blurted, unsure how many more times I'd get to say it.

He turned around and smiled. "I love you too." He shut the door and disappeared.

I felt sick to my stomach. I would spend the day packing and organizing my departure. He had no idea when he walked through that door everything would be different.

I only had one small suitcase, and I threw everything inside, not caring about tidiness. I stole one of his shirts from his drawer and kept that too, knowing I would want it when I was sleeping alone in my apartment.

When everything was put together, I called Joseph.

"What's up?" he answered.

"I was wondering if I could catch a ride from you later today…" It was hard to talk when I was on the verge of tears.

Joseph heard the sorrow in my voice. "Are you leaving him?"

"Yeah…"

"You're sure you wanna do this?"

"Yes."

"I hate the guy, but you shouldn't let some cunt tell you what to do."

"I'm not…I just know it needs to be this way."

"Well, I'm nowhere near Scotland right now. I'm in Russia, actually."

"Oh…" I assumed he was about to perform the heist that he and Crewe planned together.

"But I can have one of my men pick you up. A very trustworthy guy."

I didn't feel comfortable sitting in a car with someone I didn't know, but I didn't have any other choice. I just needed to get to the airport. "That'll be fine."

"Okay. I'll have him swing by."

"Thanks." I sat on the edge of the bed with my arms crossed over my chest. There wasn't anything else to say and Joseph wasn't interested in these types of conversations, but it felt good just to sit on the line with him.

"I don't want to be insensitive, but I need to go…"

"Oh, I understand." I knew he was busy with more important things.

"But I still think you should reconsider what you're doing. If Ariel is willing to hurt him like this, she shouldn't be in his life at all."

"I know…but I did a lot of terrible things. I understand why she doesn't trust me."

"It's fine that she doesn't trust you. But this is hurting Crewe—the man she's supposedly loyal to."

"Joseph, I appreciate what you're doing, but this is how it has to be."

He sighed. "Whatever you say."

"I'll talk to you later."

"Alright. Love you." I hardly ever heard him say anything remotely sweet, so I knew he meant it.

"I love you too."

When five o'clock came around, my heart shattered.

This was the most difficult moment of my life.

I had to let him go even if he didn't want to let me go.

Crewe walked inside and immediately peeled his jacket off, but he halted when he saw my roll-aboard suitcase at the end of the bed. "Is this a hint that you want me to take you on a vacation?"

I stood beside the suitcase and couldn't meet his gaze. It was too difficult. In a matter of seconds, I would hurt him more than I hurt right that second. "I've been doing some thinking…"

Crewe stiffened noticeably. I could see the movement in my periphery since I refused to look directly at him.

"I don't think I can sacrifice my whole life to be with you. I've always wanted to be a doctor and practice medicine, but I can't do that here. My friends are back in New York. I can't give up everything just for you. And a life of royalty…

it's just not for me." I held back the tears up until that moment, but I wouldn't be able to hold back the dam much longer.

Crewe was absolutely still. It didn't seem like he was even breathing. "I have no idea what you're talking about."

"I've decided to go back to America, Crewe. That's all I'm trying to tell you."

He stepped closer to me before his voice turned hostile. "Look at me."

I knew I would cry the second that I did. I lifted my gaze and stared into his scotch-colored eyes. Tears formed in the corners of my eyes then dripped down my face.

Crewe watched me without an ounce of sympathy. "Where is this coming from?"

"I've been thinking about it for a while."

"Didn't seem that way yesterday," he said coldly. "Or the day before. Or the day before that…"

"I just…I guess I've been waiting." I grabbed the handle to my suitcase, like that would make my intention more convincing. "I'm sorry, Crewe. I don't know what to say." I moved around him and headed to the door.

He blocked the way with his massive size. "This isn't making any sense. We were happy yesterday."

"I haven't really been happy. I stay home all day—"

"I never had a problem with you going to school."

"I know, but it's not—"

"You don't need to transfer your credits if you get your citizenship and live here forever," he said simply. "So what the fuck? This isn't making any sense. What aren't you telling me?"

"I'm not hiding anything," I said defensively. "I just…I don't want this lifestyle. I don't want to go to these fancy parties with people I'll never be good enough for. I don't want to be dressed up like a doll and reminded not to slouch. I just want a normal life, Crewe. We both know I'll never get that with you."

"You're destined to have more than a normal life," he said quietly. "Even if you're unhappy with the situation, it doesn't make sense for you to leave. You love me."

The words elicited more tears. "Don't make this harder than it needs to be."

"I'm not the one making this hard. You're giving me whiplash right now."

"I'm sorry if I've confused you…but I want to leave."

He clenched his jaw in annoyance, his eyes darkening. "This isn't making any sense."

"Crewe, I don't want to be with you." I strengthened my voice so it wouldn't shake. "I came back because I thought I loved you, but I think that was just a high. Now that I'm here as a free person, I realize I don't want to be here."

He continued to block the door, but his hostile expression softened.

"Based on the way we started, it would never work between us. We had no chance anyway. We were never going to get married, so it makes sense for me to leave sooner rather than later." The mention of marriage made me want to cry harder.

Crewe bowed his head to the floor. "I didn't realize you felt this way."

"I…I do." A part of me wanted him to catch my lie, to know I didn't want to say any of this.

"How long have you felt this way?"

I made something up. "A few weeks."

"And you aren't willing to work on it with me?"

"No," I whispered. "I want to marry a normal guy…have a normal life. I'm sorry."

He rubbed his fingers over his jawline, his shoulders stiff with pain. "And that's it?" he asked incredulously. "You're just gonna go, and we're gonna move on like nothing happened?"

I nodded.

He dragged his hand down his face then shook his head. "I guess Ariel was right. I feel like an idiot."

That was the last nail in the coffin. More tears fell.

Crewe finally stepped out of the way. He moved toward the fireplace and didn't turn around, refusing to look at me.

The path to the door was open, and now I had no reason to stay. I waited for him to say something, to understand this wasn't me at all. I hoped he would understand how much I loved him and I would never do this unless someone were forcing me. But I knew Josephine had fucked up his brain. She left him for someone else, and now I was leaving him. It wasn't the first time a woman broke his heart.

I finally opened the door and walked out, doing my best not to look at him. I made it down the hallway and to the stairs, the tears falling harder and harder. Like a sheet of rain, the moisture drizzled down my face.

When I got to the front door, Dimitri stared at me with concern. He didn't show any joy at my sadness, only confusion.

I got the door opened and ran right into Ariel. In her typical dark clothing, she looked like she had returned just to make sure I kept my word. She looked right at the tears on my face without giving the slightest reaction.

I had to steady my fist so I wouldn't punch her. Nothing I'd like to do more than break that pretty little nose of hers. "You should be ashamed of yourself." That was the best I could come up with on the spot. I moved past her, purposely shoving my shoulder into hers as I moved down the stone steps and to the driveway. There was a black SUV waiting for me, and the man got out and immediately helped me into the back seat.

I looked out the window as I waited for the car to pull away. Ariel stood at the front door with her arms crossed over her chest. She watched me with a stoic expression, my final words not leaving any kind of mark. I surveyed the windows of the tower, wondering what Crewe was thinking at that very moment. I treasured the final view of my home before I was pulled away forever, returning to my mediocre and passionless life.

When the car pulled away, I covered my face and gave in to the grief that burned inside of my heart. The driver didn't glance at me over his shoulder. He didn't ask me any questions either. He left me to cry to myself in peace, letting me express emotions that I couldn't express in words.

I didn't just lose the love of my life.

I lost my reason to live.

19

CREWE

I WAS NUMB.

Absolutely numb.

Whenever I was angry, I reached for the scotch. But I didn't do that today. Whenever I was pissed, I shoved my fist through a wall. That didn't happen either.

What I felt in that moment was different from anything else I'd ever experienced.

The first thing I did was sit down on the balcony. It was freezing cold outside and windy, but I needed the temperature to cool myself off. I rested my fingers against my chin and tried to understand what just happened.

She left me.

She didn't want me anymore, so she packed her things and took off.

I thought we were happy.

I thought she loved me.

A part of me still thought those things. There had been instances when she behaved strangely, but I assumed she was simply in a peculiar mood. I didn't think it reflected on me or her happiness in our relationship.

Maybe if I'd paid more attention, I would have noticed.

I sat there for hours until it was pitch black outside. I didn't bother turning on the lights or having dinner. I allowed the shadows to surround me and steal my soul. I almost felt indifferent, but I knew that wasn't the case. I knew I was in such distress my body didn't know how to cope with the pain.

I was going to ask her to marry me.

But she wanted to break up instead.

How would I internalize that? How would I accept that? It was hard for me to take her back to begin with. She fought for me, even moved here for me, and then she just changed her mind?

It didn't add up.

I made love to her last night, and everything seemed normal. She was drenched for me, and when she said she loved me, I could see the passion in her eyes. If you told me then that was my last night with her, I wouldn't have believed you.

But that didn't stop it from being true.

I didn't know what to do with myself. I'd given up alcoholism, my biggest habit. I'd given up my asshole attitude too. All my bad characteristics had been locked away so my good features could shine through. Without her with me, there was no reason to be a good man. There was no reason to be happy.

There was no reason for anything.

I didn't hear the knock at my door, just Dunbar's approach from the living room. "Sir?"

I didn't turn around. Even if he had a gun pointed at me, I still wouldn't turn around. "I'm listening."

"I just picked up the ring. What would you like me to do with it?"

If it hadn't belonged to my mother, I would have told him to throw it away. "Leave it on the table. Tell the rest of the staff not to disturb me."

Dunbar was smart to not ask any questions. "Yes, sir." He shut the door and disappeared.

There were only two women I'd ever intended to marry, and both of them left me without a backward glance. Not only was I wealthy and smart, but I was handsome and gentle. I had a lot of good qualities when I allowed them to shine through.

But neither of them seemed to care.

I needed to have children to pass down my lineage. If not, I would have stopped giving a fuck.

But I couldn't picture myself with anyone, letting alone being a husband. All I could think of was the woman I'd fallen madly in love with. She played me like a fool, not once, but twice.

Ariel had been right.

Why didn't I listen to her?

I stared into the darkness and tightened my hand into a fist, the kind that pierced my skin and made my knuckles turn white. "Fuck her."

Ariel walked into my office. "I just got off the phone with—"

"You can reach me by email today. I'm not taking any personal visits." I didn't look up from my laptop, not interested in seeing a human face other than my own for the foreseeable future.

Ariel lingered in the doorway. "Everything alright?"

"London left. But you already knew that."

She didn't deny it. "I'm sorry, Crewe."

"No, you aren't. You can say I told you so. Go ahead." I finally looked up, unable to hide the pissed expression on my face. All I wanted to do was destroy everything in the castle. If everything weren't a preservation of history, I would have set it on fire. I wanted to ruin anything that woman had ever touched.

"I have no interest in doing that."

"Then get out. I have shit to do."

Ariel didn't hesitate before she walked out the door.

When she was gone, I turned back to my computer and dragged my hand down my face. I wanted to flip my desk over and shatter it. When London originally left, I didn't feel anything. But now that I had a few hours of sleep, I was just pissed.

Fucking livid.

All I felt was hatred.

I wanted to grab her by the neck and strangle her.

I closed my eyes and willed the pain to go away. The rage was affecting my ability to work, and work was the only distraction I had right now. But I needed the anger. Once it was gone, there would only be depression.

And I hated being depressed.

———

Joseph was launching the attack tonight. I stayed on the line in my bedroom so I could overhear their communications.

Joseph was in charge of intercepting the wire transfer, not the actual murder. I shouldn't care if he was safe since he was London's brother, but her happiness was always something that lingered in the back of my mind.

Pissed me off.

"How are things going?" I asked him over the phone.

"Everything is on schedule. We're ready to intercept the second the line is open. Our men are staked at the house right now. The second the wife and kids are gone, we'll loot the place. The third team is in place to take him out the moment he leaves the meeting and gets into the car."

"You think he won't run the second the money is intercepted?"

"He won't know the funds have been misplaced for at least five minutes. He's done this dozens of times, so he has no reason to think it won't go through."

"For argument's sake, what if he doesn't get in the car?" I didn't care about all the money Joseph would steal from the asshole. I just wanted the asshole to be dead.

"I have a team in place if it comes to that. Don't worry, Crewe. I know what I'm doing."

"Surely, you must understand why I doubt that."

Joseph didn't strike with a comeback. "I'm gonna put you on speakerphone. Don't talk until it's over. I can't afford a distraction right now."

I expected him to mention London, but he never did. He probably expected me to mention her too, but now wasn't the time. It wasn't like Joseph had anything to say to make me feel better. He never wanted me to be with his sister anyway. "Okay."

I sat on the line and listened. Joseph's fingers hit the keyboard in the background, and I could hear our men radio in while they took their positions. We decided to split the men down the middle, fifty-fifty. It made us both equally involved and equally in charge, even though Joseph was running the operation.

"Family left," Joseph reported. "They're in and looting everything."

I could hear the men speaking over the intercom, so I was aware of the situation.

Joseph conversed with his teammates as his fingers struck the keyboard. "Wiring in place…ulterior route is in action."

I listened in silence.

"It went through," Joseph said without emotion. It didn't seem like he cared that he just received forty million dollars.

"What about him?" I asked.

Joseph conversed with his men over the line. "He just left the building. He's getting into the car."

This was the moment I'd been looking forward to. If I didn't have such a reputation, I would have pulled the trigger myself. But this was how it had to be. I had to have a concrete alibi when all of this went down.

I interlocked my fingers, and it was the first time I didn't think about London. The death of my greatest enemy was the only thing strong enough to distract me. I hardly breathed as I listened, not wanting to miss a word.

Gunshots went off in the background.

"What's your status?" Joseph asked.

A guy spoke over the intercom. "Driver is knocked out. Target is dead. Two bullets in the skull."

I leaned back in my chair and smiled, feeling the sense of revenge wash over me. If I were really cruel, I could have killed his entire family instead and allowed him to live with the heartache. If you asked me, my actions were merciful. I got the revenge I deserved, and that asshole got what was coming to him.

"Did you hear that, Crewe?" Joseph asked.

"Yes." My smile dropped once the weight of the truth had sunk in. That asshole was really gone. My family was finally avenged.

"I'll give you an update on the house—"

"Couldn't care less." The only thing I cared about had been taken care of. "Great job, Joseph. It was a pleasure working with you."

"No problem. Thanks for the muscle."

"Sure." I hung up before he could say anything. I didn't want there to be an opportunity for London to be mentioned.

She was the last thing I wanted to talk about.

"I heard the good news." Ariel walked into my office before lunchtime.

I rubbed my temple and stared out the window. "What good news?" A cold glass of scotch was in my hand—the seventh one since this morning.

"That you killed that dirtbag." She sat on the sofa across from me.

The room was spinning, and the lights were too bright. My head ached like my skull had been cracked, so I placed the glass right against my head. I closed my eyes and tried to absorb the coldness, but it didn't make a difference.

"You doing okay?"

"Fine."

Ariel opened her notebook. "I think we should talk about the offer from Constantin. I think expanding would be good."

"Who's Constantin?"

"The man we had lunch with yesterday," she said calmly.

I couldn't remember him. "Oh…whatever you think is best." I opened my eyes and looked out the window again. The room was spinning harder than before. I could barely keep my eyes open because it was so bright. Every other second, I thought of London, and that made me feel a million times worse. I slowly slid sideways and spilled the drink all over me.

"Crewe, are you sure you're okay?" Ariel leapt up and grabbed the glass out of my hand before I could spill it everywhere.

"I said I was fine." I lay back on the couch and propped my feet up. "I'm just…"

She placed her palm against my forehead.

I smacked her away. "Don't fucking touch me." Ariel hadn't done anything to me, but I was so angry at the entire world that everyone was a target. I hated all of my employees. I hated anyone who was happy. "Go touch Cassandra."

Ariel didn't rise to my anger. "I'm calling the doctor. I think you have alcohol poisoning."

"Are you a doctor now?" I snapped. "Just shut the fuck up and leave me alone."

Ariel went silent, but her anger was loud. "I suggest you watch your mouth."

"Why? Because you'll just leave me like everyone else?" I sat up quickly and got to my feet, determined to storm out and prove a point I didn't have. But I lost my balance and crashed into the table.

"Crewe!" Ariel grabbed me by the arms and helped me to the floor. "That's it, I'm calling a doctor."

"Don't."

She pulled out her phone and pressed it to her ear.

"I said, don't." I smacked her hand so the phone went flying.

"Jesus Christ, Crewe. Calm down." She left me on the ground and retrieved the phone. She made the call.

I didn't stop her because I couldn't move. Otherwise, I would have grabbed her phone again and snapped it in two.

She talked in the background, speaking to a nurse or some other medical professional.

Shortly afterward, I blacked out.

I woke up in my bed. Well, my old bed. It was the bed I used to sleep in with London.

I'd been sleeping in the other room since she left.

An IV was in my arm, and monitors on wheels were connected to my bed. A blood pressure cuff tightened on my arm uncomfortably, and that's probably why I woke up in the first place. I opened my eyes wider and found Ariel sitting at my bedside.

It suddenly dawned on me that I had no one in my life who cared about me.

All I had was Ariel.

I didn't have any friends or family.

I didn't have London.

I had nothing.

Ariel approached the bed when she realized I was awake. "Hey, Crewe. How are you feeling?"

I felt the same as I did last time I was awake. "What time is it?"

"One."

I looked out the window and saw the daylight. "So…I've been asleep for, like, an hour?"

"More like twenty-four hours."

"Oh…"

"Crewe, the doctor said your blood alcohol level was so high he's surprised you didn't slip into a coma and die."

"Damn…should have drunk more, then."

She gave me the coldest look I'd ever seen. "Crewe…"

I couldn't stand her look, so I turned my gaze to the other side of the room. "I'll cut back on the drinking, alright? Just so I don't get sick like this again. Is that what you wanted to hear?"

"I want to understand why you're behaving this way."

"Behaving like what?" I'd completely lost myself. Now all I wanted to do was be the biggest jackass in the world.

"Like you've lost your mind."

"I have lost my mind."

She scooted closer to me on the bed and rested her hand on mine.

I yanked it away, not wanting any affection from anyone— not even London.

"I know London left and it's been hard for you—"

"I don't care that she left." It was the most pathetic lie I ever told. Ariel certainly didn't believe me, not when I didn't even find myself convincing. "I hate her. I fucking hate her."

"I know…but you can't let it destroy you like this."

"It's not about her," I said quickly. "You wouldn't understand." No one would understand.

"I know you pretty well, so I might understand."

I was pretty sure I was still drunk even though I was awake. I was still a little dizzy. Even though I'd slept for twenty-four hours, I could fall back asleep if I wanted to. "I didn't realize how unhappy I was until I was happy. And that's when I realized I'd never been happy my entire life. Then when I was happy, I was so scared I was gonna lose it. I felt whole, complete. Then London left, and it was hard…really hard. But when she came back…everything was good. I finally had what I've always wanted. I finally had the kind of joy I didn't think I'd ever attain. Then she didn't want me anymore. Now I know I'll never be happy again." I couldn't believe I was telling her any of this. I sounded like such a pussy. "I'm not meant to be happy. I'm meant to be cold, cruel, and empty. But I wish I'd never been happy to begin with. I wish I'd never known such a feeling. Because living without it…is cruel."

It was the first time Ariel looked genuinely sad. She lowered her head as she processed what I said. "You could always be happy with someone else, Crewe. Someone better."

"I'll never be happy with someone else. She was everything I wanted. We were perfect together. She understood me. But it didn't matter how good I was to her. It didn't matter what I sacrificed for her. It wasn't good enough. That hurts most of all…"

She kept her head bowed.

"I know I shouldn't have lost control like I did…but what the fuck does it matter? If I die, everything goes to you. Honestly, death doesn't sound so bad. Experiencing nothing but darkness…sounds peaceful. All I'm doing with my life is making money. And fuck, money doesn't mean anything if you don't have anyone to share it with, anyone to trust. Fucking sucks." I regretted everything I said as soon as I said it. I shouldn't have spoken my mind, opened my heart. I sounded pathetic, even to my own ears. "Forget everything I said. I'll get back on my feet…just give me some time."

She leaned back in the chair and crossed her arms over her chest. She didn't feed me empty words to make me feel better. She didn't give me a stupid pep talk to get me on my feet. She just accepted me for who I was.

That was something I loved about her. I could be myself without consequence. She was all I had of a family, and I was grateful she was there. "You've always been there for me…I'm sorry I ever gave London a chance. I should have listened to you. You're my family…she never was."

She tucked her hair behind her ear and avoided eye contact with me.

I was probably making her uncomfortable by wearing my heart on my sleeve. I'd never done anything like that before because it was inappropriate and unprofessional, but the booze had clouded my judgment. I couldn't erase my stupid mistake, but I could at least prevent it from getting worse by not talking. So I didn't say anything else.

Ariel was quiet for an hour, just sitting at my bedside with me. She didn't pull out her laptop and get to work. She just sat with me.

"You don't have to wait with me," I whispered. "I'm sure you have stuff to do. In a few hours, I'll be good to go."

"I'm staying, Crewe. The doctor warned me you might vomit and choke in your sleep."

"Well, I'm awake now."

"You could fall asleep again."

I still didn't want her to waste her time with me. "Send Dunbar in instead. I know you have more important things to do."

Finally, she didn't argue with me and stood up. "Is there anything I can get you?"

My head was still spinning, but I was aware of how empty my stomach was. "Food would be nice."

"You got it." She walked to the door to let herself out.

"Ariel?"

She turned around. "Hmm?"

"I'm sorry if I said anything rude before…I know I have a problem with that." I did it to London one too many times.

She gave me a pained smile. "Don't worry about it."

———

I didn't stop drinking, but I didn't push myself that far again. Anytime I thought I was getting too close to my threshold, I cut myself off.

But I was definitely drunk every single day.

When the anger passed, I was left with pure misery. My life became filled with sleepless nights, productive work days, and pure emptiness. I didn't go out and find a woman, and I didn't call up a woman who would jump into bed with me.

I couldn't get hard if I tried.

As days passed, I kept rethinking my final conversation with London. It was hard to believe because we seemed happy. The sex was great, the conversation was good... everything felt right. Or did I feel something she never did?

I felt like I was missing something, but I had no idea what it was.

I knew she took her phone because I hadn't seen it lying around the house. I could call her if I wanted to, but I had way too much pride for that. If she didn't want to be with me, I wasn't going to try to convince her otherwise.

No matter how much I loved her.

I spent my time working a lot more than usual and also exercising more than I did before. Now that I had nothing to do with my free time except battle my depression, I tried to stay busy, but there was only so much I could do besides work, drink, and exercise.

Would I ever get over her?

I really thought she was the woman I could spend my life with. I really thought marrying her would be worth the sacrifice of diluting my royal bloodline. I gave up more for her than she realized, and I wondered if she ever grasped that.

Probably not.

There were days when I hated her.

Then there were days when I was in love with her again.

But then I hated her and loved her at the same time.

I wondered if I would ever feel better again, if I would ever feel whole. Spending my life as a manwhore and terminal bachelor didn't seem so bad, but I'd always wanted to have children. I wanted to make my family grow to fill the sorrow in my chest. I wanted to replace the family that I lost.

Looked like I couldn't marry for love.

I'd have to find someone as broken as I was.

I was working in my office when Ariel walked inside. She and I hadn't talked much over the past few days. After that alcohol poisoning disaster, we'd kept our distance from one another. I said some things I shouldn't have said, and she obviously wished she hadn't heard them. "What can I do for you?" I skipped the pleasantries altogether.

"You have a minute?" She sat down in the chair in front of my desk. It was the only time I'd seen her without her folder. She wasn't in her work attire either, just jeans and a t-shirt. Her aura of confidence was snuffed out, and she could barely meet my look.

"Of course. If this is about everything I said when I was in bed, I'm sorry. I—"

"No, Crewe," she said quickly. "There's something I need to tell you. It's difficult because…I know things for us aren't going to end well."

I shut my laptop because the email I was writing became irrelevant. Ariel never expressed fear or doubt, so when she did, I knew it was serious. "I'm listening."

She took a deep breath before she spoke. "Well…I made my feelings for London very clear—"

My phone rang on the desk.

"You can get that," she said quickly.

I glanced at the screen. "I wonder why Joseph is calling me…" I felt bad interrupting Ariel when this was clearly important, but Joseph didn't call me unless he had a reason to. Maybe London was hurt. Maybe she needed help. "Sorry, I have to take this." I placed the phone against my ear. "It's Crewe. What's up?"

"I need to talk to you," he said. "I'm not supposed to say anything or get involved. London said she would kill me. But I feel like I should say something as her older brother."

I didn't know what he was talking about, but now I needed to know. "What is it?"

"She left because of that little cunt of yours, Ariel."

My eyes moved to Ariel. When I saw the guilty look on her face along with all the fidgeting, I knew she could hear every word Joseph was saying. "What about her?"

"Ariel told London she would only stay if London promised not to marry you. When Ariel found out you were going to propose, she told London and sent her away. London doesn't want to be in America right now. She just did it because she knew how devastated you would be without Ariel by your side. She knows she's family to you—all you've got. I just wanted to tell you that…" Joseph kept talking, but I didn't listen to a word he said.

All I could do was stare at Ariel.

Slight tears formed in her eyes. I'd never seen Ariel cry, but she was on the verge of breaking down.

Joseph kept rambling in my ear as my hand tightened into a fist. My knuckles turned white, and I felt rage like I'd never known before. I'd never wanted to hit a woman so much in my life. I wanted to break my desk into pieces just to have something to throw at her. Good thing I didn't have a gun anywhere nearby. I'd probably shoot her in the goddamn face. "Thanks for letting me know. I have to go."

"Wait, what are you—"

I hung up on him and tossed the phone on my desk. Then I stared at her.

She stared at me.

I didn't move or speak. It was one of those moments when I was so mad I couldn't even think. All I could do was feel ferocious rage. Not only did she purposely sabotage my happiness, but she severed her loyalty to me. Any trust I had for her evaporated like hot steam from a boiling pot. All I could see was red.

Ariel blinked her tears away and hid them as best she could. She still didn't say anything, probably because she had no defense.

I rubbed my fingers along my jaw, feeling my heart pound in my chest. I should have trusted my instincts when London behaved strangely. She told me she wanted to leave, but everything she said contradicted the way she was with me.

She did love me.

She did want to be with me.

The realization dimmed my anger, but only slightly. The sooner I got on a plane, the sooner I could be with her.

But first, I had to take care of this bitch. "Looks like you're the snake in the garden."

Ariel's eyes looked slightly bigger with the black frames on her nose. Her expression wasn't so professional anymore.

Now she had emotions, reactions. Above all else, she looked scared. "Let me explain myself…"

"Sure. I'd like to see you try." There was nothing she could say to justify what she did. Not a single thing.

"I don't need to remind you of everything she did to us…"

"No," I said coldly. "I was there. I remember."

"She's not trustworthy, and I didn't want to work in a business where she could benefit from it. I've never trusted her feelings toward you. I've never trusted that she would be a good partner for you. I didn't want you to throw away everything you worked for by choosing the wrong wife."

That only made it worse because those reasons were bullshit. "I understand you like to be in control of everything around you. But I'm not something that can be controlled, Ariel. I'll fuck who I want to fuck. And I'll marry who I want to marry. I'd definitely prefer to leave you behind than sacrifice the love of my life. You had no right to do what you did. I'll never forgive you. And I'll certainly never trust you."

When she blinked, a small tear emerged. "I understand, Crewe. I didn't realize how much you loved her until she was gone. That's when I realized I made a mistake. I came in here to tell you that."

"Looks like her brother beat you to the punch."

"And if he hadn't, I would have told you myself. I admit what I did was wrong, and I came in here to make it right. I understand if you don't want to work with me anymore, but I promise I'll never do anything like that again. I promise I'll make this right and get her back here. I promise—"

"Fuck you, Ariel. I don't want you within three miles of me at any times. You hate London because of what she did, but your actions are far worse. She was the victim of a kidnapping, and she was trying to survive. You were just a brat who wanted to get your way." I shook my head and ground my teeth. "The world isn't accepting of who you love, but I've always been supportive of that. You know I would defend you and stand up for you, even to the fucking Queen of England. I thought we had each other's backs, Ariel. I thought we loved each other—"

"We do."

"Shut the fuck up. You threatened to leave our business because you didn't accept who I loved. And then London sacrificed me just to get you to stay. I find it very odd that my relationship revolves around you. I find it very odd that the person I trust most stabbed me in the back like that. It's so selfish I can't even stomach it."

"I know what I did was wrong—"

"I'll never forgive you." We could argue for a week straight, and I wouldn't change my position. Ariel was corrupt and cruel. She claimed she did everything to protect me, but she did it for her own self-interests. "I never want to see you again. I'll talk to my lawyer, and he'll take care of all your shit. All communication can be done through him."

Now she cried harder and wiped the tears away with her fingertips. "Crewe—"

I rose out of my chair and snatched my phone on the way out. "I have to go get my woman now. I don't have time for any more of this bullshit."

20

LONDON

I WAS LIVING off my savings and sleeping in a motel room.

It wasn't nice, but I didn't need nice right now.

I hadn't bothered to find an apartment yet. I hadn't even bothered to find a job. I'd never been this lazy in my life, but it was hard for me to get out of bed. I only ate when my stomach wouldn't stop growling and I felt light-headed. There was a deli just next door, so I walked there to get a sandwich.

I'd been watching a lot of daytime TV, most soap operas. Every time a couple broke up, I thought of Crewe and shed my own tears. I constantly checked my phone to see if he texted or called me and I just happened not to hear it.

But he never did.

I tried to convince myself this was for the best. He deserved someone better than me. But those words did little to make me feel better. Honestly, I loved him so much that I wanted him to myself.

Did that make me a terrible person?

I'd never hated someone before, but I truly hated Ariel. If she weren't so close to Crewe, I would have told her to fuck off then gave her a black eye. She had a lot of nerve pulling the stunt she did. When I disliked her before, at least I respected her. But now I just thought she was a manipulative bitch who controlled Crewe like a puppet with invisible strings. The only family I had was Joseph, and I knew Ariel was all Crewe had. If it weren't for that fact, things would have turned out completely differently.

A knock sounded on the door.

I was lying in a bed that had only been made once, with the light from the TV shining on the wall. It was nearly nine in the evening, so I assumed it wasn't housekeeping. I felt perfectly safe in New York, but I wasn't naïve either.

I crept to the door and looked through the peephole.

I knew I was losing my mind when I saw a man who looked just like Crewe on the other side. With the same five-o'clock shadow, the same mocha brown eyes, and the same powerful shoulders.

Maybe this was a dream.

"Lovely," he spoke through the door. "It's me."

I inhaled a sharp breath before my hands began to shake. I tried to get the latch off the door, but I couldn't slide it through the metal. My movements were too jerky because I couldn't keep my body still. "One second…I'm trying to get the lock." I finally slid it over and unlocked the handle. When I pulled the door open, the cold air rushed inside, bringing the smell of frost from winter.

I hadn't even thought about changing. I was in sweatpants and his old shirt with a messy bun planted on the top of my head. I looked terrible, but I was so excited to see him that I didn't think twice before opening the door.

I'd been thinking about him nonstop, and now that he was here, I didn't think. I said the dumbest thing. "Can I get you some water?"

Crewe stepped inside and shut the door behind him.

"I mean…sorry. I just can't believe you're here. I… Why are you here?"

His hands went to my waist, and he moved in close to me. "Ariel told me the truth. Now I'm here to take you home."

"She did…?" She put me through all that misery just to come clean about it?

He nodded. "You'll never see her again. She's gone."

"Really?" I whispered, tears springing to my eyes.

"Yeah. And I apologize in advance for this…I didn't want to ask you this in a run-down hotel in Manhattan, but since you already know…" He pulled the ring from his pocket and slipped it on my left ring finger. "Please say yes. I don't want anything to come between us again. I've already lost you twice, and I can't do it again."

I eyed the beautiful ring with a red stone in the middle with tears in my eyes. It was unlike any other ring I'd ever seen. Without question, I knew it was special. I knew it wasn't a ring he simply picked up at the store.

"It was my mother's," he explained. "And my grandmother's before that…"

"I'm so honored."

"Then do me the honor of saying yes." He grabbed my wrist and placed his hand over my chest. "Say yes."

"Yes." A new wave of tears spilled down my face. "Yes."

He cupped my face and kissed me like he never had before. A combination of hard and soft, his lips moved with mine with desperation. He slowly backed me farther into the room, his fingers sliding into my hair then down my shoulders. My tears stuck to his cheeks, but that didn't slow him down. He wiped one drop away with the pad of his thumb before he broke the kiss. "You wanna spend the night here or head back home?"

New York wasn't home to me. This hotel was just a room stuffed with my misery. Scotland was the only place I wanted to be, the home away from home that became permanent. I wanted to be exactly where I belonged—not stuck here for a minute longer. "Let's go home."

It was nice to be home again.

I'd only been gone for a week, but it felt like a lifetime. Misery was suffocating, a blanket of sadness that nearly smothered me. I couldn't do anything but exist. I wasn't sure when I would have finally left that hotel room and found an apartment and a job. Probably a while.

My belongings were returned to the room I shared with Crewe, but now that we planned to spend our lives together, everything felt different—in a good way. I loved my ring, and it made me feel special knowing his mother had worn it as well.

Crewe didn't go to work like he normally would have. He took time off to be with me, to make up for the time we lost. It was only a week, but for both of us, it felt like an eternity. There wasn't much talking involved, just a lot of sex.

He didn't mention Ariel.

I didn't either.

We managed to stay in bed all day, having our meals left by the door while we were wrapped up in the sheets. The only time we left was to eat and shower. The rest of the time, our naked bodies were wrapped together.

Crewe placed my left hand on his chest and ran his finger over the red ruby in the center of my engagement ring. "It looks great on you."

"I think we go pretty well together, actually."

"You're right." He brought my hand to his lips and kissed the back of my knuckles. "So, when do you want to get married?"

"I don't care. Don't you have to have a royal ceremony and all that stuff?"

He shrugged. "I'm supposed to. I probably should...but I don't want to."

"What would you like to do?"

"Something with just the two of us. Maybe a few witnesses."

"Like on Fair Isle?" I asked with a smile.

He smiled back. "That sounds perfect, actually. It'll be a little cold, but if the sun is out, it'll be beautiful."

"That sounds nice to me. Maybe we could have our own ceremony then do the big royal thing later?"

"That sounds fair. Let's do that."

"Perfect." I cuddled into his side and wrapped my arm around his waist. "You sure you want to marry a peasant?"

"Absolutely."

"That means I'll be a duchess?"

"Yep."

"That's kinda weird…"

"Not really. All you have to do is look pretty. It's the easiest job in the world."

"You're oversimplifying it."

"Oh, and fuck your husband every chance you get. Forgot that one."

I pressed a kiss to his chest. "That doesn't sound so bad. I'd do that even if he weren't my husband."

"Good answer."

As much as I enjoyed him spending time with me, I knew he couldn't neglect his business forever, especially since Ariel was no longer around to help him with anything. "Are you sure you don't need to get back to work?"

"Trying to get rid of me already?" he asked with a smile.

"No. I just don't want to make your life more complicated."

"Maybe I like complicated. I did ask you to marry me."

"Hey." I gave him a playful slap.

"You should let Joseph know what's going on. I'm sure he's curious."

"Why would he be curious?" Last time he knew, I was in New York. My phone was in my bag somewhere because I forgot about it the second Crewe whisked me into his arms. The battery probably had died by now.

"Well…he called me and told me why you left."

"He did?" My natural response was to be furious, but seeing how things worked out, I guess it didn't matter.

"Ariel was in the process of telling me herself, so I would have found out anyway. He'd probably like to know you're here."

It was a sweet thing for Joseph to do, considering the fact that he didn't like Crewe. I guess that was the best blessing I was going to get. "I'll call him later."

Crewe sat up in bed and looked at the clock. "I should probably get in the shower. Unless you'd like to join me?"

I loved to see that hot and naked body under the warm water any day. "I would, but I should probably call my brother."

"You can always take a peek some other time." He winked then fished his phone out of his pocket. He tossed it on the bed beside me before he walked into the bathroom.

When I called Joseph, I barely heard it ring once before he answered. "Crewe?"

"Actually, it's me."

"London?" he asked excitedly. "Looks like my message went a long way. I called you a few times, but it kept going straight to voice mail. I assumed you just didn't feel like talking."

"No, my phone died. Crewe and I have been busy…"

Joseph ignored the awkward thing I'd just said. "Well, I'm glad you're happy again. I almost didn't say anything, but I'm grateful I did. You're probably pissed at me, but I don't care."

"Actually, Ariel was in the process of telling him when you called, so I can't be mad."

"She told him?" he asked in surprise. "So the bitch has a heart, after all…"

"Or some form of one."

"Crewe fired her?"

"Yeah. I haven't heard anything about her."

"Good. She got what's coming to her."

I eyed my beautiful engagement ring, pregnant with ancient history. Duchesses had worn it before me. Even the Queen of Scotland probably wore it centuries ago. "So…Crewe asked me to marry him."

"He did?" Joseph blurted. "Oh, shit. Did you say yes?"

"What do you think I said, dumbass? No?"

"Damn. Well…I'm happy for you. I can't believe that guy is gonna be my brother-in-law. Weird."

"It doesn't have to be weird if you both make an effort."

Joseph was quiet for a long time. "He's got a lot of resources and a great reputation. So I guess I can make it work."

"I'm sure he feels the same."

"So, when's the wedding?"

"We'll have a small ceremony soon. Then we'll have the big royal one in about a year."

"Do I have to go to the big royal one?" he asked with a groan.

"No. But there'll probably be a lot of beautiful women there…"

"Ooh…maybe I'll go after all."

I rolled my eyes. "I'll let you know when we do the small ceremony. It'll be in Fair Isle."

"I'll definitely make it to that. I'm gonna give you away, right?"

I smiled. "I assumed so."

"Alright. I'll get my finest suit. And I'll even be nice to you all day."

"Whoa, that's a serious wedding gift."

"Yep. A one-time thing."

I chuckled. "Well, I guess I'll talk to you later."

"What are you guys gonna do about Ariel?"

"What do you mean?"

"She's just gone? Like off the map?"

"Sounds like Crewe fired her."

"You said they were really close, so I guess I'm surprised."

Crewe had been in a good mood since he picked me up in New York. It didn't seem like he missed her, not like before. But her actions probably erased any affection he had for her.

"I'm not saying what she did was okay—by any means. I'll always think she's a cunt. But I saw the way Crewe was protective of her. She's really important to him. You betrayed him, I shot him…maybe she should get a second chance too."

After what she did, I wasn't so inclined. But I shouldn't lose sight to why I went to New York in the first place. I wanted Ariel to be in his life. She was what Joseph was to me. Without her, all Crewe had was me. I tried to make it work with Ariel, but she refused to meet me halfway. That said, my prejudice shouldn't stop me from doing what was best for Crewe. "I've never heard you be so wise."

"I'm not just a pretty face."

I chuckled. "We have very different definitions of pretty."

"Are you gonna do anything about her?"

"I don't know…I'll think about it."

"Well, let me know what happens. It's unfortunate she's a lesbian because she's pretty sexy."

"Don't be gross, Joseph."

"I'm wise and gross. Deal with it." He hung up.

I opened Crewe's contacts and saw Ariel at the top of his favorites list. She was by far the person he called the most. He hadn't deleted her from his phone book, so she wasn't completely wiped from his existence.

I pressed the number and held the phone to my ear.

It rang four times before she answered. With her voice so weak, I hardly recognized her when she spoke. "Crewe?"

"Actually, it's London." I felt a wave of anger once our conversation was engaged. She'd caused me a lot of unnecessary pain. For an instant, I forgot why I was even bothering to do this.

"Oh…"

I sat on the phone in silence, unable to form words. I chewed on my inner cheek and cleared the anger from my blood. "I'm back in Scotland. Crewe asked me to marry him."

"Congratulations…" She still sounded frail. "I know you don't believe me and that's perfectly fine, but I'm sorry for everything. I shouldn't have overstepped my boundaries. I shouldn't have done any of the things I did. Please take care of Crewe. He's a good man."

I shouldn't pity her, but I did. "Crewe told me you told him the truth."

"He went through a hard time when you left. Got blood poisoning from drinking too much. Lost his way…it was bad. I realized I made a terrible mistake, and I had to make it right. But telling him the truth doesn't erase what I did. I understand that."

When I pictured Crewe drinking himself into a coma, I wanted to burst into tears. When we were face-to-face, he took my departure calmly. But I should have known how disturbed he would have been once I was gone.

"Thank you for giving me the chance to apologize," she said. "I'll let you go now."

"Wait, Ariel."

"Yes?"

No one would judge me if I never spoke to her again. No one would think less of me if I let Crewe lose her. But I didn't want Crewe to lose someone he cared so much about because of me. If I'd never come into the picture, none of this would have happened. "Can you come to the castle today? I want the three of us to talk."

"London, he doesn't want to see me. I accept that."

"I've never wanted him to lose you. I know you're important to him, even now. There's no reason it can't be the three of us. You were always loyal to him until I came around. I want the two of you to have that relationship again."

Ariel was quiet.

"Can you come to the castle?"

"I want to work it out with Crewe more than anything, but I don't think I can watch him kick me out again. It broke my heart enough the first time."

"We have to try. Crewe is stubborn, but if you give him enough time, he'll come around."

"I can be there in twenty minutes."

"Perfect. I'll tell Dunbar to put you in the office, and I'll come down with Crewe."

She sighed over the phone. "I hope this goes well, but my expectations are low."

"My expectations are high."

CREWE

"WE NEED to get out of this room." After I got dressed, London pulled me by the hand into the hallway.

"Do we?" I asked seriously. "Food is delivered to us whenever we want. We get plenty of exercise. And we're naked all the time."

"We have all night. Come on." Hand in hand, we took the stairs together to the ground floor. Dunbar looked at me, but he didn't wear a look of contempt for London. After my misery and blackout, he obviously thought London's presence was essential.

London headed for my office.

I didn't care about work right now. The business could wait until I started to care again. Without Ariel, the work was seriously piling up. It was so overwhelming I didn't even want to bother. I'd need to get a replacement for her, but I didn't want to deal with that either. "I hope the only reason we're going in there is to fuck on my desk."

"We'll see." She walked inside first then shut the door once I was inside.

I saw Ariel sitting on the leather sofa, in her jeans and t-shirt. Her glasses were gone because she was wearing contacts. When she looked at me, she wore the same expression of sadness that she did the last time we spoke. I distinctly told her I never wanted to see her again, so she must be here because of London.

I glared at Ariel, just as pissed off as I was the last time I saw her.

"Crewe." London grabbed my hand. "Let's sit down."

"I told you I never wanted to see you again. You thought that was a joke?" My fury burned right through my skin.

Ariel looked down.

"Crewe, calm down." London pulled me to the couch and sat down. She patted the cushion beside her. "Take a seat."

Furious, all I could was stare at her.

"Crewe," she whispered. "Come on. Let's be calm about this."

"No." I wasn't going to be calm, not after the person I trusted most betrayed me.

"Then sit for me," London said. "Please."

Only London's beautiful voice could get me to cooperate. I resisted for a second before I lowered myself into the chair.

London grabbed my hand, her engagement ring brilliant as the sunlight filtered through the large window. "I asked Ariel to come today. She resisted because she knew how upset you were, but I pressured her to join us. So, don't be mad at her. And you better not be mad at me."

I watched Ariel avoid both of our gazes. She never backed down from any kind of confrontation, but now she yielded the authority to me.

"Crewe, Ariel is an important person in your life—"

"Was an important person," I corrected. "Now she's a stranger to me."

London squeezed my hand. "I want the two of you to work this out. I want her in our lives."

I yanked my hand away. "How can you possibly say that? After what she did to both of us?"

"I can say it because we all make mistakes," London said calmly. "I betrayed you too. Then I came back. Joseph betrayed you, but you gave him another chance."

"I never gave him another chance," I argued. "I just put up with him for you."

"Well, put up with her for me."

This was ridiculous. "Why are you doing this, London? Ariel has been nothing but terrible to you. You don't owe her a damn thing."

"She's family, Crewe. She's family to you."

"Was," I corrected again.

"And family has their ups and downs, but they always find their way back to each other."

"It's not like we had a disagreement about something petty," I said. "She made the woman I love leave. She never accepted you. She went behind my back and betrayed me. That's not the kind of thing you just forgive."

"She thought she was doing the best thing for you," London said calmly.

"That's bullshit, and you know it," I snapped. "She was doing the best thing for herself."

Ariel didn't say a single word.

"Crewe, calm down," London said. "I understand you're upset—"

"Upset doesn't begin to describe it." When I looked at Ariel, I still wanted to strangle her.

"Ariel apologized," London said. "She seems sincere about it. I'm sure nothing like this would ever happen again. She'd be so grateful to have another chance that she would be even more loyal to you."

I shook my head. "Forget it."

"Crewe." Ariel finally met my gaze. She didn't cry like last time, but she looked just as devastated. "If you don't want me to be your business partner again, I understand. I don't blame you for feeling this way. But…I don't want to lose you. You're my closest friend. I don't think I can live my life without you in it in some capacity. I want to be at your wedding. I want you to be at mine. I love you…"

I was ashamed to admit her words got to me. Only a decade of respect and adoration could get me to soften. If I didn't think the world of her, I wouldn't have cared about anything she just said.

London stared at me, expecting me to say something.

But I couldn't say anything.

"I've forgiven Ariel," London whispered. "Ariel accepts me as the woman in your life. Our relationship isn't perfect, but in time, I'm sure we can be great friends. If she and I can come to this understanding, I think the two of you can work this out."

I stared at the floor.

"Crewe," London pressed. "This is what I want. And I know you want it too."

I raised my head and looked at Ariel. "You know how my family's death has bothered me. You know how hurt I was when Josephine left me. You're the last person I expected to turn against me…I can't get over that."

"I know," Ariel whispered. "I really thought I was doing the best thing for you."

"But you left," I reminded her. "You left when I wouldn't give up London."

"Because I thought you were going into financial ruin," Ariel said. "But now that I've gotten to know London, I realize she's the most compassionate, smart, and selfless person on the planet. She would do anything for you, even if she doesn't agree with it herself. You couldn't find anyone better. I mean that."

London looked at me. "We can take things slow. Trust doesn't need to be rebuilt in a day. But if I can forgive her, so can you."

I couldn't believe I was doing this. "If you ever do anything to London again—"

"I'll show her nothing but respect, Crewe," Ariel said quickly. "I'll treat her the way she deserves to be treated. I'm not one to admit when I'm wrong, but I was very wrong about her."

"Okay, I'll give you another chance. But this wouldn't have happened without London."

Ariel took a deep breath, her eyes watering. "You have no idea how grateful I am."

We sat in awkward silence, sitting on opposite couches and staring at one another.

London let go of my hand and excused herself from the room. "I'll give you two a minute…"

Ariel and I didn't speak. Everything had already been said, but the heavy tension still remained. It would probably be awkward like this for a long time.

Ariel cleared her throat. "I guess I'll start again tomorrow, if that's okay."

I nodded, unsure what else to say.

"I'll make up for what I did," she whispered. "Somehow, someway."

"I hope so. You're my closest friend. I'm angry with what you did…but you'll always be important to me."

"You've always been important to me too."

When there was nothing left to say, I rose to my feet. "I'm going to spend the rest of the day with London. We'll get back to work tomorrow."

"Sounds good." She stood up as well and looked at me.

I stared at her, but I didn't know what else to do. It seemed like something was missing, but I didn't know what. After what she did, I shouldn't forgive her, but I found myself feeling better after we had the conversation.

Ariel came closer to me then moved her arms around my waist. She hugged me gently even though I didn't reciprocate. "Congratulations, Crewe." She dropped her embrace and turned away.

It was hard for me to stay angry when she seemed sincere. Ariel and I had so many memories that it was difficult not to think about them. If I let her go, I would be throwing away a friendship filled with a decade of happiness. "Thank you."

London sat across from me on the terrace, avoiding my gaze because she knew this conversation wouldn't be pleasant. "I know you feel like I ambushed you—"

"Because you did."

"But I did it because you two needed to make up. What she did was wrong and I won't defend her, but I think it's best if we let it go. You two are great together. You shouldn't throw away all those years when we can work it out now. She and I are on good terms."

I knew London never would have done this if she weren't so infatuated with me. She put aside her own feelings of irritation for a woman who constantly insulted her just to make me happy. I considered myself to be a very lucky man to know that kind of love. I had a woman who would do anything for me. And I would do anything for her. "Are you sure you want this?"

"Yes," she said immediately. "I want us to start over—all of us."

"You give her a lot more compassion than she ever gave you."

"And now I'm certain she's a more compassionate person because of it. So…are we okay?"

We would always be okay. "Yes, Lovely. Nothing can come between us."

"Ariel will be back at work tomorrow?"

I nodded. "It'll take a long time for the trust to come back… if it ever does. But our friendship is certainly there. Baby steps."

"It'll return to what it was in no time."

There was nothing else to say about Ariel. We were moving forward, all three of us. "So, when are we gonna get married?"

"You tell me."

"Well, I want to get married as soon as possible?"

"As soon as possible, huh? What's the rush?"

"Babies," I said honestly.

"Babies?" she asked in surprise. "You want to have kids right away?"

"I've always wanted my own family."

"Well…that's a lot of pressure on my ovaries."

"We can wait if you want. But I'd rather not."

"I've always wanted to have kids," she said. "It just wasn't in my five-year plan."

"Well, I can't wait five years, that's for sure. I want to have little ones running around by then."

"So if you had it your way, on our wedding night you'd be trying to knock me up?"

I smiled. "Damn right."

"Wow. Think of the royal scandal…"

I chuckled. "We'll wait until after the official ceremony, then. That gives us eight months together. Sounds fair."

"Eight months is still pretty soon…but I'll consider it."

I couldn't push her much further. She already gave up her life to be with me. If she needed another year before getting pregnant, I could be patient. "I'll have Ariel prepare everything. As soon as you can get a dress, I'd like to tie the knot. The world won't know we're married, but we do— that's all that matters to me."

Her eyes softened. "I never thought you could be so romantic."

"I'm not romantic," I said honestly. "I just like being romantic with you." London changed my life when she came to me as a prisoner. She taught me not to be bitter, to let my anger go, and to live life to the fullest and be happy. Without her, I'd still be the hateful person I once was. Now I'd finally closed the book on my past, and I opened a new chapter in my life. "I'll always be romantic with you."

EPILOGUE

CREWE

LONDON HAD her arm tucked in the crook of mine as I guided her through the party. We already said our pleasantries to most of the guests, but we had a few more on our list. London looked beautiful in a strapless gold gown. With her deep brown hair and emerald eyes, she looked like a jewel.

When I turned to the right, I came face-to-face with Josephine. With thick cheeks and a neck not nearly as elegant as before, she looked at me with the same look of guilt. Her stomach was extended through her dress, her belly swollen with her first child. When I heard about her pregnancy, I couldn't have cared less. "Hello, Lady Josephine." I always addressed her formally because there was nothing informal between us. It was strange to think she could have given birth to my child.

Thank god that never happened.

"Hello, Lord Donoghue." She leaned in and accepted the kiss I gave her on the cheek. "Nice to see you." She turned to London next, her dislike written in her expression.

"Nice to see you, Lady London," I corrected, demanding that my wife get the same respect I received.

Josephine's cheeks reddened in embarrassment. "Of course…Lady."

I eyed her stomach. "Congratulations. This must be an exciting time for you."

"It is," Josephine answered. "Andrew and I are very excited." She looked around the room to find him, and to no one's surprise, he was speaking with one of the young waitresses. She turned back to us like she hadn't noticed.

I actually felt bad for her. "Have a good evening. My wife and I have a few more people to say hello to."

"Of course." Josephine moved her hand to her stomach then turned away.

London moved farther into me. "Karma's a bitch, ain't it?" After all this time, my wife was still fiercely protective of me. "Looks like she can't keep that husband of hers on a tight leash."

"It doesn't surprise me." The queen had just finished greeting the Duke of Rosenthal and she had an opening. I pulled London with me, and we said our greetings.

London was an expert at royalty. She knew exactly what to say and how to carry herself. Even the queen didn't intimidate her. London belonged in this life more than I did. After chatting for ten minutes, I excused us so we wouldn't overstay our welcome. "Having a good time?"

"I am…" She sighed and looked down at her wine.

"Doesn't sound like it," I said with a smile.

"I guess I just miss the kids. Is that stupid?"

"No." I rubbed her back then pulled her into me, planting a kiss on her hairline. "Not at all."

"I'm with them all the time, but when they're gone, I can't stop thinking about them."

"I miss them too."

"So…can we blow off this party?"

I took a look around, realizing I'd said hello to all the important people who mattered. "Yeah, I think that would be fine."

London's face lit up like I'd just said the magic words to make her the happiest woman in the world. "I'll tell Dunbar to get the car."

London walked through the doors first then headed into the grand living room where the enormous hearth sat underneath the TV. Joseph had the baby on his chest while Christopher played with his blocks on the floor.

"You look so comfortable right now," London said with a chuckle.

Joseph's eyes were lidded and heavy, and he didn't seem to be watching the TV even though it was still on. "It took me, like, an hour to change his diaper. And that shit smelled."

"No cussing around the kids." London grabbed Alan and held him against his chest. "How's my baby?" She spoke in a soft voice, in a way she only did with the kids. "Mommy and Daddy missed you." She rubbed her nose against his and made him giggle.

I watched my wife, transfixed by the blessing I had right in front of me. I had a perfect wife and two healthy kids. Christopher had my eyes and facial features. Alan looked more like London, with soft features that were still masculine.

"They were pretty good," Joseph said. "Christopher played with the blocks the whole time."

"You had fun with Uncle Joseph?" London asked Alan.

"Of course he did." Joseph stood up and gave Alan's foot a gentle squeeze. "They love their uncle. They'll love me even more when I take them driving and to pick up women."

"I hope you'll have a family of your own when they're that age, Joseph." London sat down and laid the baby in her lap.

She touched both of his hands then smiled down at our son. "I'd be concerned if you didn't."

Joseph walked up to me and extended his hand. "How was the ball?"

I shook it. "It wasn't a ball. A birthday party."

"Sounds like a ball to me." He nodded to Christopher. "They were both good kids. Pretty damn cute too."

"They get that from your sister." I kneeled down and picked up Christopher. "Hey, little guy." He was two years old, walking around the house and saying a few words here and there. While I worked during the day, London watched them and taught them everything under the sun. Sometimes I hated being at work because I missed out on finger painting, story time, exercise. "Have fun."

He stared at me before he reached his hand out and grabbed my nose.

I let him do whatever he wanted, being a pushover father like London predicted.

Christopher let out a giggle when I smiled.

Joseph patted me on the back. "I'm gonna head out. I'll see you guys later."

"Bye," I said without taking my eyes off my son.

"Bye, Joey." London didn't look at him either. "Let's get these kids to bed. They're already up later than they should be."

"Thanks to their asshole uncle," I jabbed.

"Hey," Joseph said as he walked out of the living room. "I'm the best uncle in the world, and you both know it."

We carried the kids upstairs, placing Christopher in the crib in his bedroom and the baby in the bed with us. I didn't like giving up my alone time with London. We usually made love before we went to sleep and again in the morning. Fortunately, we made time during the day just for the two of us. We took a long lunch in our bedroom, eating in private and fucking when we were full. It wasn't so bad.

London took off her makeup and got undressed while I watched Alan. I changed his diaper, putting him in his pajamas, and placed him in the center of the bed where he couldn't roll away.

London got into bed a moment later, wearing one of my t-shirts with her hair pulled up. She wasn't in lingerie like she used to be, but she was still beautiful. She got under the covers and snuggled next to the baby, her hand resting on his stomach so she could feel him at all times. Her eyes closed, and she immediately drifted off.

Instead of turning off the bedside lamp, I left it on so I could watch London and Alan sleep together. Their chests rose and fell at the exact same rate, and I thought it was the most beautiful thing I'd ever seen.

I had my own family.

I missed my parents and my brother, but their absence didn't feel so painful anymore. Now that hole didn't feel so deep. It had been filled with the family London gave to me. I had two incredible sons, and I intended to have two more children when she was ready to make more babies.

I was a king.

Now I had a queen.

And two perfect little princes.

This castle felt like a home. I still ran the scotch business, dominated the world of liquor, but now, I was so much more. With more money than I knew what to do with, I was a very lucky man.

But I truly felt privileged with this family.

I was the scotch king—and I was definitely blessed.

———

I hate when series end, but the good news is that the next series is ready for you to get started. Siena is on a mission to save her father. But that means winning over the most powerful and paranoid man in Italy. Read all about it in **The Banker**.

What happened after Christian and Ana got their happily ever after in Fifty Shades Freed? **Find out in this full-length novel**, written by Penelope Sky herself!

Printed in Great Britain
by Amazon